# FINDING FOREVER

## BOOK 6 OUTLASTING SERIES


LK MAGILL


FIRST HALE PRESS

**Finding Forever/ LK Magill** – 1st ed.

Ebook ISBN 978-1-950928-17-0

Paperback ISBN 978-1-950928-18-7

Hardcover ISBN 978-1-950928-19-4

DEDICATION_


*To God, thank you for allowing me to write another.*

THIS IS BOOK 6 IN A CONNECTED SERIES...
If you haven't already, please make sure to start with Book 1, OUTLASTING AFTER.

CHAPTER ONE_
ELIJAH ROE

"WHAT'S THE FIRST THING YOU REMEMBER?" LIAM'S VOICE WAS
steady, his gaze calm and direct.

Eli rolled his shoulders and glanced away. They'd done
this before, more than once.

"You don't have to worry about her," Liam went on. "She's
not watching."

At this, Eli smiled.

His hazel eyes bounced all around the tiny room that the
two of them were currently crammed in, as if searching for
Shelby.

It was standard interrogation style, with a small wooden
table, two stiff-backed chairs positioned opposite each other,
and blank gray walls. Off to Eli's right there was a single glass
mirror sunk into one wall... somehow he knew that it was
most likely made up of one-way glass.

The legs of his chair scraped across the floor as Eli pushed
out of his seat and stalked over to the mirror. Tilting his head
to one side, he stared hard at his own reflection.

3

Instinctively he knew that Liam was lying… she was back there, watching.

Lifting his right hand up to his face, Eli studied the fresh scar that ran between his thumb and pointer finger. He had no memory of how he'd gotten it. Cass (the woman everyone said was his sister) told Eli that Liam had removed something called a "microchip" from his body. That's why he couldn't think like a normal person. It was the microchip.

Then there were the tattoos. Odd geometric designs covering both of his forearms from wrists to elbows. He had no memory of getting those either.

"We've done this already," Eli said, and stretched his hand out toward the glass. "Nothing has changed. When I remember something, I'll tell you."

"Let's just talk," Liam replied easily, he was still sitting in his chair. "It might shake something loose for you."

With a slight frown, Eli touched the glass with the tip of his index finger. If it was a normal mirror, then there would be a tiny gap of space between the tip of his actual finger and the reflection of his finger. If the mirror was one-way glass however, then the tip of his actual finger would connect with the reflected image of said finger… which it now did.

Bingo.

Dropping his hand down to his side, Eli took a step back and blinked at his own reflection in the glass. There were people behind there, watching him. Shelby for certain, and maybe Cole and Cass too. They'd all been at the baseball field when the soldiers had come for him, so it made sense they might be back there now.

"She's not there," Liam tried again, as if reading Eli's thoughts.

With a huff, Eli shook his head.

The Good Doctor, as Liam often referred to her, would not miss this. She was tenacious and stubborn, and Eli (with his unexplainable tattoos and vacant brain) was her personal pet project. Not that Eli minded. With Shelby, he'd take any sort of attention he could get, even if it was purely scientific in nature.

"I've got nothing to hide," Eli said, and ignored the small twist of doubt in his belly. "I don't mind if she listens."

Flashing a wide grin then, he winked at his own reflection before retreating back to the table. When he sat down, he planted his feet on the gray cement flooring and rocked back in his chair. The two front legs of the chair left the ground.

"What's the first thing you remember?" Liam tried his original question again. His hands were folded calmly in his lap, he observed Eli with dark, intelligent eyes.

Ignoring him, Eli teetered for a bit, clenching his abs and finding his center before finally lifting his feet entirely off the ground. For a few seconds he was just hovering there on the back legs of his chair.

"You're going to fall," Liam commented dryly.

"No, I'm not," Eli countered and flashed another one of his triumphant grins.

Liam, as usual, looked unimpressed. "I can do this all day," he added.

"The first thing I remember is my sister in the back of the Jeep," Eli supplied.

The memory of that particular moment was branded like fire inside his brain. The dark-haired woman with blood all over her. The rocking of the vehicle. The roar of the engine. Confusion. Fear.

Eli didn't particularly like to relive it, over and over. But what else could he do? What else could he say?

Bracing one knee beneath the table now, Eli attempted to bring his arms up behind his head. He tried to keep his body perfectly still, with the chair tipped back and his legs stretched out, like he didn't care about this conversation, like he didn't care about anything in the world.

"Did you know she was your sister at the time?" Liam asked.

"No." Eli pursed his lips. He didn't like to admit that.

"But you knew you were riding in a Jeep," Liam supplied. "You knew the name of it, and that it was a vehicle with a motor and how it worked."

"Yeah." Eli's stomach muscles clenched as he worked to keep the chair balanced on its rear legs.

"How do you explain that?" Liam again. "You know the name of the vehicle you're riding in, but not the name of your own flesh and blood?"

Frowning, Eli held his breath. His heart began tapping at him and the chair was shifting beneath him. One false move and this balancing act was over.

Liam cocked a brow then, and stared.

"I don't know," Eli spat finally.

With a huff, he sat up straight and sent the chair slamming forward into its proper place. His feet hit the ground and his hands hit the tabletop and he rolled his eyes.

"Come on Liam, this is repetitive as hell. Nothing has changed," Eli argued, before swinging his eyes over to the glass. "At least... nothing for *me* has changed. I just don't remember anything. I don't know what to say. I'm doing everything you guys want me to do."

Nodding, Liam tapped on the tabletop with his fingers and drew Eli's attention back over to him.

"There's something I want you to hear," he said. "I want you to tell me if it triggers anything for you."

"Something on *your* end has changed," Eli stated, gesturing vaguely around the room. "That's what this is all about."

"Will you listen to it?" Liam asked, unblinking. "And tell me if you remember anything?"

"Shelby's not back there?" Eli jerked a thumb at the window. "Because this sounds a lot like an experiment, and I know how she is about those. She wouldn't want to miss it."

Shrugging, Liam refused to answer. The dark-haired, dark-eyed man who sat across from him gave nothing away.

Eli could never be sure of Liam. Eli could never be sure of anybody. But what choice did he really have? It's not like he could say no right now. It's not like he could get up and walk away.

With an answering shrug of his own, Eli eased back in his chair, like he could not care less, like this didn't have his insides twisting.

Liam lifted his left hand in the air and motioned with one finger.

A speaker crackled with static, and then a voice filled the room.

*If anyone's out there. I'm calling for help. We have women and children in need of food and...*

Static.

*Our location is just south of Provo, Utah. If you can hear this message, please bring food and any medical supplies you may have.*

Static.

*If anyone's out there. I'm calling for help. We have women and children in need of food and...*

Eli's brow furrowed.

The voice... it was... familiar.

Eli's eyes popped up to lock on Liam's. He was met with an utterly blank expression. Cold eyes sat in a quiet, controlled face. They were measured and intelligent, and gave nothing away.

*If anyone's out there. I'm calling for help.*

"That's me," Eli exhaled the words as the room began to spin.

Squeezing his eyes shut, his fingers gripped the edge of the table. His head throbbed and his breath hitched in his lungs. It was him. The voice on the recording... was Eli.

But it didn't make any sense. Eli didn't remember saying those words. He didn't know what Provo was, or Utah, or anything about needing help.

Eli's heart slammed against his ribs. The room began to swirl and sink. Sweat gathered on his upper lip as a wave of dizziness overtook him, pulling him under. Saliva flooded his mouth and his stomach clenched unhappily.

He was going to be sick.

He was going to throw up.

"Eli!" Someone called out to him... a woman. "Eli! Stay with us!"

The voice was rushing closer, but then Eli's eyes were rolling back and his face went slack.

In that moment, Eli was pushed forward into the gray swirl of memories. In that moment, Eli succumbed.

THE TIP OF ELI'S FINGER TOUCHED THE ONE-WAY GLASS AND HE tilted his head slightly to the side.

Shelby stood stalk still and watched. Eli's glittering hazel eyes bounced down to his own hand, and then back up to the mirror, before he took a single step back.

The cocky grin that spread out across his face then had her heart skipping a beat, even when she didn't want it to.

"What's he doing?" She asked, and tucked a wayward red curl behind one ear.

It was like he could see her, the way that he stared at the glass and smiled. She'd gotten used to that smile during the past two months of working with him. He was a charmer, that much was for sure.

"Testing the glass," Cass supplied, her arms were folded across her chest. "He knows someone is back here. He knows he's being watched."

"How would he know about one-way glass?" Uriah Linfield cut in.

The Commander was standing off to the right. A pair of

his soldiers were leaning against the far wall.

"He was a poor kid attending a rich kids' school." Cass gestured to the mirror. "This isn't his first time being interrogated. If anything went wrong, then they questioned Eli first."

"I thought he was their star quarterback?" Uriah frowned.

Shrugging, Cass sighed before answering, "He was."

On the other side of the glass, Liam kept talking and Eli made his way back to the small wooden table. When he took his seat, he stretched his long body out and leaned back in his chair.

As broody and intimidating as Liam was, Eli seemed equally nonplussed. Instead of swallowing hard and wringing his hands (like pretty much everyone else living behind the Wall would do), he was pushing his chair up on its rear legs and screwing around.

"He's relaxed and comfortable," Shelby pointed out. "He has nothing to hide because he literally can't access any of his memories beyond about nine weeks ago. This is pointless."

"Let's let Officer Byrne do his job," Uriah countered. "I have an audio recording of Eli that says he's currently in Utah. I need answers."

Rolling her eyes, Cass limped her way towards Uriah. Her curly brown hair was tied back in a messy pony tail, and her cheeks were flushed.

Shelby's eyes narrowed and she pursed her lips. Cass and she had been roommates not so very long ago, and now Shelby was concerned. Cass was over-exerting herself after the surgery on her leg. She should be taking it easy.

"Obviously he's not in Utah right now," Cass growled. "It's a recording, so it was clearly made *before* we found him in Oregon."

Blinking slowly at her, Uriah folded his arms across his chest and said nothing. The soldiers behind him shifted slightly.

"Again…" Shelby cut in. "I don't think it's wise to play this recording for Eli while his brain is in its current recovery state."

"We've been actively trying to jar his memory for weeks now," Uriah countered. "This might finally do the trick."

"Or it could completely overwhelm him," Shelby argued. "This is too soon in the process. I think we need to wait, give his brain a few more months to heal."

"Well, I don't agree." Uriah swiped a hand through the air. "I have men out in the field flying blind right now and I need all the information I can get. We're moving forward. He'll be fine."

Biting her lip, Shelby's gaze drifted back to Eli.

His dark hair was cut short, but even so it curled slightly at the ends. The resemblance between he and his sister was uncanny.

For her part, Cass shifted slowly to face the glass once more. Her right leg was obviously bothering her. Like her brother's brain, it would take a few more months to heal.

Internally, Shelby noted all of these things because she was a doctor. Technically speaking, her specialty was in genetics and research, but she'd been trained clinically first, and so she had some experience with the practice of medicine.

Cass should be sitting down right now. All of this walking and standing would result in an increase in inflammation and painful swelling later on.

"Cass, you should sit," Shelby whispered, but Cass just waved her off.

On the other side of the glass, Liam lifted a hand in the air and gestured for them to play the recording. Stepping over to the wall, Uriah pushed a button. The sound of Eli's voice calling for help filled the space.

Pressing her lips together, Shelby held her breath. Her eyes focused on Eli's stunned face as it drained slowly of color. She tried to keep her observations clinical. She ignored the uncomfortable thumping of her heart and the subsequent tightening in her chest as the impact of the recording on Eli became clear. He was listening to himself say words that he didn't remember ever saying.

"He's going to pass out," Shelby announced. "He might hit his head."

Whirling on Uriah, Cass hissed, "Turn it off!"

But it was too late.

"He's going down," Shelby spat, and bolted for the door.

She was out of the observation room and inside the interrogation room before she knew it.

"Eli!" Shelby called. "Eli! Stay with us!"

But for once, he didn't turn at the sound of her voice. He didn't acknowledge that he'd heard her. He didn't acknowledge that he could hear anything at all.

Liam was jumping up from his chair then, just as Eli's entire body went slack.

"Grab him!" Shelby shouted, as she darted forward.

Liam lunged across the table. His long arms shot out and his hips bumped hard against the edge of the wood. It was no use though, he was too far away.

Eli's shoulders slumped and his body melted to one side. He fell to the right, like a freshly cut tree in the forest. The sound of his head impacting the cement was sickly and ominous.

"Shit!" Liam spat and scrambled right over the top of the table.

Shelby slid to a stop beside Eli's crumpled body and placed two fingers at the base of his neck.

"He's got a pulse," she announced.

Her voice sounded so calm and in control, which was in direct contrast to the panic bubbling in her throat.

As Liam climbed down to her and Uriah arrived at her back, Shelby continued speaking, "Let's lay him out flat. I need to check his head."

"He's having a memory," Uriah murmured. "That's what they look like, right?"

"Not always," Shelby countered, trying hard to keep the bite from her voice.

She didn't want him to be right. She didn't want Uriah Linfield's rash decision to be rewarded.

Liam said nothing as he and Uriah worked to lift Eli, and drag him to where he was flat on his back. Shelby shifted along with them, removing her hand from Eli's neck in order to cradle his head. He wasn't bleeding, so that was good.

At her back, a door slammed open and other people entered the room.

"Eli!" Cass cried.

"Have her sit," Shelby snapped, without turning to look. "Cass, you're injuring yourself."

Whatever response Cass had for her was blocked out though. Suddenly, everything around Shelby was background noise. Her vision narrowed. Her focus sharpened.

Leaning down, Shelby lifted Eli's eyelids, one then the other. She checked his pulse again, then combed her fingers through his thick brown hair. There was a bump growing where his skull had impacted the floor. It was definitely a concern, something to keep an eye on, but there was no laceration.

"How long will he be out?" Uriah asked, he was crouched just beside her now, observing.

"Hard to say." Shelby frowned.

Eli's mouth was slightly parted as his lungs drew in air. Was it wrong that she stared at his perfect pink lips? Definitely.

He was a research assignment, a sort of patient. She'd always been the consummate professional, youngest in her class at med school by about four years. This attraction he brought out in her was wrong, and she would squash it. She would.

On the ground, Eli began to stir. His fingers moved first. His fists clenched and relaxed. His right foot twitched.

"He's coming around," Shelby announced, and moved her hand to his wrist.

She meant to monitor his pulse, but at that very moment Eli came alive. His eyes popped open and his body went rigid. Rotating quickly, his hand grabbed onto hers and he squeezed... hard.

"Ow!" Shelby yelped at the unexpected strength of his grip, but was unable to pull her hand away.

Her eyes locked on his then, and widened. Liam hovered, trying to brace Eli's body, while Uriah worked to pry Eli's fingers loose. For a moment, Eli's gaze was distant. He stared at her, seemingly without seeing her, and his bruising grip did not loosen.

But then all at once those hazel eyes of his cleared. A smile took over, and the dark look from moments earlier, melted away.

"Doc," he muttered, as his hand gentled and released. "I can't breathe."

Frowning, Shelby leaned in closer.

"You can speak," Shelby pointed out. "Therefore you can breathe. Are you hurt? Can you describe the sensation?"

"I can't get enough air," Eli whispered. "You're going to have to do CPR."

That's when he hit her with a broad smile and doubled down with a wink.

Groaning, Uriah eased back and dusted his hands together. Liam gave a huff and rolled his eyes.

"Stop flirting with my doctor," Uriah spat. "What's the last thing you remember Eli? This is important."

Biting at his lip then, Eli kept his eyes glued to Shelby's face. Her heart skipped in her chest as his hand reached up to curl around hers once more, softly this time. His thumb worked tiny circles against her skin in the exact spot he'd hurt moments before.

After a moment's hesitation, Shelby pulled her hand from his and tucked it at her waist.

Eli sighed.

"I remember my baby sister bleeding out in the back of a Jeep," he said and turned his head to look at Uriah. "But I'm an asshole, so I didn't know who she was at the time. That's my first memory... of being a clueless loser. Satisfied?"

"No." Uriah rocked up to his feet and stared down. "No, Eli. I'm not satisfied."

CHAPTER THREE_
ELI

HE WAS A LIAR.

Sweat poured down his back, tickled along his spine and soaked through his gray shirt. Eli puffed out a breath and ignored the discomfort. He ignored the pain.

Keeping his grip on the bar, Eli continued to count his reps. Fifty-one. Fifty-two. Fifty-three. The muscles in his arms and shoulders screamed at him, but he didn't have to think much about the weight he was lifting. His brain was working on autopilot as his eyes tracked his sister's progress across the gym.

Cass was doing her physical therapy, which consisted mostly of stretching on the mat and then a few mild floor exercises. Her brow was furrowed in concentration and her lips pressed together in a thin line. She was in pain. She was sitting on the mat, leaning over her injured thigh and it caused just as much sweat to bead on her forehead as it did for Eli to lift her entire body weight on the ends of this bar.

Guilt and concern swamped him.

He may not remember who she was with 100% clarity, but there was something about Cass that triggered an emotional response in him. Eli looked at his little sister and he saw something of himself wrapped up in a tiny female package. When he looked at Cass, he *knew* that she belonged to him, that it was his job to protect her and to keep her safe.

But instead of doing that, he'd caused her to re-injure herself yesterday.

He'd listened to that stupid recording and passed out like a little bitch. When he came back around, Cass was sitting in a chair with her head bent and her hands clutching her leg. She'd overdone it because of him.

If Jameson were still here, then it never would've happened. That guy (Cass's boyfriend who was also supposedly Eli's best friend) would never had allowed her to get hurt. Eli had watched them together for weeks. The guy was head over heels for her, no doubt about that.

"You're gonna hurt yourself," Liam's voice crept into Eli's space, causing him to frown.

"Go away," Eli huffed and kept lifting.

"Do you have a rep count in mind, or are you just going till failure?" Liam again, his tall body was looming off to the left.

Gritting his teeth, Eli ignored the guy and kept watching Cass.

He kept lifting the bar and grunting against the vibration of his muscles. She was in pain, so he was in pain. It *felt* right. It felt like something he'd been doing for a really, really long time... matching their pain together.

It wasn't until Liam stepped directly in front of him and blocked his view, that Eli blew out a hot breath and set the bar down. The sounds of the gym continued all around them. Weights clunked. Machines whirred. People breathed... loudly.

Stepping back, Eli dusted his hands together and sucked in some much needed oxygen. His body was zinging and his head was swimming but still... it wasn't all that hard to shift from anger at himself, to anger at Liam.

"Do you mind?" Eli spat and swiped the back of his hand along his forehead.

He was damp and sticky, unlike Liam who looked like he had yet to begin.

Tilting his head to one side, Eli examined the man who had been as much of a shadow to him these past weeks as he'd been to Cass. They were about the same height and build, with more similarities than differences. Square jaw, straight nose, broad shoulders, trim hips. In another life they could have been brothers.

Their eyes were different though, Eli noted. His were a greenish-brown where Liam's were pure darkness, laced with ice.

"Did we know each other?" Eli asked, gesturing between them. "Before?"

Shaking his head, Liam looked away.

"No," he said simply. "We didn't."

Nodding, Eli accepted the answer and took a giant step to one side. Cass came into view once more and his heart rate began to decrease.

Even if Jameson hadn't left explicit instructions about watching over her, Eli figured he'd naturally be almost as protective. There was something instinctual about it, like a silent warning winding through his DNA. Watch Cass's back, it seemed to say, it's you against the world.

"You're going to be late," Liam commented dryly.

"For what?" Eli spared him a glance.

"Your appointment with the Good Doc." Liam tapped his finger on his wrist. "I'll hang with Cass until you're done."

And there was that double-edged sword again. Liam the friend. Liam the foe. According to Jameson, Liam could be trusted implicitly to watch Cass. Also according to Jameson he was some sort of an interrogation expert.

Trust him.

Don't trust him.

"Something goes there," Eli stated, and pointed at Liam's wrist. "Something that says what time it is."

"That's right." Liam's eyes became laser focused. "Can you remember the word?"

*Watch, motherfucker. It's called a watch.*

"Nah." Eli shook his head and flashed a grin. "Wish I could, man. Wish I could."

"Hmph," Liam grunted and his nostrils flared. "It's a shame that recording yesterday didn't shake anything loose for you. I know Shelby was really counting on it. If she can't get anything from you soon, then Uriah is going to pull her from your case."

"Is that so?" Eli arched a brow and placed one wide palm over his chest.

When he'd come to yesterday, Shelby had looked mad as hell, and *not* at Eli. Nope. The daggers in her intelligent blue eyes were all aimed at Uriah Linfield.

"Yeah." Liam nodded. "Like I said, she's all work. She's going to need answers from you, that's what makes her tick."

"Well, I better remember something soon then," Eli drawled, and bent to remove the weights from the bar. "And thanks for keeping an eye on Cass."

"Sure," Liam answered. "No problem."

Sucking in a breath, Eli worked methodically. He returned the gym's equipment to its proper place, wiped it down and headed for the showers. All the while, his stomach swirled and his thoughts grew gray and hazy.

He could feel Liam's eyes on him, tracking him, studying him. And it wasn't an unfamiliar feeling. Eli got the sense that he'd lived most of his life under some sort of scrutiny. Because he was able to keep a relaxed sort of expression on his face, even as the images he'd recalled from yesterday fought their way to the front of his mind.

Heading for the men's locker room, Eli stripped out of his sweat-soaked clothes and stalked into an empty shower stall. His heart was jumping in his chest now and his throat had gone dry. Flipping the water to cold, he let the shock of it stream over his head, pour down his face, and spray against the clean tile walls of the shower.

He remembered something yesterday when he'd passed out.

He remembered something bad.

He'd killed people.

At least… he thought he had. In his memory, he'd felt such intense sorrow. And then there were the bodies. There were so many bodies in his memory. Stacks and stacks of dead people. Women. Children. And then there was a shovel in his hands, which was stained with old blood.

He was digging. In his memory, he was breathing through

a bulky black gas mask and he was digging a massive fucking grave with a dozen other men beside him.

Squeezing his eyes shut now, Eli leaned his forehead against the stark white tiles of the shower, and fought back the images. His head throbbed and his stomach clenched but this time, he refused to pass out.

## CHAPTER FOUR_
SHELBY

Flipping through the pages of the text book, Shelby leaned forward over the long wooden table. Her flaming red hair fell down to frame her face as her brow furrowed in concentration.

This warehouse was one of many buildings located inside the Wall. It was about two stories high, with corrugated metal sheeting covering the entire exterior.

On the inside, the other buildings were used to store military equipment, medical supplies, food, seeds, clothing, shoes, etc. And from the outside, it was hard to tell one giant metal warehouse from another.

But *this* particular warehouse, the one Shelby was currently sitting in, was different. Inside *this* warehouse, was an expansive fully furnished library.

Clean white walls, overhead lighting, climate control, and floor to ceiling wooden shelves stocked with books, manuals, texts, maps, and paper. Not tablets. Not computers. Real. Touchable. Books.

For Shelby, it was like walking into the past.

It was every Ivy League college she'd ever stepped foot in. It was real and perfect. The source (despite all of its many faults) had at least done this thing right.

It made sure to stockpile as much of the world's knowledge in written form... *before* it proceeded to end humanity. And blessedly, none of the content was digital. Nope. This library was packed with carefully organized and catalogued *printed* information.

You didn't need power. You didn't need internet access. You just needed light to see by, and your brain.

The smell alone was intoxicating. There was something about the scent of books that was heady, something about the ink and the crinkly paper pages and the hardbound covers that did you in.

There were no windows at all in the warehouse, but between the overhead lighting and the little lamps situated on each of the long wooden tables, Shelby never lacked for light.

It was heaven for a nerd like her, and also a bit lonely.

It reminded her of medical school... and well, high school too. She'd been ten years old when she'd started as a Freshman. Being escorted around by your mother to class made it sort of hard to make friends. Solitary time in the library was a given. Mom would take lunch at the end of one table and Shelby would study at the other. No giggling girlfriends. No makeup. No dance team or cheerleading or prom.

But that was the cost of excellence, right?

That was the cost of flying through school at an alarming rate. Add in her bright red hair, too many freckles and awkward silver braces and Shelby had indeed been a winning combination.

No friends. No boys. *Plenty* of time to study.

"Is this seat taken?" Eli's voice broke the silence in the air.

Shelby jumped a little, and rocked forward over the table. Her hands came down to brace on the textbook she'd been engrossed in, just as her stomach did that uncomfortable flutter thing it tended to do around Eli.

Huffing a breath, Shelby tipped her face up and gave Eli what she hoped was a confident smile. Gesturing to the chair opposite her, she nodded.

"Eli," she said. "You caught me off guard."

"I'm sorry Doc," he replied easily, and shot her a wink. "Didn't mean to scare ya."

Instead of taking the seat indicated though, the guy sauntered around the end of the table and pulled out the chair right beside Shelby. Before she could so much as speak, Eli was flopping down and making himself comfortable. He ran a hand through his damp hair, stretched out his impossibly long legs and sighed.

"How is your head?" Shelby asked.

Her eyes zeroed in on the area of impact from yesterday, and her hands itched to reach out and examine him. Eli watched her for a moment before biting at his lower lip. Leaning forward, he bent his head so she could see the bump clearly.

"Kinda hurts," he stated. "Maybe you should check it out."

Turning to face him fully, Shelby scooted to the edge of her seat and did just that. Her fingers combed carefully through his damp hair and her brow furrowed in concentration. There was definitely a decent sized lump, but she judged a contusion was as far as things went.

Inhaling, it was hard not to take in the scent of fresh soap mixed with the very male smell of his skin. It had something primal curling up inside of her.

Suddenly uncomfortable, Shelby retracted her hands and cleared her throat. Scooting back in her chair she smoothed her hands along her simple blue jeans and glanced around. There was no one else here, as usual.

"So Doc," Eli said as he lifted his head. "What are we doing today?"

"Well…" Shelby turned her attention to the array of textbooks before her and tried to look busy. "After what happened yesterday, I thought we should revisit your tattoos. I've been researching ancient code origins and I have a few new ideas."

"Ancient code origins?" Eli arched a brow and shot her one of his crooked grins. "Sounds fascinating."

"No, it doesn't," Shelby countered and rolled her eyes. "At least, not to most people. I know what I am, you don't have to humor me."

"Oh?" Eli frowned and inched his chair closer to hers. "And what are you, exactly?"

"Uh…" Shelby's mouth parted slightly as he crowded her space.

Bringing his tattooed forearms up between them, Eli braced one against the table and offered the other one for her inspection. After a moment's hesitation, Shelby took the offered arm in her hands. Tracing her fingers over the black geometric designs, her brows drew together.

"I'm a nerd," she answered finally. "I like boring things. You don't have to pretend what I do is interesting to save my feelings. I'm used to it."

Reaching for a pencil with one hand, she began scribbling

on a nearby pad of paper. They'd been at this for over two months now and she still didn't have the slightest clue as to what the Command Code meant. It was beyond her. It was beyond Cole Tanner as well, and he actually had some limited training on the subject. Fact was, the code design on Eli's arms was beyond everyone who lived inside the Wall.

"Forgive me, but..." Eli exhaled the words on a laugh. Shelby could smell the minty freshness of his breath. "What is a nerd, exactly?"

"Oh, right." Shelby's eyes flitted up to lock with Eli's. "A nerd is... well... a nerd is someone who is *not* cool."

"Not cool?" Eli blinked slowly at her, with that same grin twitching at the edge of his perfect mouth.

"Nerds, by definition, are boringly studious," Shelby huffed her explanation, and returned her attention to his tattoos. "I am a nerd. You are cool, which is the opposite. I'm sure on some subconscious level, you understand this. In my experience it seems people are predisposed to either grouping and divide accordingly at an early age."

"Wow. I see." Eli bobbed his head and in doing so caused the muscles in his arm to move beneath her touch. "So if I'm the opposite of a nerd, then that would make me excitingly *not* studious. Is that right?"

"That's right." Shelby nodded absently before making several additional notes.

There was definitely a pattern of some kind, with squares and ovals and little lines. But just when she thought she'd figured out a reason for the sequence, it dissolved into nonsense on her. It wasn't locations. It wasn't names. It wasn't stats or dates or times.

If only Uriah would consent to turning on an electronic

scanner, then they could have the answer to what these tattoos meant in less than a heartbeat. But he was adamant. The use of electronics was expressly banned. The risk of reigniting the source was too great, and so this particular mystery must be solved by old fashioned means.

Long hours. Attempts. Failures. Research. Repeat.

"Is there something wrong with being excitingly not studious?" Eli asked.

"Hmmm?" Shelby continued making notes.

"Cool. You said I'm cool," Eli stated, shifting around on his chair. "Is there something wrong with being cool?"

"Huh?" Shelby glanced up at him and gave her head a slight shake. "No, of course not."

"Well, why did you say it like that?" Eli again.

"Like what?" Shelby's brow rose.

"Like they don't go together." Eli frowned. Picking up his free hand, he gestured between them. "Like you're one and I'm the other and that's it."

Sitting up straighter, Shelby let loose a long sigh. She didn't know quite how to respond. Over the years she'd observed dozens of handsome, charismatic, popular men like Eli. When they walked into a room, heads turned and people gathered around. They never wanted for attention or admiration and very rarely did they make an effort to approach her. On the scant occasions that sort of thing had happened, Shelby quickly learned exactly what men like Eli were after. Once they got it… they soon disappeared.

"Eli…" Shelby glanced between his tattoos and his face, searching for the right thing to say.

"I could be studious." Eli wiggled his eyebrows. "You don't know who I was before, I could be the world's biggest nerd."

"I highly doubt that."

"Ah, so judgy," Eli scoffed.

Reaching for one of the massive textbooks on the table, Eli pulled it closer. Shelby leaned back in her chair and folded her arms over her chest. It was becoming hard to observe him like this while keeping a straight face. Her cheeks wanted to turn pink, so she bit the inside of her cheek and crossed her legs.

Humming to himself like he hadn't a care in the universe, Eli flipped casually through the pages. His chiseled jaw had just a touch of dark scruff coming in and Shelby found her eyes were drawn to it.

For several moments, they sat there quietly together. The sound of pages turning and the absent tapping of Eli's foot against the floor was all that could be heard.

"Any insights?" Shelby asked finally.

Letting her gaze fall to his forearms, she resumed her relentless scrutiny. She'd tried tracing the tattoos, writing them on paper and then laying it all out flat. She'd rearranged it, top to bottom, bottom to top, inside to outside and vice versa. Nothing. Nothing made sense.

Suddenly, Eli's body jolted. His body shifted back, and he was snapping the heavy book closed. Frowning, Shelby looked up into his face. A line of sweat had beaded on his upper lip. Quickly, he swiped it away.

"Eli?" Shelby's voice was low.

"Guess you're right." He forced a laugh then, and stood up. "I'm not boringly studious."

Narrowing her gaze, Shelby's heart thumped in her chest as she watched him pace away. Eli's hands came up to run roughly through his hair. His entire body was taut, from the line of his broad shoulders, to the flex in his calves as he stalked along the floor.

"What did you see in there?" Shelby's blue eyes darted over Eli's figure.

Stopping in his tracks, he rotated to face her. His expression was a mask of charm now, from the crinkly smile lines at the corners of his eyes to the up turn of those full pink lips.

"Nothing." He shrugged and then glanced away, stuffing his hands into the pockets of his pants. "I just can't sit still anymore."

"Okaaaay." Shelby blew out a long breath. That was a lie.

Reaching for the text he'd been reading, Shelby pulled it in close. Her eyes examined the cover briefly before she began to turn the pages.

"What page were you on?" She asked, looking for a crease or seam that would give her the answer.

"Shelby." Eli huffed a laugh and strode back over to the table. "Go for a walk with me?"

Continuing to turn the pages, Shelby's eyes darted over the words, searching for something… she didn't know what.

"Shelby." Eli's large hand came down and tugged at the ends of her red hair. "I've got something I want to show you."

"Huh?" Looking up at him, Shelby gave her head a little shake.

"Come with me," Eli coaxed, and offered her his palm. "You want me to remember, right?"

"Uh… yes." Shelby swallowed and stared at his hand. "Yes, I want to help you remember."

"Great." Eli wiggled his fingers. "Then come with me."

CHAPTER FIVE_
ELI


"THAT'S CRAZY, WHAT YOU DID BACK THERE." THE SOLDIER SITTING beside him shook his head.

"Is it?" Eli asked.

Staring down at his own hands, he watched them shake. The skin of his palms, for the most part, was clean.

It was the backs of his hands that gave him away. That, and his uniform, and his weapon (which now sat propped at his side), even his hair was sprayed red with dried blood. Everything. Every single part of him felt coated in thick, sticky death.

Cass hadn't been on that transport train, or the one before that, or the one before that. Cass was nowhere. Cass was dead.

"Yeah," the soldier kept talking, kept shaking his head, as the vehicle they were riding in kept driving. "You guys aren't supposed to be able to do that. I mean... you aren't supposed to be able to do anything remotely close to that."

Nodding slowly, Eli pursed his lips and blinked down at his hands. His palms. They were so damn clean.

"Did you hit the two trains before that one?" The soldier asked. "Was that all you? By yourself?"

*Eli failed to answer.*

*"Because if so..." The guy hesitated a moment before continuing. "We've been looking for you."*

With a jerk, Eli came back to himself. He flipped the textbook on the table closed with a decided thump and sat up straight. A line of perspiration had collected around his mouth. Reaching up, he swiped it away.

"Eli?" Shelby's voice came out low and quiet, but the sound sent an electric current through him so strong that he had to stand up.

He'd forgotten she was here.

He'd forgotten the present and instead, he'd remembered a tiny piece of his past. And just like yesterday, it filled him with an immense weight of dread. He didn't want this to be his life. This *couldn't* be his life, he wouldn't allow it.

"Guess you're right." He forced a laugh. "I'm not boringly studious."

"What did you see in there?" Shelby asked.

"Nothing." *Too much.*

Pacing away, Eli ran his hands roughly through his hair and tried to manage the swirl of sickness churning in his gut. Shelby kept talking and he kept answering her, but his responses were like an automated message running in the background of his mind.

He had to get away from here. He had to get some fresh air.

"Shelby." Eli strode back over to the table. "Go for a walk with me?"

His heart thumped loudly in his chest as the beautiful

redhead before him kept flipping through pages. She was so damn tenacious and intelligent, and from now on he knew he would have to be extra careful around her. The smart thing would be for him to avoid her altogether, the smart thing would be for him to go his own way, the smart thing would be for him to leave the Wall.

But as she sat there, with a little bump of concentration forming between her slender eyebrows, Eli couldn't help the impulse flowing through him.

He couldn't leave her well enough alone. He was playing with fire. Red hot flames in the form of gorgeous soft curls, flowing like silk beneath his fingers. He itched to touch her. He wondered what it would be like to make her his.

Swallowing, Eli tried again.

"Shelby," he said, as his hand came down to tug at the ends of her hair, he couldn't stop himself. "I've got something I want to show you."

"Huh?" Looking up at him, Shelby gave her head a little shake.

"Come with me," Eli coaxed, and offered her his palm. "You want me to remember, right?"

"Uh… yes." Shelby looked at his open hand. "Yes, I want to help you remember."

"Great." Eli wiggled his fingers and coaxed the smallest of smiles from her lips. "Then come with me."

Taking his hand, Shelby scooted her chair back and stood up. They moved through the library like that for several seconds, hand in hand. And it didn't escape his notice that she waited longer than necessary before finally pulling hers away.

As they left the library and stepped out into the fresh air, Eli had to hold a hand up to shade his eyes. The sun was bright overhead and the air thick with late summer heat. He needed a ball cap or sunglasses but those items were in short supply inside the Wall.

"Where are we going?" Shelby asked as she fell into step beside him.

"You'll see," Eli answered easily.

They crossed a wide green lawn and moved beneath a few shady trees. As they left the warehouses behind, people began showing up in greater numbers. There were men and women both, heading to their jobs or out to grab lunch in the cafeteria. Young children screamed and ran on the grass. Bicycles buzzed by, then a few joggers.

Eli's brain absorbed all of these things as the sun warmed the skin of his bare arms and the sickness in his soul began to dissipate.

Beside him, Shelby walked in silence. He knew from experience that she was thinking. He also knew from experience he shouldn't leave her alone with her thoughts for too long. It often ended in another experiment, another attempt at getting him to recall a past he increasingly felt was best left unknown.

"Over here," Eli said, and gestured to a small door located in the side of the massive gleaming metal wall that surrounded this place.

"What's in there?" Shelby asked, but Eli just smiled and pulled the door wide.

Inside, it was cool and dim, with little overhead lights situated every so often. When the door thunked closed behind them, Eli took the lead and headed for a nearby stairwell.

Up, up, up they ascended until Shelby's breath puffed out

into the air, joining the clang of their steps echoing in the enclosed metal space.

When they got to the top, Eli pulled open yet another door and stepped back.

Sunshine flooded the threshold. Shelby hesitated a moment before eventually walking through.

With a sigh, Eli joined her in the open air. They were on the very top of the wall, with the world stretching out in perpetuity all around them.

"It's beautiful," Shelby commented quietly and Eli couldn't help but agree.

Forests and fields unfurled in all directions, stretching to crawl up the sides of great mountains in the not so far distance. The sky was an enormous blue blanket, bright and unyielding in its intensity.

"Not a cloud in the sky," Shelby again, observing, always observing.

"That's not what I wanted to show you," Eli commented and started walking.

There was a narrow catwalk of sorts running along the top rim of the wall. It didn't have railings. It was just a two foot wide flat space you could walk, and every hundred yards or so, there was another door that led back down inside.

Eli moved along effortlessly. Head held high, arms swinging easily.

Heights (apparently) did not bother him, so it took him a little while to realize that Shelby was not the same. It took him a little while to realize that she wasn't trailing behind him.

Rotating around, Eli spied her standing stock still where

he'd left her. She was frozen in time, staring straight down at the ground so very many stories below.

"Shelby," Eli called, and she lifted her head. "You coming?"

"I… um…" Shelby looked up at him and then back down at the ground once more.

When she didn't say anything else, Eli frowned.

"You afraid?" He called.

In answer, Shelby swallowed. After a beat, Eli walked back over to her and bent to peer into her face. She was slightly pale.

"Hey," he coaxed. "Just don't look down."

"That's easier said than done," she huffed, and lifted her eyes to meet his.

"Do you trust me?" He asked and cocked his head to one side. "I won't let you fall, promise."

"That's why they call it an accident," Shelby countered. "You don't mean for it to happen."

Huffing a laugh then, Eli straightened and looked around. The reflection of the sun bouncing off the metal caused the already warm air to heat considerably. Sweat was beginning to collect along his spine and beneath his arms. A cool breeze would be welcome, but so far there was none to be had.

"Just hold my hand," he said. "I swear I won't let you fall. The walkway is two feet wide, if it was a sidewalk on the ground down there, you wouldn't have a problem."

"True." Shelby nodded and pursed her lips.

It was so hard for her to fight against logic. Eli used it against her often.

Turning away from her then, he stuck his hand out behind him and waited. After the count of five, she took it.

Moving slower than usual, he guided her along the rim of

the wall. They walked and walked without saying a word. Her hand was gripped tightly in his… and he found that he loved it. He didn't want to let go. He wanted to keep touching her.

When they arrived at the landing of the next doorway, Eli leaned his back up against the closed door and slid down to sit. Without hesitation, Shelby plunked down beside him. Her body was pressed up against his side, and he flung a long arm around her delicate shoulders.

The landing itself was wider than the walkway by several feet so that when someone opened the door there was room to shift around and close it without falling to your death. Even so, Eli's long legs had his ankles hanging over the edge.

They were facing south-west and so the frame of the door cast their bodies in a swath of shade. Eli inhaled the velvet air and sighed. Shelby shifted against him as her eyes took in the view. He could feel her start to settle. He could feel her starting to relax.

"Were you from there?" Eli asked, and pointed his finger out at the horizon.

"From the West Coast you mean?" Shelby asked.

Eli nodded.

"I know what an ocean looks like, but I don't remember a specific time when I saw one," he said. "Isn't that strange?"

"No." Shelby shook her head. "That's typical of your condition."

"A condition you had too," he qualified.

"Yes."

"When you didn't remember who you were," Eli went on. "Did you make up a past in your mind?"

"What?" Shelby slanted a look at him.

"Like… did you guess about what you were like?" Eli

looked down at her pretty face. "Did you think you were a doctor? Or was it a famous painter? Who were you? Who did you think you were before you found out who you actually were?"

"Oh." Shelby gave her shoulders a slight shrug and huffed a laugh. "I thought maybe I was a writer."

"A writer?" Eli couldn't help but smile. "Why?"

"Well, because I love to read, and I ended up spending so much time in the library. I figured maybe I'd written one of the books there," Shelby offered. "Maybe under a secret pen name or something."

"And when you remembered you were a doctor," Eli prompted. "Did that all go away? The writer part?"

"Yes. I guess it did." Shelby frowned.

"Don't you think that maybe… being a writer, being whatever you thought you were before you remembered, is actually your true self?" Eli's eyes darted over the side of Shelby's face.

Nibbling on her lip, Shelby considered. "I don't know."

"Like that was your natural state," Eli rushed on. "Without the world influencing you and your past and your circumstances… Shelby the writer is who you *really* are."

"Eli…"

"Do you think bad people, evil people, are born that way?" Eli asked, his eyes left her face to drift off to the horizon. "Like… if a bad person were to forget everything they ever did, do you think they'd still be bad? Or would they default to being good?"

"I don't know," Shelby commented. "It would be an interesting experiment."

"Yeah… an experiment," Eli echoed.

*That's all I am to you, a giant fucking scientific experiment.*

"Eli, you weren't a bad person," Shelby ventured. "Cass and I lived together for a long time and we've talked a lot about you since she got her memories back. I can assure you, you were good."

*You're wrong.*

Lifting his right arm, Eli pointed at the thing that he'd brought Shelby all the way up here to see. His finger traced the faraway path of tracks snaking and winding their way towards the Wall. The metal rails crossed with wooden planks appeared to get bigger as they got closer, coming all the way up the metal perimeter before stopping short.

"Whenever I see those," Eli said. "I can smell smoke."

"The train tracks?" Shelby asked, leaning forward and chancing a glance down.

"Yeah." Eli nodded. "I can smell burning."

"Smell association," she commented. "We can try to do more with that."

"What if I don't want to do more?" He asked, swallowing. "What if I just want to live my life from this point on? Don't I have that right? The right to forget?"

"Eli…" Shelby patted at his thigh reassuringly. "I promise, you'll be fine when you remember everything. Perfectly fine."

Pursing his lips, Eli let the conversation die.

*Burning bodies, Shelby.*

*When I look at the tracks of the train, I smell the burning of human fucking bodies. When I remember everything… my chance at a good life will be gone.*

IT'D BEEN A WEEK SINCE SHE'D SEEN HIM.

Lifting her fist to the door, Shelby blew out a long breath before knocking. The tall white door in front of her was a familiar one. She'd been to this particular apartment plenty of times before.

Eli wasn't the only one who lived here, Cass did too. And so the fact that Shelby was standing here waiting for the apartment door to open, shouldn't have made her nervous.

And yet... it did.

Stepping back, Shelby let her arm drop to her side. She glanced down the empty hallway and shifted the strap of her bag on her shoulder.

This past week, Shelby had cancelled all of her appointments with Eli. The reason she'd given him, was that she had other projects that needed her focus, other work she needed to do.

She refused to tell him that their walk along the top of the wall had unnerved her. She refused to admit that sitting so close to him, having their bodies wedged up together, caused all sorts of tingles to dance along her skin. Nope.

She was a professional. She had other duties, other priorities.

After all, it was the source that originally brought her here to further its research in genetic modifications that resulted in disease prevention. And even after everything that had happened, that speciality was still her passion. Preventing disease was still a worthwhile cause.

So this past week, she'd let herself be sucked down the rabbit hole of said research once more. She needed to focus. She needed to gain some professional perspective.

When Eli came to the lab looking for her, Shelby's assistant had sent him away.

Rude? Yes.

Was she sorry? Also, yes.

But it'd given her the time and the space she'd needed in order to settle. Eli was handsome and charismatic, and Shelby was not dumb. She knew that when he remembered exactly who he was, he'd be on to the next woman, and then another after that. She'd seen it before, experienced it before.

There was no need to go getting her heart all smashed up in that nonsense again.

So tonight, she was the one coming to him with her best professional shield in place. She'd brought along a pad of paper, a few pens, and some fresh ideas. There were some new things she wanted to try with his code tattoos.

But when the door opened, Shelby lifted her brow in surprise at the man standing in the threshold.

"Shelby," Cole Tanner said with a smile. "How's it going?"

A chorus of women's voices and the sound of a baby

screaming flowed out from behind him. Frowning, Shelby glanced at the number beside the door once more. 115... she had it right.

"Um..." Shelby managed, and tried to look past him.

"Come on in." Cole stepped aside and made a sweeping gesture with his arm. "They're in the living room."

"They?" Shelby asked.

Sliding past him, she traversed the short entrance hall and stopped short as the room opened up. Three women sat lounging on the blue living room sofa while a chubby baby boy took swaying steps across the thick carpet at their feet.

Shelby smiled then and stepped fully into the room, she recognized them all.

Cass, with her flowing curls and injured leg propped up on the wooden coffee table. Lena, with her bright-blue eyes and raven-black hair. It was her baby boy that was clapping his little hands and falling back to his bottom on the carpet. And Hannah, with her golden hair and Cheshire Cat grin; her hand was propped lazily on her growing belly.

"Shelby!" Cass's face lit and she patted a hand on the arm of the sofa. "Come sit."

"Oh yes!" Lena waved a glass of red wine in the air. "Come join us! It's girls' night!"

"Girls' night?" Shelby arched a brow. That always spelled trouble, and didn't usually involve a baby. "Actually, I was looking for Eli."

"Of course you are." Cass nodded and slid Hannah a knowing look.

Hannah smirked.

"Not like that," Shelby rushed, even as heat flooded her

cheeks. "I have some work I need to catch up on with him. I've been busy this week."

"So I've heard," Cass intoned. "Well, he's not here."

"Oh." Shelby frowned and glanced around, as if Eli would step out at any moment.

"But you could join us." Lena leaned forward and ran a hand gently over her baby's dark hair.

"Yeah you could join them," Cole spoke from behind her. "I'll get you a glass of wine."

Glancing over her shoulder at him, Shelby frowned.

"You're here for girls' night?" She asked and he cracked a grin.

"Wouldn't miss it," he stated easily. "This is where all the best stuff happens anyway. Guys' night sucks."

"Guys' night?" Shelby's eyes narrowed.

"He's lying," Hannah put in. "He'd way rather be out with the guys, but he drew the short straw, so he's stuck."

"I drew the short straw on purpose." Cole flashed a wicked grin and retreated to the kitchen. "Plus, I'm on baby watch."

"The baby isn't due for another few months," Hannah pointed out. "You're hovering."

"So?" Cole shot Shelby a wink.

On the floor, Ian began to gurgle and fuss. He clapped his hands together a few times before dropping to all fours and starting to cry.

Pursing her lips, Lena began looking for a place to set her half-empty glass of wine. Shelby's heart softened.

"Oh, I'll play with him," she offered.

Slipping her bag off her shoulder, Shelby got down on all fours too and began crawling over to the him.

Immediately, Ian stilled. His big brown eyes blinked at the

strange woman entering his space and for a moment, he forgot about his crying. Shelby's red curls bobbled down in front of her face as she moved. Knowing that was part of his interest, she gave her head a little shake.

When she got close to him, Shelby rocked back onto her own butt and folded her legs beneath her. There was a collection of wooden toys strewn about, and so she busied herself gathering them close.

Deliberately, she placed some brightly painted square blocks on top of each other until they formed a tantalizing tower.

Ian's body bobbled then, as he balanced himself. For now, he was thinking and watching. Shelby continued to stack the blocks, higher and higher still, until Ian simply couldn't resist. Slowly, he crawled towards her.

"Oh, hey Ian," Shelby cooed and set one red block directly in front of his chubby hands on the carpet.

Instantly, his mighty fist came down on it and he batted it to the side. Shelby made an approving sound, and then delivered him another. He swatted the second one even more quickly than the first, and she repeated the game.

"You're hired Shelby," Lena announced suddenly. "Seriously, tell Uri you are no longer under his employ. You belong to me and the baby."

Laughing, Shelby glanced up at the three women gawking down at her, then shrugged.

"They're fascinating," she admitted. "The way their brains grow during this time, it truly is a wonder of science."

"What's a wonder of science is how anyone can go this long without sleep," Lena chuckled and then sipped at her glass. "But I wouldn't change it," she added quickly, and nodded to Hannah. "It's hard to explain, the love, it makes everything worth it."

"No, it's fine." Hannah waved her off. "I think I get it."

"Oh, you'll get it," Lena mumbled. "Boy, will you get it."

"Alright," Cole cut in. "Maybe I should've gone with the guys after all. Shelby can be on baby watch."

"Too late now." Cass shifted on the couch. "Their little experiment is well under way, and besides, who else will get us more popcorn? We can't make Shelby our slave, she's one of us."

"More popcorn?" Cole blew out a breath. "How can you want more? I've made three batches already."

"Wait." Shelby interrupted, her hand stilling as she clutched a yellow block. "What little experiment?"

Biting at her lower lip now, Cass glanced over at Hannah who pointed to Cole.

"It was his idea," she accused and had Shelby glancing over her shoulder at the handsome man.

"Alcohol." Cole lifted a shoulder. "You've been neck deep in your research this week, and Uriah was getting impatient. I figured maybe a little drinking would help loosen things up for Eli."

Shelby's brow hit her hairline then, and she dropped the block. Ian squealed in delight.

"You're getting Eli drunk," she said slowly. "Without consulting me?"

At that, Cole outright grinned.

"You can still observe," he pointed out. "But you'll have to hustle. He and Liam have been at it for a few hours now. If you hadn't noticed, it's past nine o'clock."

With a huff of indignation, Shelby shoved up off the floor and crossed over to where Cole was standing.

Initially, they'd worked together on Eli's tattoos because Cole had some informal training with Command Code. The actual project of recovering Eli's memory however, had been assigned solely to her, and she resented not being consulted. This was her work, her job, and she wasn't about to let Cole and Liam interfere.

"I don't appreciate you inserting yourself into my project," she accused and fisted both hands on her hips. "It might not seem like it from the outside, but all of the work I do with Eli has an affect on his brain development. Maybe you and your buddy need to step back and leave the heavy lifting to the person best suited to the task... the *trained* scientist."

Spreading his arms out wide, Cole looked past her at the other women in the room. His face was much too relaxed for a man getting dressed down, in Shelby's opinion.

"My bad," he said. "Won't happen again."

The other women murmured and chuckled. Shelby's jaw ticked.

"Better not," she grumbled, and spun away from him.

Grabbing her bag off the floor, Shelby swung it over her shoulder and gave the girls on the sofa a nod. Ian began to fuss. Lena groaned.

"Go get em' Shelby!" Hannah called.

"They're at the Rec Center," Cass added. "Oh... I'm sure you'll get more out of Eli if you let him buy you a drink."

"Hmph." Shelby threw a hand up over her head in salute and headed for the front door. "Thanks."

## CHAPTER SEVEN_
## ELI

Bringing the amber-colored bottle to his lips, Eli sipped... slowly. His eyes were locked on Liam, who was doing the same.

All round them, the strings of an electric guitar vibrated through the air. The live band rocking on the far end of the crowded room was loud and good. The male singer's voice had this raspy, haunting quality to it. When you paired it with the beat of the drums and the swing of the bass, it sent an excited sort of tension straight to your heart.

Everyone else in the auditorium could feel that same sort of buzzing, Eli was certain. Hundreds of people were dancing and laughing and shouting at each other, in an effort to be heard over the demands of the song.

Eli could be one of them, he thought, if not for the task at hand.

"It works better if you don't drink it like a little bitch," Liam commented, his back was leaned up against a long bar, his legs crossed casually at the ankle.

Liam (as always) was the picture of predatory cool. Blue

jeans. White t-shirt. Lace-up boots. His dark eyes seemed to glide over the room, not really zeroing in on any one particular thing, before coming back to Eli with a bored sort of gleam.

Behind him, bartenders ran back and forth between waiting customers and ice chests filled with bottles of beer and wine.

"I'm drinking the same as you," Eli pointed out and grinned.

Bringing the bottle up to his lips once more, Eli took what appeared to be a generous swig. In reality, he let the beer wash over his lips before sliding right back where it came from.

Liam rolled his eyes and followed suit. Whether he actually drank from the bottle or not wasn't something Eli could tell. They'd been playing this slow sort of cat and mouse game with each other for several hours now and were about six beers deep each.

The original object here had been to get drunk fast. Think, direct injection of alcohol to the brain, as much as possible, to get things moving so to speak. Cole had suggested it, and Liam had pushed it, and so Eli could do nothing but follow along.

But the thing was... Eli *knew* about alcohol. Instinctively, he was aware that it took away your self-control. And despite the fact he'd been trying to drag this thing out, he could feel it working, loosening his muscles and warming him from the inside out.

Which kindled the darkness.

The drifting gray voices of memories that he absolutely did not want to recall... were flitting about at the edge of his consciousness now. He didn't want to let them forward. He didn't want to hear them speak or smell the smells or see the sights.

He just wanted to be free and innocent... like he was before.

He just wanted to ditch Liam and get lost in the crowd, maybe find a certain redhead who'd been avoiding him for the past seven days (not that he'd been counting).

"It's a shame there's no whiskey left," Liam commented. "That would hurry this crap along."

"You in a rush?" Eli's brow arched in question but he knew perfectly well the answer.

Liam would much rather be at home with his woman, then here waiting for Eli to get shit-faced and suddenly remember all about his tattoos.

"Hello gentlemen," a female voice entered their space and had both men looking down.

A pretty girl stood between them, one hand propped on her hip and the other stretched out to brace against the nearby bar. Eli cocked his head to one side as his eyes noted the closeness between them, maybe a few inches at the most.

"Care to buy me a drink?" She asked and flashed a confident smile.

Eli took her in, cataloguing her features carefully, but only in such a way as to compare them to Shelby. He didn't mean to do it, but at this point, he couldn't seem to help himself.

This woman was curvy, where Shelby was petite. This woman had smooth caramel skin, where Shelby's was pale and covered in a million tiny freckles. This woman had a sweep of thick dark hair, where Shelby's was all red curls.

This woman was alluring, and her confidence made her even more so. But alas, she wasn't the Good Doc that had so taken over Eli's mind, and so his chest deflated just a little bit.

Disappointment. What was it about the human race that made you want something you couldn't have?

"I'm married." Liam wiggled the ring finger of his left hand and nodded at Eli. "But he's not."

"Lucky girl," the woman sighed and turned her attention fully to Eli. "Are you two brothers? You look so much alike."

Eli's face screwed up and he gave his head a little shake.

"No," he replied and huffed a laugh. "We're not related."

"Oh." The woman cocked her head to one side and batted her extra long eyelashes at him. "Coulda' fooled me. So how about that drink?"

"Um." Eli gaped a moment. In the background, he heard Liam clear his throat.

"I don't have any money," Eli managed finally and swallowed.

"He's a charity case," Liam offered. "No job, just a freeloader."

The woman laughed and Eli frowned.

"Hey," he protested, even though it was basically true.

Grumbling, Eli was about to remove the crumpled bills that his sister had given him from his pocket and go ahead and buy the lady a drink, but just then... up stormed Doctor Shelby Sullivan in all her angry glory.

Eli froze, his hand still stuffed into his back pocket, and gaped.

Her perfect pixie face was all flushed, her chin was tipped up, and those brilliant blue eyes of hers were bursting with angry daggers.

Liam straightened, Eli stepped back, and the woman

they'd been talking to glanced over her shoulder.

"These belong to you?" She asked and gestured at the two men.

"In a strange sort of way…" Shelby locked eyes with Liam first before pivoting to Eli. "They do."

"Well then, they're all yours." The woman bowed her head graciously and sauntered off into the crowd. She would have no problem getting that drink, Eli was certain.

Folding her arms over her chest now, Shelby took the spot the woman had vacated. Eli's eyes dropped down to her toes and then did a quick sweep up her body, all the way back to her face. She was so damn beautiful, with those tight blue jeans and a loose black top that slipped off one shoulder before tucking in at her waist.

He couldn't help the look of appreciation that took over his face. She was flame itself, he thought, the way she made him burn.

"What's this I hear about an experiment?" Shelby accused, her gaze leveling once more on Liam. "Last I checked, you weren't a scientist."

"This isn't an experiment," Liam countered and lifted his beer. "This is two guys out on the town. Want a drink?"

"Is that so?" Shelby rocked back and huffed a laugh. "You expect me to believe that nonsense? I've heard all about it… from your *wife*."

Liam's mouth twitched then, and his dark eyes narrowed.

"She's got you there," Eli chuckled and ran a hand back casually through his hair. That is, until Shelby turned her fury in his direction.

"What?" He asked with a shrug.

"*What?*" Shelby seethed. "The question is *what* are you

doing agreeing to this without consulting me? This is *my* project!"

Eli's gut sank and his heart kicked at him unhappily. Project. He was her *project*. In the background, he heard Liam let loose a low whistle.

"Right," Eli spat the word out of his mouth, his tongue tasted sour all of a sudden. "I'm a *project* to you. Something to test and poke and observe."

Bringing the bottle of half-drunk beer to his lips, Eli slugged it down. Seeking to cover the unwelcome taste that had gathered in his mouth.

Liam nodded his head then as if in agreement, and did the same.

"Another?" He asked, smacking his lips together.

"Yeah," Eli confirmed. *What the hell.*

His heart was pounding and his chest was growing tight. Stepping into Shelby's space, Eli let his chest bump against her shoulder as he set his empty beer bottle down on the bar top. She was so tiny compared to him, that he was looking down on the very top of her head.

Inhaling, he took in the scent of her, despite himself.

Candy. She smelled like cotton fucking candy and he wanted to lick every last inch of her. But she didn't feel the same. She wasn't jealous over that girl or pissed that he was drinking without her. She was upset because he was an experiment to her and Liam was screwing with her results.

When Eli stepped back, he let his eyes do one last sweep of her body before forcing himself to look away.

His lungs were squeezing in smaller now and his lips automatically turned down. Fuck it. Guess he was getting drunk tonight after all. Come what may.

## CHAPTER EIGHT_
SHELBY

She hadn't meant to chastise them publicly. That was not in her original plan. She knew it was embarrassing, and making a scene wasn't something she normally did.

No. She intended on finding them and putting a quiet stop to their drinking.

If they were going to try to jog Eli's memory using alcohol, then it was best done in a controlled setting. She needed to document how much he consumed and over what length of time. It would be helpful to monitor his vitals as well, especially if the alcohol worked. How could you duplicate a process if you didn't understand it properly?

But then she'd walked into the auditorium and seen the two of them.

Being so tall, they weren't hard to spot. The unexpected part had been the woman wedged between them. The mysterious brunette was sexy and dynamic and everything Shelby was not. And seeing Eli smiling down at the pretty woman, is what had Shelby losing her cool.

It wasn't a proud moment.

But now the woman was gone, and Eli was upset. Liam kept ordering beer after beer and an awkward sort of uncomfortable feeling settled in the air. Shelby regretted her actions, and she regretted seeing Eli with the other woman even more.

"Another two!" Liam called to one of the bartenders, before slapping paper bills on the sticky bar top.

Eli chugged at his beer. His eyes were hot, but aimed away from her, over the crowd. He refused to meet Shelby's gaze, even when it was clear she wanted to talk to him. That fact alone had her stomach churning, though she didn't know why.

"How many have you had so far?" She asked finally, raising her voice to be heard over the music.

Eli continued to ignore her.

Shelby pursed her lips.

Liam eyed her for several silent moments. "That one he's got will make eight," he said finally.

"Over what period of time?" Shelby shifted her bag and pulled out a small pad of paper and a pen.

Eli swung his eyes over to her then, and scowled. His lips thinned and his nostrils flared.

After a beat, Liam smiled. Like he actually, genuinely smiled. It was the first time Shelby had witnessed it, and it had her mouth dropping.

"About four hours," he answered, then flicked his dark eyes over to Eli and shot the guy a wink.

Eli's chest rumbled then, before he thrust his now empty bottle of beer straight into Liam's chest. The other man laughed as he grabbed the bottle and set it easily behind him on the bar. Liam never smiled, Shelby noted, and he never laughed.

The effects of alcohol were impossible to fight. This just might work.

Swallowing, Shelby clicked the end of her pen and began to scribble notes. Her right elbow stuck out as she balanced the small pad of paper awkwardly in the palm of her left hand. Eli's chest bumped against her arm then and she could literally feel him take a breath. Her palm grew sweaty and her tongue darted out to wet her lips.

"All the same type of alcohol?" She asked, refusing to glance up at him.

"Yup." Liam was the one to answer.

Shelby cleared her throat, but Eli did not step back. His eyes lingered on her skin. She could almost feel it like a caress against her neck. Shelby's pulse spiked and heat gathered in her core. So much for a professional demeanor, it was all she could do not to pant.

A bar tender came over then and set down two freshly opened bottles of beer. Liam accepted them both in his large hands while the barkeep scooped up the paper money and shoved the bills into the front pocket of his small black apron.

"What are the ounces on those bottles?" Shelby attempted to focus, as Liam passed one over to Eli.

Leaning down into her space, Eli lifted the bottle to his full lips and sipped. Shelby's eyes darted up to his face quickly and then away once more, back down to her paper. The words she'd been about to write disappeared from her mind. Instead, her eyes closed and she breathed him in. She could smell the masculine scent of his skin, it was mixed now with beer and soap.

"Did you bring a breathalyzer with you *Officer*?" Eli

rumbled. "Would you like me to blow in that next? Maybe draw my blood too?"

Hmmm, Shelby thought. That would be an excellent idea, if they had a breathalyzer somewhere within the Wall, which she wasn't sure if they did. Her brows drew together as she tried to assess the possibilities now leaping into her mind. She could standardize everything in her lab. From the amount of alcohol consumed to the length of time between drinks, then monitor with blood draws and a breathalyzer to compare results.

"Wait... how'd you know that?" Liam's voice cut the air, and had Shelby glancing over at him. "About the breathalyzer, and that a police officer would be the one to use it?"

Straightening slowly, Eli rose to his full height and squared his shoulders. He brought the bottle of beer lazily to his mouth and sucked down more of its dark bubbly contents. Liam stared and Shelby stared. Behind Eli, the band let loose a guitar solo that had the entire place bursting with energy and sound.

"Eli..." Liam warned. His voice was barely audible now over the music.

With an arrogant shrug, Eli lowered the bottle from his lips. He brought his left hand up to his head and tapped a single finger against his temple.

"Don't know!" He called out, before shooting Shelby a hot look. "This game sucks. I'm not playing anymore."

Shelby's brow rose and she glanced between the two men. But before Liam could say anything more, Eli was turning on his heel and stalking off through the crowd.

"Where are you going?!" Shelby called, but he didn't stop

and he didn't turn around. "Where's he going?" Shelby gave her question to Liam, who sighed.

"You've got a good memory, yeah?" Liam asked.

Shelby nodded.

"Probably a photographic one," Liam continued, and again Shelby nodded. "Then put away the pen and paper. Go after him and remember what he says, instead of writing it all down. No more scientific type questions, got it? You're just a chick and he's just a guy."

"But…"

"*You've* just gotta listen," Liam insisted and stepped closer. "He just wants you to listen, like you give a crap about him as more than one of your lab rats. Understood?"

"Okay." Shelby blew out a long breath and stuffed her pen and paper back into her bag. Her hands were shaking slightly, but she hid it. "Are you sure he wants me to follow him? He seems pretty mad."

"Oh yeah." Liam shot her a dubious look. "He wants you to follow. Trust me."

Straightening slowly, Shelby smoothed her hands down the front of her blouse. Her palms were slick and a fresh burst of nerves erupted like butterflies in her bloodstream. Adjusting the bag on her shoulder, she had to rise up on her tiptoes to search for Eli in the crowd.

"In fact," Liam cut in and stripped the bag from her. "I'll hold onto this for you."

"But…"

"Trust me," Liam insisted, and looped the bag over his own shoulder. "I'm good at holding a purse."

Opening her mouth, Shelby was about to protest when Liam cut her off.

"Better go," he said and gestured to the dance floor. "Before he finishes that beer and finds another redhead. It won't be the same, but at this point he may not care."

"What?" Shelby's face twisted, but Liam shooed her away.

With a growl of frustration, she stomped off in the direction he'd indicated.

People were packed in tight, their bodies swaying and bouncing to the music. Men and women moved together, in pairs or in large groups. Laughter and raised voices fought together to be heard as the band's singer stepped up to the microphone and belted lyrics that apparently everyone knew.

Shelby was soon swallowed up.

She couldn't see past the people in front of her. Her hands came up as she weaved through the bodies, forced to sway and jump along to the beat. People came up and brushed against her unintentionally. They were dancing and laughing and smiling. Shelby nodded her head and nibbled at her lower lip.

Then all of sudden, Eli was there. He was stepping into her space and she stopped short.

"Good Doc!" He shouted above the crowd, he no longer held a beer. "Where's your notebook?!"

"I left it!" Shelby called back, rocking up to her tiptoes to get closer to him.

Eli bent his head down, lowering his ear so that her lips were only an inch away.

"What?" He asked again, his hands came out to steady her hips as the people all around kept dancing and jostling them.

"I left it!" Shelby repeated.

Pulling his face away just far enough to look directly into her face, Eli studied her.

"You come to dance?" He asked finally.

Shelby's heart beat harder and she swallowed. They were the only two people standing still in a sea of bodies that wouldn't stop moving. Even the air seemed to vibrate, and the floor beneath their feet.

Glancing around quickly, Shelby's nerves tried to work their way up into her throat. Eli's hands were still on her hips and his face was a breath away from hers. If she wanted to, she could lean in ever so slightly and kiss him.

"Yeah," she answered finally, her breath coming out short. "I want to dance."

"Alright." Eli straightened and drew her body flush up against his. "Let's dance."

For that, Shelby had no response.

Her hands flattened against his broad chest, and he began moving them to the music. Their bodies pressed and rubbed together. One of his hands cruised to her lower back, the other reached up to take one of her hands in his.

Shelby's lips parted slightly, but no words came out.

The beat was fast and Eli moved her effortlessly. He created space between them, spun her in a tiny circle, then brought her back up against him. Everywhere his hands went, her body tingled and heated. She became hyper-aware of every single movement, every brush of his body against hers.

They didn't talk.

The music was too loud, and Shelby found suddenly she had absolutely nothing to say. Her mind emptied of everything except Eli, of everything except the smell of him so close and the way his muscles moved beneath her touch.

When she glanced up into his face, her eyes widened. Eli was watching her, his sparkly hazel eyes were intense.

Huffing out a breath, Shelby had to look away. Her stomach flipped and his grip on her tightened.

The band transitioned to another song. People shifted around them, backs bumping into other backs lightly. Laughter. Sweat. No one seemed to mind. No one seemed to care.

Eli didn't stop and he didn't let go. His hold on her was firm, but not tight. The way he moved against her was intoxicating. If Shelby didn't know better, she'd of thought herself the drunk one and not him.

Leaning down suddenly, Eli framed her face in both of his large hands. Her hair was a tangle of red curls and he frowned at her a moment.

Bringing his mouth over to the side of her face, his lips brushed the shell of her ear as he spoke. "Don't let me kiss you," he said.

Instantly, Shelby's cheeks burned red. Her tummy flipped as something coiled deep inside of her.

"What?" She gasped the word.

"I want to kiss you," Eli said and then pulled back slightly to look into her face. "But I've been drinking too much. I can't tell if it's the right move. So don't let me."

Shelby managed a feeble nod before Eli shot her a wicked grin. It sent a shock wave through her. She wanted him to kiss her. There was no denying it now, she just did.

Straightening then, Eli took her hand and spun her around before pulling her back up against him. The music blasted on and on. Their dance continued. Shelby ached... and she wondered about the aching.

She wanted to ask him a million questions just then. She wanted to drag Eli out into the quiet, sit him down and stare into his face. But Liam told her she was just supposed to listen. He'd been very clear on that part, and so Shelby kept her mouth shut and she waited.

And she danced.

And she waited some more.

But for all the listening she was prepared to do… Eli didn't do anymore talking, or any kissing for that matter.

CHAPTER NINE_
ELI

IT WAS THE SAME DREAM EVERY TIME HE HAD IT, BUT THE
alcohol coursing through his system made it worse, more real,
more intense. Eli tossed uncomfortably in his bed. His mind
leapt and stuttered. It wanted to show him more, further,
longer, and this time… he wasn't able to hold it back.

So more is what he got.

*The Jeep rolled down the open road. Its tires hummed against the
black asphalt highway. The sound was all his brain could fixate on,
the humming. The sky overhead was turning dusky now and the
radio crackled with empty static.*

*The driver (Ricky? Ronnie?) had stopped talking awhile ago.
Maybe he'd grown tired of Eli's inability to answer. Maybe he'd
grown tired of Eli's vacant stare. But as the light all around them
waned, something changed. The driver shifted in his seat, and
reached to tune the radio.*

*Eli wondered what the point was. Radio stations had stopped* working months ago. So many of the towers were abandoned. So many more had burned.

"I don't blame you," the driver said suddenly.

Eli gave his head a little shake and met the man's bland brown eyes briefly in the rearview mirror.

"That's why you aren't in cuffs," Ricky/Ronnie continued. "If I could just let you go here, then I would."

Looking down at his hands, Eli rotated them palms down so he could stare at the blood spatter once more.

Let him go? It was the first time Eli had thought about what they were doing together in this Jeep. After the train... well... he'd ceased thinking for awhile.

This solider had shown up, stuffed Eli in the back of the Jeep and they'd started driving. It was just the two of them.

"I still can't get over how you managed it though," the guy huffed and pursed his lips.

"How I did what?" Eli lifted his eyes and stared at the back of Ricky/Ronnie's head.

"How you defied orders. How you went against protocol. You aren't supposed to be able to do that. I gotta know... how did you do it? Didn't it hurt?"

"Hurt?" Eli's brows drew together and his mind rolled through all the death in those train cars. Everything about it fucking hurt. Everything.

The smell and the sounds. The people screaming. The pop of bullets. Then the soldiers all around him screaming. The cry of human death was a distinct sound all its own. A man's voice echoing in terror through the rubber of a gas mask was haunting.

Eli's stomach rolled slowly inside of him and his throat ached. If he'd of had anything in his belly, he was sure at that moment it all *would've come up. In a sense, he wished he could puke everywhere. He wished he could vomit it all out.*

*"Yeah man," the solider went on. His hands rested comfortably on the steering wheel as the Jeep kept cruising the empty highway. "The chip in your hand. It should have fucking stopped you. It stops the rest of us cold."*

*"Chip?" Eli's face screwed up in confusion.*

*Ricky/Ronnie lifted his own right hand from the steering wheel and waved it in the air. The sleeve of his shirt slipped down just enough to reveal a tangle of black tattoos. Squares. Dots. Dashes. Lines. So permanent and distinct.*

*"Unless you don't fucking have one," the guy stated suddenly. "Do you?"*

*His brown eyes jumped to the rearview mirror, then darted back to the roadway. His hand went to the radio and switched it off. Eli sucked in a breath as his heart reminded him he was still in fact living, and that despite his brain's agony, his body wanted to continue to do so.*

*Eli's gaze darted to his rifle, still resting beside him. He was out of ammo. He'd pulled that trigger and reloaded until there hadn't been a bullet left to fire within a mile of that train station.*

*"Will you send help?" Eli asked quietly. "To the rest of the people. The ones that survived?"*

*Ricky/Ronnie's eyes shut briefly and the Jeep did a little jog to the left. But just as quickly as they swerved, Ricky/Ronnie opened his eyes again and guided them gently to the center of their lane. Although seeing as there were no other vehicles around, it wasn't technically necessary. They could've driven on the opposite side and never encountered a car.*

*"They're already dead, bro," the guy answered. "I was sent to*

collect you, and the replacement crew should've arrived after I picked you up. By now they've taken care of everyone. I'm sorry."

"Fuck," Eli spat the word as his chest heaved. "Why? Why the fuck are you doing this?"

"I don't know," the guy shook his head. "They're sick. They're contagious and dying. We've got to eliminate them before they spread it."

"Spread what?" Eli leaned forward in his seat, his voice strained. "What the fuck is happening?"

"How did you even get on that crew?" Ricky/Ronnie asked. "No chip. No tattoos. Nothing. How did you get on it?"

Flopping back in his seat, Eli ran both hands down the front of his face. "My sister was put on one of those trains," he whispered. "I'm trying to find her. I just walked the tracks until I found a station."

"Ah. Fuck." Ricky/Ronnie dipped his head. "I'm sorry. You look like a soldier with the uniform and everything. I just figured..."

"I was one." Eli blew out a sick breath. "South-West Side."

"That's good." Ricky/Ronnie licked his lips. "Keep with that then, and maybe you should forget everything else."

"Forget?" Eli frowned. "I don't understand..."

"You want to find your sister? If she's still alive?"

"Well... yeah." Eli sat up straight, his brain focusing again for the first time in hours.

"Then I'm gonna pull us over and knock you the fuck out." Ricky/Ronnie began to slow the vehicle, his foot pressed down on the brake and the two men rocked forward. "And when you come to with a nice big shiner, you're gonna forget everything that happened on that train. Alright? If anyone asks you a question, you're gonna stare at them like you're a dumb piece of shit."

"But..."

"And when they give you the tattoos and they inject you with the chip, then you're gonna do everything they tell you to do," Ricky/Ronnie cut him off, his eyes boring into Eli's.

"How can I find my sister?" Eli licked his lips, they were so chapped and dry.

"You'll have to figure it out yourself," Ricky/Ronnie stated and hesitated before continuing, "You know she's probably already dead, right?"

Bringing the Jeep to a complete stop, the guy shifted into park and turned around in his seat. Eli's mouth parted and his heart tapped hard against his ribcage.

"And you're going to forget we had this conversation. In fact, you're going to forget you know my name."

Nodding, Eli fought against the dread building within his system.

"That won't be a problem," Eli assured him.

He'd do anything. He'd do anything at all if it gave him the slightest chance of finding Cass.

Holding perfectly still, Eli held his breath as the driver pulled out his pistol. Keeping his eyes wide, he didn't flinch as the guy flipped it around and slammed the butt end as hard as he could into the side of Eli's head.

CHAPTER TEN_
SHELBY

HER BLACK HIGH HEELS CLICKED ACROSS THE CEMENT FLOORING in the lab. She was the only one working right now. She had the place to herself. But still, the ridiculously female sound had Shelby second guessing her life choices.

She usually wore sneakers. When you work on your feet all day, measuring, testing, pursuing results, heels were the absolute last thing you wanted to wear.

But today was different. She'd slipped into a dress, put her white lab coat on over it and then stepped into *the* sexiest pair of shoes she had.

Ridiculous? Why, yes. Because she was a professional woman for gosh sakes and she knew better than to let one night of dancing distract her.

But still… it had been two weeks since she'd last seen Eli.

You'd think after such a long time she'd have stopped thinking about him. The sad truth was that if she were to shut her eyes right now, she could feel his hands on her hips, his smell in her nose, his words coming out in whispers against the shell of her ear.

With a growl, Shelby rolled her shoulders and tapped her way over to her pad of paper. Flipping through the pages, she jotted down a few notes.

It was unprofessional of her to entertain thoughts of her patient/project in a romantic way.

"You're better than this," Shelby muttered to herself.

Pushing back from her notes, Shelby spun and assessed the space. In the center of the room, there were two long counters running parallel to each other. Typically thcy were covered in open text books, note pads, microscopes and various other technical equipment. But not today.

For the past two weeks, she'd been researching and then drafting protocols for a new experiment in olfactory and its impact on memory. She'd gathered scents for Eli to smell in an effort to see if they triggered his brain into recalling specific events in his past.

On the countertops were carefully spaced and sealed glass jars. Each one contained a different scent. She didn't want his sight or preconceived notions about the scent to influence the experiment and so she wrapped each jar with thick black paper. In addition, she planned on blindfolding her subject.

Now said subject just had to show up.

Looking up at the wall, Shelby frowned at the old-style analog clock. Two black hands ticked away the time against a round white face. Two thirty-five. He was late.

Just then the silver door handle dipped and the door to her lab swung wide. In walked almost six and a half feet of masculine beauty. There. She said it. Or thought it. Or whatever.

"Hey Doc." Eli flashed his signature grin before entering the space. "Sorry I'm late."

"Oh, you are?" Shelby huffed a fake laugh and looked away. "I didn't realize." *Stop.*

Walking over to one of her jars, she adjusted its position on the counter unnecessarily. The door clicked shut of its own accord and Eli's footsteps strolled slowly over to her across the floor. Why was it she could suddenly sense him coming? Her body primed, just like on the dance floor, anticipating heat and touch and tingles.

Drumming her fingers against the glass jar a moment, Shelby swallowed before she smoothed at her lab coat.

"You seem taller," Eli commented and came to a stop beside her.

Shelby straightened and shoved her hands into the front pockets of her coat.

"I do?" She feigned ignorance once again and immediately hated her choice in shoes.

"Yeah." Eli gave her a once over and then tilted his head to the side. "It's the heels. I've never seen you in heels."

"Oh well..." Shelby stared down at her own feet like a complete idiot. "I have plans later, so..."

"You do?" Eli's bright face darkened, and he took a step closer. "Like a dinner date or something?"

"Yup." Shelby's mouth popped on the *p* sound. *No! I'm lying so I don't have to admit that I wore these for you!* "Shall we get started?"

"I guess," Eli grumbled.

His tall frame kicked to one side as he folded those extra long arms of his over his chest. His hip leaned against the counter, and his plump lips pursed together.

Turning away, Shelby blew out a silent breath and picked up the blindfold.

"What's that?" Eli asked.

"A blindfold," Shelby stated confidently, and rotated back to offer it to him.

An amused expression transformed Eli's face and his hazel eyes began to sparkle.

"What game are we playing today, Doc?" He asked. "Do you have some handcuffs back there too? Maybe a bit of rope?"

Stopping short, Shelby's cheeks burst with red heat and her neck flushed pink.

"I… ah… no," she sputtered. "No, I do not."

"You sure?" Eli pushed off the counter and stalked towards her. There was a cocky set to his shoulders and she couldn't help but notice the rough stubble gracing his jawline. "I won't tell anyone… if that's what you're into. Promise."

"Eli…" Shelby held up both her hands and sucked in a breath. Her body was zinging as she pressed her thighs together. "This is a serious experiment, okay? So… be… be serious."

Biting at that impossibly full bottom lip of his, Eli came to a stop directly in front of her and stared down. His short brown curls fell onto his forehead and he brushed them back without so much as a thought.

Even with the high heels, Shelby's head was only level with his chest. She had to tilt her chin up to meet his gaze. But the gesture itself helped to remind her of who was supposed to be in charge here. One thing was for certain, it absolutely could not be him.

"Don't give me that look." Eli reached out and played with the ends of her hair. "I'm only teasing."

"Fine." Shelby exhaled. "Then let's get down to business.

Let me put this on you and we can begin. I'll be leading you to each jar where I will open it and then let you smell the contents. I want you to tell me anything that comes to your mind, anything at all."

"Oh God." Eli chuckled and took the blindfold from her hands. "Tell me one of these jars isn't filled with shit."

"Eli!" Shelby laughed as all the tension fled her body.

"Well?" Eli tied the blindfold around his own head carefully and then reached his hands out towards her. "I'm all yours Doc."

CHAPTER ELEVEN_
ELI


THE BLINDFOLD COMPLICATED MATTERS. IT WAS MADE OF THICK black cloth and Eli couldn't see through it at all. Around the edges, of course, light filtered in. But for all intents and purposes he couldn't see his hand if he held it up in front of his face.

Which was the point, he supposed, of Shelby's experiment.

She was going to have him smell things, and then document if a memory leapt forward. Only… Eli was going to have to lie about that last part. After the alcohol induced dream from a few weeks ago, there was no way in hell he was going to tell the truth.

So he would have to work really hard not to pass out.

The gray grainy voices were already on the outskirts of his consciousness, just begging to be set free. It was a daily battle now, with him fighting against the tide of violence and despair he knew was coming.

Reaching out, Eli braced himself against the counter. His shoulders tightened and he dropped his head. Eliminating his sight and replacing it with darkness seemed to weaken his ability to ward them off. The memories. He hated them.

"Oh, are you alright?" Shelby's delicate hand came out to wrap his forearm, sending a hit of desire coursing through his system.

Eli grabbed ahold of the feelings she brought on. The heat. The curling in his body. Wanting her was like the slow winding of a spring, all aching tension and anticipation. His heart thumped heavily in his chest and the awful memories were pushed quickly away.

"Just hard to balance," he lied and cracked a grin. "Without being able to see."

"It can be disorienting." Shelby's other hand came out to brace his lower back. "But I'll be right here and we can stop anytime you need."

*I don't want to stop with you. I only ever want more.*

"Sounds good," Eli answered and absorbed her closeness.

Without the benefit of sight, his other senses began to sharpen. He could feel the press of her body so close to his, smell the scent of her skin and unruly hair. He wanted to inhale *her*, instead of whatever she'd cooked up in these jars.

"Alright just take a few steps to your left," Shelby coaxed.

Her hands urged him to move and Eli complied. When her grip tightened, he came to a stop. He was beginning to like this game, she had to always be touching him. But then her hands dropped away and he heard the clink of a glass jar being opened.

"I'll hold it just beneath your nose," she said. "And you breathe in."

Eli pursed his lips and did as she asked.

"Strawberries." He huffed a laugh.

He listened as she set the glass jar back on the counter with a pop and then shuffled through a pad of paper. That notorious blue pen of hers clicked and he could almost visualize her frowning. She got this adorable little bump right between her eyes when she wrote, and it made him want to press his thumb there, to ease her tension. He could think of a million other ways he could ease her tension.

"What comes to mind?" She asked. "Tell me everything."

Smirking, Eli did as she asked.

"I see myself feeding strawberries to you," he said honestly. *Blush for me baby, I wish I could see.* "They're ripe and sweet. After you take a bite of one, I see the juice on your lips. Makes me want to lick the taste off of you..."

"Okay, stop." Shelby exhaled a harsh breath. The shocked little sound made Eli's insides jump and his smile even broader. "That's not what I meant and you know it. You need to take this seriously Elijah."

"Oooo using the full name now?" He lifted a brow and caused the blindfold to shift slightly against his face. He still couldn't see anything, but the sound of his full name on her lips made the strawberry fantasy intensify.

"This is important," Shelby reminded him.

The pen clicked and he heard the snap of the notepad being placed roughly down on the counter. The sound of a lid being replaced on the glass jar was next, followed by a few extra huffy noises from the Good Doc. He wanted to laugh out loud now, but he knew better.

Then her hands came back to his body and she was urging him to scoot down another step. Eli's tongue snuck out to wet his lips as he complied.

"Alright," Shelby announced. "Let's try that again, but serious this time. Okay? Agreed?"

"Yes Ma'am." Eli sniffed and rolled his shoulders. "Let's do it."

Placing his palms flat on the countertop, he drummed his fingers as the sound pattern repeated. Shelby opened a glass jar and held it up to him. Eli inhaled.

"Grass," he said. "It's green."

"And what else…" Shelby's pen clicked in anticipation.

"Rolling lawns, outdoors, a picnic," he rattled off thoughts as they came to him. "You know… we should have a picnic or something. Would you like that? Maybe instead of this mysterious date of yours tonight, you could have dinner with me."

"Eli…" Shelby warned.

"Who is he?" Eli frowned suddenly as he remembered her high heels and the way her sexy as hell legs disappeared beneath her lab coat. She had shorts on under there or maybe even a dress. He detested the idea of her dressing up for anyone else.

"Look, Eli…"

"Do I know him?" His frown deepened as his brain worked through the possibilities.

He'd been avoiding her after the dance because of his memories, but she hadn't sought him out either. He'd tried not to let it bother him. After all, he was clearly a bad man, and he'd done awful things in his past. He didn't deserve Shelby and he didn't want to put her at risk. She was good and tenacious and smart and pretty.

Eli had been determined that he was going to let the idea of her and him getting together go, but now…

The thought that some other fucker was going to have her

instead, was going to touch her instead, was going to kiss her instead, had his blood positively heating. His fingers gripped against the counter and his jaw clenched down tight.

"You don't know him, there is no *him*." Shelby sighed. "It's a girls' night out, okay? So just stop playing around now and focus. Please. This is serious. My work is serious."

The pen began scribbling ferociously against the paper again and then the lid to a glass jar was clinking and all the typical busy background noises were sounding, but they were nothing compared to the flood of relief that overtook him. Girls' night out? Hell. Yes. He could get behind that. In fact... he was going to have to crash that party, if at all possible.

Eli let loose a long breath then, and tipped his face up towards the ceiling. He could feel the warmth of the lights shining down on him and the darkness of the blindfold lifted just a bit.

"Alright, next jar," Shelby grumbled.

Her hands came out to guide him again and Eli relaxed beneath her touch. He took another step to the side. His hands slid along the cool countertop before she brought him to a stop.

"I take your work seriously," he said.

"Yeah, I can see that," Shelby countered.

"No really, I do," he insisted.

He had to smooth over the ripples he'd just caused when that spike of jealousy hit him. He needed her happy again if he was ever going to make his move and actually take her out to dinner.

Which he now decided he should definitely do. He hadn't remembered all his badness just yet. Maybe he could stop things here and be good from now on. Plus, it was better that

Eli be with her, rather than some other schmuck. What if this other guy was an asshole? Eli didn't think he could stand for that.

But then Shelby was opening the jar and holding it under his nose. Eli inhaled like a good little boy.

"Smoke," he managed, as his breath fled him. "Burning."

*Fuck.*

All around him, the gray voices rushed forward. Churning. Racing. Impossible to stop.

Eli's knees buckled. A split second later and he felt the impact of the counter against his head... but vaguely. His lungs were seizing. He tried to take in oxygen, but futilely so. He gasped for air. He was sucked under.

*The smoke was getting thick now, laying low in the surrounding streets, making it hard to breathe, making it hard to see.*

*Stumbling a few feet forward, Eli collapsed to his hands and knees on the yellowed lawn and threw up. His arms were shaking as his stomach punched up into his throat. Again. Then again.*

*Behind him, he felt Garrett approaching. He could sense his friend. He could hear him calling out to him, but the words he said were jumbled in Eli's mind.*

*Cass. His sister. His only real family. The little kid he'd taken care of night after night, day after day, for as long as he could remember, was dead. She'd been taken from him, ripped away and delivered to the devil, by his best friend. By Garrett Jameson.*

*"How could you?" Eli rasped the question. His throat burned from the vomit as his sickness gave way to white hot rage.*

*"I loaded her on the train myself, I made sure it was safe."*

*Garrett was kneeling beside him now. "I swear she's safer now than either you or I could make her."*

*"Fuck. You." Eli spat the words as he sucked in air. His head was clearing. His muscles were beginning to burn as his hands clenched into fists in the grass. "Those trains go nowhere. Everyone on those trains dies. I've seen it myself. I've buried the bodies."*

*"Wha... what?" Garrett shook his head. "That's not... no."*

*Sitting up, Eli wiped the leftover puke from his lips and looked Garrett square in the eye. "Did you hurt her first?"*

*Garrett's mouth dropped and he huffed a half-indignant breath.*

*But Eli had known the man long enough. And he'd known the teenage boy version before that. Guilt. Avoidance. There was something here, and it had Eli's whole body priming.*

*"Look me in the eye, and tell me that you've never crossed the line with my sister," Eli demanded. "Look at me and tell me you've never laid a finger on her."*

*"Eli... I..." Garrett's blue eyes popped up and locked with Eli's hazel ones.*

*There.*

*It was all right there for anyone who wanted to see. Garrett had crossed that line. He'd done everything that guy from across the street said he had.*

*Eli lost it.*

*He was on top of his old buddy before he even knew what he was doing. His fists rained down on Garrett's face. His legs straddled Garrett's body.*

*Over and over, he drilled the guy into the ground. Blood began to spray. It was coming from Garrett's face and covering Eli's fists.*

*He kept swinging down until his arms grew weary from slamming into Garrett's face and his breath started coming out short.*

*Eli's hands slipped down around Garrett's throat then, and began to squeeze.*

*Automatically, he applied pressure. Eli's thumbs dug into the soft flesh of Garrett's neck, until the guy's eyes were bulging and his body was twisting and writhing beneath him.*

Eli's eyes popped open, but he couldn't see. His body was contorted on the ground and Shelby was calling to him. He began to twist and gasp. His hands clawed at the blindfold, trying to rip it off... but then the voices were coming for him again and his eyes rolled back in his head... and he gone.

*"What." Eli stepped into the space and slammed the door behind him. "The fuck. Neal."*

*"Hey now, Eli boy." Neal puffed up his chest and turned to him. The short fucker had to look up. "You may have grown a few inches the past year or so, but that don't mean you can talk to me like that."*

*"Oh yeah?" Eli's eyes shot to Cass, then back to Neal. "Get in the bathroom Cass."*

*"I..." Cass's mouth dropped and she began to shake.*

*"Bathroom, Cass." Eli shucked his backpack on the floor, followed by his duffle bag full of football gear. "Now."*

*Ducking her head, Cass did as she was told. She slipped into the tiny bathroom and locked the door behind her.*

*"You put your filthy fucking hands on my sister?" Eli's chest heaved with hatred. "She's twelve you sick fuck."*

*"Hey," Neal's voice grew cocky. "She came after me."*

*"Yeah, right," Eli sneered. Cass was young and innocent and he was damn sure going to keep her that way, or die trying.*

*Stalking forward, Eli felt his shoulders square and his chest* expand with the rapid beat of his heart. The sound of his wet sneakers squeaking along the worn linoleum floor of their shitty apartment echoed in the tiny space.

"You need to go," Eli growled. "Get your shit and get the fuck out. I don't wanna ever catch you back here again."

"Nah, boy," Neal countered. "Your mama still owes me for tonight. She ain't paid, yet."

"I said get out," Eli spat, his stomach twisted with the sick thought of his mother and what she kept doing to herself. "You're not getting that kind of payment anymore, not from her and definitely not from my sister."

"Oh, you wanna step up to me, boy?" Neal chuckled and had Eli's hands balling into fists "You may have a bit of height to ya, but you're scrawny as hell. Back up Junior, before you hurt yourself."

Eli's jaw clenched and he kept on coming, and his body kept on priming. He was six foot two already and stronger than he looked, but Neal was right, he was skinny and underweight, mainly because he didn't get enough to eat.

"Leave, old man," Eli hissed.

"I'm gonna come back for my payment," Neal countered. "You can't watch that little sister of yours all the time. Hell, maybe I'll have 'em both. Huh? What do ya think about that?"

That's when the first hit came, Eli didn't even think about it. His right arm cocked back and swung down automatically. Almost instantly, he felt the sweet impact of his fist against Neal's face ripple up his wrist and arm. The smack of flesh echoed in the ugly apartment, along with a satisfying grunt of pain as Neal stumbled back a few steps.

Eli hesitated then, for just the tiniest of seconds. His lungs sucked in air and he felt the flood of power and need to crush this disgusting person into dust.

*That's when Neal's eyes narrowed, and he charged.*

*Eli met him halfway, already swinging, already grunting. Neal landed a couple blows, but it was like Eli couldn't really feel it, he couldn't feel any pain. He was immune. Time rushed forward.*

*Neal tackled him and all of a sudden, they were on the ground, rolling and struggling.*

*Neal was on top. Then Eli. Then Neal again.*

*That's when the first wave of pain broke through Eli's barrier of adrenaline. His left eye started to swell shut and his nose dripped with blood. He was scrambling back until he came up hard against the bathroom door. Eli's head impacted the thin wood and Neal pounced.*

*Gripping Eli's hair, Neal slammed his head back against the door, over and over.*

*Eli's chest heaved as he tried to wedge his arms up between them. Eli was the only barrier between this ugly piece of trash and his baby sister. He was the only thing keeping her safe in this world.*

*And that was it.*

*Eli lost it.*

*Sucking in a breath, his entire body bucked and he switched their positions. Wrapping his hands around Neal's slimy throat, Eli held on.*

*Neal's eyes widened. His legs kicked out and his fingers scratched channels into Eli's cheeks.*

*Pressing down as hard as he could, Eli ignored the pain and dug his thumbs deep into Neal's windpipe.*

*Slowly.*

*Ever so slowly.*

*Eli watched the other man turn red, then purple... then blue. He felt Neal's body buck and wriggle beneath him. Felt Neal's arms weaken and those fingers of his drop to claw uselessly at Eli's arms.*

*In the end, he was covered in scratches and blood. But it didn't matter.*

*Eli didn't stop.*

*He didn't let go until Neal's arms flopped out uselessly to the floor and his eyes got that glassy vacant stare. Even then, he didn't really want to let go.*

*"Eli?!" Cass screeched his name, and it was like a shock to the system.*

*Eli inhaled and rocked back onto his butt.*

*The back of Neal's lifeless head hit the bathroom door a final time before lolling to one side.*

*"Eli!" Cass screamed again. "Eli! Answer me!"*

*Eli drew his knees to his chest then as a wave of nausea hit him. He hung his head and tried not to puke. He'd just killed a man.*

*"Eli," Cass's voice wavered then, she was so damn scared.*

*"Yeah, Cass." Eli sucked in air between his words. "I'm here."*

*"Oh thank God."*

*Eli listened to her flip the lock on the door handle and pull it open.*

*"Don't. Look." Eli panted. He didn't raise his head. "Just get back in the bathroom." Coughing, he shook his head. "I'll take care of this."*

*"Eli..."*

*"Just stay where I put you!" Eli screamed the words now, his face still tilted towards the floor.*

*He listened as Cass retreated into the bathroom and shut the door once more. Then she flipped the lock. It had his heart aching. He'd done this. He'd fucked up so bad. She was scared of him now too.*

*"When I tell you to stay," Eli managed finally. "Just. Stay. I will always come for you, Cass. Always."*

"ELI?" SHELBY LIFTED ONE EYELID AND STUDIED HIS PUPIL. "Come back to me now. It's time to come back Eli."

He was crumpled on the floor of her lab. His large body was wedged awkwardly against the cabinets. She tried to straighten him as best she could, but he was heavy and only a minute before he'd been thrashing around wildly.

She ripped the blindfold off of him, but by then, he'd already passed out. Shelby's hand dropped to his wrist now, and she timed his pulse. It was steady and strong. His breathing was even and good.

There was no doubt in her mind that he was having memory recurrence. No doubt whatsoever.

"Eli?" Shelby spoke again, willing him to come back to consciousness.

Unlike his, her own heartbeat was pounding way too fast. She could feel her pulse hammering up in her throat, causing her breathing to strain. Forcing a slow exhale, she briefly closed her eyes.

Before the war, she would have called for help. She would have pulled a cell phone from her pocket and dialed 911.

Even after the war, and before the fall of the source, she would have been able to use a tablet to contact the hospital within the Wall. That wouldn't have been necessary of course, the source was always watching. It would have sent help before Eli's head impacted the countertop on his way to the floor.

But there were no electronics to assist her now. She didn't even have one of the handheld radios. They were in too short a supply, needing batteries and charging and all of that.

Sucking in a breath suddenly, Eli's head flopped to one side. His brows pulled down and his face twisted.

"I killed him," he said. "I killed him."

Shelby's lips pursed and her hands rushed to grab his. He was twisting again, his legs kicking out and his heavy body shifting.

"You're alright," Shelby said, leaning down to peer into his face. "You're alright, Eli. Come on now. Come back."

And in that moment, he did.

Eli's glittery hazel eyes flew open and locked onto her face. His hands grabbed ahold of hers and he squeezed.

"Shelby?" He asked.

"Yes." She nodded and blew out a shaky breath. "Yes, I'm here. You fell."

"What?" Eli frowned.

"You fell," she repeated and forced what she hoped was a reassuring smile to appear on her face. "We're in my lab. Remember?"

For several silent seconds, Eli simply stared. His eyes

darted over her face and his hands clutched tightly onto hers. Shelby's breath stopped dead in her lungs.

But then Eli was shutting his eyes and letting loose a low groan. His hands broke free and he reached up to rub at the side of his head. Another large lump, the second one in a month, was already forming.

"It's just a contusion," she said and held herself back from running her hands through his hair again. "You aren't bleeding. There's no laceration."

"Mmm." Eli's lips pressed together as his hand found the spot and pressed too hard.

"Don't do that," Shelby admonished.

Grabbing for him, she took his hand in both of hers and brought it down to rest on his chest. Eli's eyes opened then and he looked at her once more. His gaze was soft and speculative, his breathing was calm.

Shelby glanced away. She couldn't help the heat that came to tinge her cheeks.

She was worried for him. She was worried about that hit to his head. She was guilty because this was all her fault. She should've kept him seated the entire time and brought the jars to him to smell, instead of keeping him standing.

"Hey," Eli exhaled the word as his hand came up to brush at her face.

Tracing a single finger slowly down the side of her cheek, Eli forced her to look at him.

"I'm sorry," she managed. "I shouldn't have had you standing. It was…"

"It's fine," Eli cut her off.

His finger lingered against her skin. His eyes dropped to her lips. Shelby's insides summersaulted.

"You had a memory," she blurted, causing him to frown.

"I didn't remember anything," he countered and dropped his hand from her face.

"Elijah…" Shelby tried, but he was already maneuvering his body to sit up. "No, just stay lying down for awhile. You might pass out again."

"I'm not going to pass out," he said.

His hands braced against the floor. His knees came up and his body twisted. Shelby was forced to scoot back. Her palms came to rest on her thighs as she sat and stared.

*I killed him.* Eli's words echoed in her mind.

"Eli, you can tell me anything," she tried. "You know that right? You can trust me."

Refusing to look at her, Eli's jaw clenched and his nostrils flared. In another two seconds he was shoving up to standing.

Shelby remained kneeling on the floor. Her heart was pounding and her mind was scrambling. He was having memory recurrence. She knew that for a fact now. He showed all the signs, and today he'd been triggered by the smell of smoke.

Leaning back against the counter, Eli cocked his head to one side. His fingers gripped the countertop behind him and his face attempted that same old cocky grin he always wore. Except now, Shelby saw the strain in it.

"I do trust you," he lied straight to her face, and had her chest aching. "I'm sorry Doc, but I just don't remember anything."

Ducking her head, Shelby swallowed. Her damp palms wiped along her lab coat before she too struggled to stand. Her bare knees were dusty from the ground and her high heels caused her ankles to throb.

"Alright, Eli." Shelby's eyes traveled over the remaining eighteen jars that she'd so carefully prepared.

An impartial scientist would have him keep going.

An impartial scientist would document everything that had just happened, then sit him down in a chair, and continue to present him with each and every other scent, hoping for another trigger.

But there in lied the real problem didn't it?

Shelby's mouth drew down and she fought against the feeling coursing through her system. She fought... and she lost.

"Looks like we should stop here then," she said finally. "I guess the olfactory triggers don't work."

## CHAPTER THIRTEEN_
SHELBY

"HE'S READY FOR YOU NOW."

Shelby stood from the plastic chair in the hallway and crossed to the door of Uriah Linfield's office.

Replacing the old-style black telephone on its receiver, the receptionist rose from behind her wooden desk and smiled. Her bob of brown hair dipped as she gestured for Shelby to open the door herself.

Swallowing, Shelby did just that.

Commander Linfield was already standing when she entered the space. He was positioned behind his wide wooden desk, a single unadorned window at his back. With a nod, he indicated for her to take the seat opposite him. His golden hair, so like his sister's, was cut short. His brown eyes glittered with intelligence.

"Please," he said, and brushed at the front of his button-down gray shirt. "Sit."

Nodding, Shelby complied. Her hands came out to grip the arms of the chair impulsively before she rearranged them in her lap.

Glancing quickly around the room, she noted its vacant-ness. There was only the one window and absolutely no artwork or color of any kind on the walls. The space was utilitarian, like the Commander himself, save for one glaring exception.

Books. He had shelves and shelves filled to overflowing with books.

Shelby itched to touch them. She itched to get up and run her fingers over their spines, listing the titles in her head before pulling out one or two for closer examination. But that wasn't to be. The Commander drew her attention over to him with a gently cleared throat.

"I've read your latest report," he said, and settled back into his oversized leather office chair.

"Yes," Shelby replied, because she had no other response.

"It seems you've been unable to make headway with Mr. Roe," he continued, steepling his fingers and frowning slightly.

Sitting straight in her chair, Shelby's mouth firmed as her belly dipped.

"It is rare for memory recurrence to resume so quickly after a chip is removed," she stated. "I warned you of this when we first began."

"I know." Uriah sighed and dropped his hands to his desk. "It's just… I hate putting peoples' lives at risk. Especially when we have the answers sitting right here, waiting to be released."

"Eli has participated in a number of experiments," Shelby reminded him. "Just because he isn't able to remember anything right now, doesn't mean he won't in the future. We need to give him more time."

"Time," Uriah repeated the word before huffing a small

breath. "The thing is Doctor, I have men out there right now running a mission that could result in some of them dying. What's worse, I'm running this mission blind. I don't really know what we're up against.

We could be bringing attention to ourselves in the worst possible way right now, exposing the Wall and all of its thousands of inhabitants to whoever controls the men with the tattoos… the men like Elijah Roe."

"I'm doing all that I can."

"I'm sure you are." Uriah leaned forward then, his chocolate-brown eyes boring into hers. "Because if you weren't, then *you'd* be the one putting all these children's lives in danger. If you were holding back in any way, then you'd be the one responsible."

Shelby's jaw clenched down tight and her chin tipped up. She wanted to eliminate the quaking of her heart, but it had a mind of its own these days.

"Liam tells me that Mr. Roe showed up with a fresh bump on his head recently," Uriah stated. His brow rose and he tilted his head slightly to one side. His eyes never left Shelby's face.

"I could examine it," she deflected, and kept her features plain.

"When questioned, Mr. Roe stated that he fell while in the shower," Uriah went on. "That he slipped in some extra soap."

Shelby's fingers flexed involuntarily in her lap. She gave no answer.

Drumming his fingers against the desk, Uriah pursed his lips.

"You know what, Doctor?" Uriah asked finally.

"What?" Shelby gave the obligatory response.

"I don't believe him. I think he passed out again, just like when he heard that recording of himself."

"We were both there," Shelby pointed out. "He didn't remember anything."

"He *says* he doesn't remember," Uriah countered, then eased back into his seat. "But I think he does, or at the very least that he's remembering some things."

Spreading out her hands, Shelby gave an exasperated huff. "I have no way of…"

"I need you to get him to talk," Uriah cut her off. "He likes you, we all know that, we've all seen that."

"But…"

"I need you to get him to confide in you," Uriah went on. "For the sake of all of us. You took an oath."

"Yes, I did take an oath…"

"Then you need to put the children first, the community first," Uriah resumed, his eyes burning like a laser straight into her soul. "Do I have your word on that? As a doctor? That you will protect our children? The last of the world's children?"

Swallowing, Shelby fought the flood of heat that took over her skin. The flush swept up her chest, into her neck and cheeks. He was asking her to sacrifice the trust of one man, for the sake of thousands of others.

"You have my word," she agreed, and hated herself.

Pushing slowly up to standing, Uriah reached a hand across the desk towards her.

Staring at it a moment, Shelby swallowed. Her eyes flicked from his hand to his face, then back. But in the end, Shelby leaned forward and clasped it tightly in her own.

LYING BACK ON THE BLUE COUCH IN HIS SISTER'S APARTMENT, Eli tucked one arm behind his head. Cass was in the kitchen, limping her way back and forth between the refrigerator and the counter. She was determined to bake something... anything... and Eli was content to watch.

He knew now just how rare this experience was.

This apartment was clean. There was no drug addict mother slumped at the rickety kitchen table. There was no drug dealer junkie waiting to put his hands all over her.

Cass was safe, and for now, so was he.

"I'm thinking sugar cookies," his sister announced, and fisted one hand on her hip. "I have all the ingredients for that, and according to this book, the recipe should be easy."

"Sounds good," Eli grunted.

When Cass shot him a dubious look, Eli cracked a grin, just for her.

"I can do this," she told him and nodded her head.

"I'm sure you can," he agreed and watched her smile.

When she turned her back on him, and started rummaging around for bowls and spoons and such, Eli let his face fall.

Was I too late that day? He wondered. Did Neal ever hurt you before? What about after, did I ever fail? Was there a time I didn't protect you?

The questions swamped him and his lungs heaved inside his chest a moment.

There was pain intertwined with the benefit of memories. He had a better appreciation for this particular day now. He could take the time to relish this safe apartment and happy sister. But on the other hand, the anguish of not knowing the rest of the story was haunting him.

He'd killed a man with his bare hands.

And yes, the asshole had damn sure deserved it. But Eli was only fourteen years old at the time. He got that tiny snippet of information, the flashback of the killing, and not much else.

He was aware though, in a way he hadn't been before. He knew about his awful mother. He realized that Cass was more like a daughter to him than a sister, because of their mother's neglect.

"Ah!" Cass straightened and plopped a ceramic bowl on the counter. "Found it."

"Yay!" Eli teased, and had her outright laughing.

"You're an ass, you know that?" She commented.

"I know," he agreed and sighed.

Shifting on the couch, Eli watched quietly for several minutes. Cass wandered around, muttering to herself and adding ingredients to the bowl.

Firming his lips, he thought about the other memory that had come to him with the smell of smoke. He'd tried to kill

Garrett. And the only reason he knew he hadn't succeeded was because he'd seen Garrett with his own eyes, not so very long ago.

In that moment, he wanted to ask Cass about it. But at the same time, he knew he couldn't.

*I tried to kill Garrett because I thought he hurt you the way Neal tried to.*

*But clearly... he didn't.*

*Because he loves you and you love him.*

*So how did that happen? How did you two come to be together, without me there?*

*Why am I covered in tattoos and Garrett is not? How did we get separated? Who the hell am I?*

If he got up and went to his sister right now, if he sat on one of the barstools at the center island, and asked her all the questions zooming through his brain, then she would know he was getting his memories back. That knowledge would put her at risk. Eli wasn't ready to tell anyone, which meant Cass would have to lie. Eli felt that was simply too dangerous. It was too dangerous for them both.

If anyone ever questioned Cass, Eli wanted her to be able to say she didn't know anything. He wanted her to be protected by ignorance.

Letting loose a low sigh, Eli adjusted the pillow behind his head and let his body sink further into the comfortable cushions of the sofa.

On the outskirts of his mind, the gray voices fluttered. They were like tiny soft butterflies this time... memories... wanting to come forward.

Exhaling, Eli weighed the cost of allowing them to surface. He wanted to know more. He wanted to remember more.

If he just closed his eyes briefly, could he control it? If he just relaxed right here and let his sister think he was taking a nap, could he wake up quietly? With no one the wiser?

"Now you're going to have to tell me honestly," Cass was saying. "If they're good or not."

"I'll tell you," Eli assured her and closed his eyes.

## CHAPTER FIFTEEN_
SHELBY

THE SUN BEAT DOWN ON HER SHOULDERS, WARMING THE BARE
skin of her arms and face. Shelby walked along the winding
cement path on her way to the gym. She didn't normally work
out, and that wasn't her plan for today either.

Yes, she was wearing shorts and a tank top and sneakers,
but that was only because it was the height of summer and she
couldn't bear the heat otherwise.

Glancing down, she studied her arms and legs. Other
people tan in the sun, but she only seemed to produce more
freckles.

With a sigh, Shelby dismissed the thought and tipped her
chin up. She'd already tried Eli's apartment and no one had
been home. He wasn't at the cafeteria having lunch and he
wasn't in the dress shop where Cass made clothes (neither
was Cass for that matter).

Tucking an errant red curl behind one ear, Shelby
trudged on.

At this point, she'd hiked all over the Wall with no luck.
Her feet ached and her tummy was rumbling for some lunch

of her own. Looking on the bright side, she was certain that she'd far exceeded her exercise criteria for the day.

A part of her longed to grab a quick snack and retreat to the coolness of her lab, but alas, Commander Linfield was watching her closely now and she had to make some sort of effort to work with Eli on his memories.

Shifting the bag on her shoulder, Shelby crested the stone steps that led to the gym and pulled open the glass double doors. Cass sometimes had physical therapy here, so Shelby figured she may as well give it a search too, before calling it a day.

Nose wrinkling, Shelby stepped fully inside.

The place was packed with sweaty people and blasting music. Machines clinked and whirred. People panted and groaned.

"It's hot," Shelby muttered to herself. She'd forgotten there was no air conditioning in this building.

Taking a few moments to survey the space, her eyes traveled over spin bikes, treadmills and weights. Places like this inside the Wall were almost surreal. It was like stepping into a time warp that slingshotted you back before the war. It was just so… normal, or it had been, once upon a time.

"Shelby!" A familiar voice called her name and had Shelby looking to her left.

"Cass," Shelby exhaled in relief. Her search was over, maybe.

Weaving her way through the gym, Shelby skirted around equipment and crossed a large blue mat. Cass was standing beside an elevated boxing ring with a crowd of other people. It didn't take Shelby long to figure out why.

In the center of the ring, stood two men. Both were tall,

with bronze skin, dark hair and broad shoulders. Shelby's mouth dropped as she took them in.

They wore nothing but gym shorts, headgear and gloves as they sweated and circled one another. All she saw were slick muscles, long limbs and narrowed eyes.

"What are they doing?" Shelby stopped beside Cass and stared.

"Um… isn't is obvious?" Cass bumped her shoulder playfully against Shelby's. "Their fighting."

"But why?" Shelby continued to gape, she couldn't help it.

Liam was circling Eli slowly, his hands raised, his eyes intent.

Eli stood in the center of the ring, rocking ever so slightly on the balls of his feet. His body appeared relaxed, and yet the muscles in his shoulders tensed and rippled.

Shelby's eyes dropped along his arms and chest before coming to rest on the defined flat of his stomach.

She'd never seen him with his shirt off before, and well… he was certainly a sight to see. Her body warmed and tingled in response, forcing her to fidget on her feet.

"They're testing him," Cass explained. "To see what training he's had, and hoping that maybe it will jog his memory too."

"Oh." Shelby swallowed.

And that's when it began.

Liam lunged forward, quick as anything. His right arm came swinging for the left side of Eli's head.

Shelby sucked in a breath and jumped back, as if she were the one about to be hit. Beside her, Cass shouted and stepped closer to the ring.

"Take him down!" Cass called, along with half a dozen other people. "Take him to the mat!"

Shelby's hand went to her throat and her breath caught in her lungs. She didn't know if Eli actually heard his sister's screeching or not, but in any event he didn't seem to need it.

Fainting back, he dodged the blow easily.

Liam's momentum brought him forward and his fist swiped at open air. That's when Eli changed directions.

Stepping into his opponent's space, Eli grabbed the back of Liam's neck and pulled him closer. His eyes were dark and focused, his lips turned down in a grim line.

Every movement was fast. Her eyes widened, trying to take it all in.

Eli's knee came up and drilled the side of Liam's ribcage. Shelby heard the heavy thump of impact and the answering grunt of pain.

Liam wrapped his arms around Eli's waist and their legs tangled together. They both went down quick in a twisting, punching, ball of limbs.

"Get his arm!" Cass was gripping the ropes of the ring now and screaming. "That's it! Don't let him on top!"

Other people crowded into the space, jostling and jockeying to get closer. Shelby was shuffled to the side and then back. She danced up on her tiptoes as the shouts kept coming and the sound of fists impacting flesh continued.

"He fights dirty," someone commented.

"He fights to win," another answered.

"Enough of this," Shelby growled.

Lowering her shoulder, she shoved her way through. When the ring came into view once more, Eli was on top of

Liam. The two men were locked together, still straining and wrestling as hard as they could.

"Tap!" Cass screamed. "Tap Liam! He's got you!"

Shelby's eyes widened. Eli had Liam's arm bent at an awful angle. Sweat poured down both their faces. Their chests heaved and their eyes were equally dark.

"He's lifting his hip!" Cass again, right beside her.

In that instant, Liam broke free. He worked his arm out from Eli's grip and the two men were rolling once more.

Shelby's eyes were fixed then, she couldn't look away if she tried.

In the corner of the ring, Cole Tanner stepped forward and clapped his hands. "Fucking go!" He yelled.

Liam scrambled to his feet and Eli was soon following.

The two circled each other once more. Chests heaving. Eyes smoldering.

Liam lanced forward, landing a blow to Eli's chest.

The crowd cheered. Cass booed.

Rocking back, Eli absorbed the hit and then dove for Liam's knees. He ducked low just as Liam slammed a heavy fist into the back of Eli's head, but then Eli was lifting Liam's entire body up in the air.

Slam.

They impacted the mat hard, Liam on his back, Eli on top.

The shock wave had the entire ring shaking. Shelby stepped forward this time instead of back. She spread her palms flat on the floor of the boxing ring and held her breath.

Eli was facing her, but looking down. She could see his eyes clearly as he stared hard at Liam who was pinned on his back. The later was bucking his hips and throwing punch after punch into Eli's side.

But it was like Eli didn't even feel it. He bore down, his thick gloved hands coming to Liam's neck where they fumbled a moment before pressing hard against his throat… harder.

"Can you do that?" Shelby whispered.

"No… yes…" Cass stammered. "There are no rules here. There are no rules anymore."

Eli's eyes grew fixed and glassy. His shoulders were taut and his arms locked straight.

Liam was slamming his fists over and over into Eli's ribs as his face began to turn red. But it was like Eli couldn't feel any of it, couldn't see any of it. He didn't grunt in pain, he didn't shift or react.

"Alright!" Cole announced and stepped forward. "I'm calling it!"

A chorus of boos and cheers erupted from the people standing all around. Cass attempted to climb into the ring before stopping short and grabbing at her leg. Clearly, she'd forgotten it was still hurt.

Shelby glanced between her former roommate and Eli.

He wasn't stopping.

Liam's gloved hands were at his own throat now, trying to shove Eli away. Shelby's eyes narrowed. Eli's face was ashen, all the color had drained from it. But then Cole was stomping over and ripping him off.

Eli landed on his side on the ground and Liam sat up, laughing.

"I need my knife," he panted, and then grinned up at Cole who rolled his eyes.

"He's too fast for you," Cole observed.

"Fuck that." Liam shoved up to standing and paced away. "Let's go again."

As the two of them stalked to the corner, Eli sat back on his haunches and gave his head a slight shake. His chest was heaving as sweat dripped from the end of his nose and chin. His tussle of short brown curls fell wet and slick to stick on his forehead.

He was pale and shaking, then he glanced up.

His eyes came straight to Shelby, and locked on.

That's when she knew.

Her belly clenched and she watched him swallow hard. The color was just now coming back to his cheeks, which had been gray only moments before.

He'd been about to pass out, she realized. He'd been about to succumb to another memory.

"Again Eli," Cole tossed the words over his shoulder. "Best three out of five."

Eli's hazel eyes widened just a touch. His gloved hands were braced against his thighs. He was still kneeling on the ground where they'd left him, his bare chest working to draw in air.

Shelby's heart lurched inside of her and she shoved up into the boxing ring. Ducking between the ropes, she heard Cass protesting behind her, but she didn't stop and she didn't look back.

Eli was rocking up onto his feet now. His gaze switching nervously between her and the men off to his left.

"Excuse me," Shelby announced and had both Cole and Liam turning. "What do you boys think you're doing?"

"Ah..." Cole's face screwed up in confusion, but beside him, Liam smirked.

"I'm getting more than a little bit tired of your interference," she continued, and came to a stop beside Eli.

"We aren't interfering." Cole huffed a light laugh. "We're training."

"Not anymore you're not." Shelby fisted one hand on her hip and cocked her head.

Liam's smirk turned to an eyebrow raise. Cole's mouth dropped slightly.

"I've been looking everywhere for Eli," Shelby stated and gestured vaguely at the man himself. "He's late for an appointment with me."

"He is?" Cole frowned.

"Is he?" Liam asked, the corner of his mouth twitching slightly.

"Yes, he is." Shelby doubled down, her blue eyes drilling a hole straight into Liam's forehead

Beside her, Eli ducked his head. "I'm really sorry I forgot," he said, and rubbed at the back of his neck. "My bad."

Folding his arms over his chest, Liam rocked back on his heels and lifted his chin. "I bet you are," he commented.

"Can't it wait?" Cole spread his arms out, gesturing to the gym at large. "We're kind of in the middle of something."

"Are you implying that my time is worth less than yours Officer Tanner?" Shelby's voice lowered as she leaned in. "Because I'm getting really sick of the two of you undermining me."

"We haven't…" Cole shook his head. "We aren't…"

"You have," Shelby insisted. "And you are. First with the drinking and now trying to jog his memory with fighting. By the time you two idiots are done pounding on him, it could be a year or more before his brain recovers enough to restore memory."

"Alright. Alright." Cole brought his palms up between them. "He's all yours."

"Thank you." Shelby flashed them a triumphant smile before turning to Eli. "Don't make me search for you again."

"I won't." Eli's eyes darted over her face. "Let me get cleaned up, then we can go."

With a short nod, Shelby kept herself from releasing a long breath. She couldn't let anyone see the nerves bundled inside of her. She couldn't let Liam, of all people, see the lies written all over her face.

"I'll wait outside," she announced with a sniff, and rolled her shoulders. "It stinks in here."

At that, Eli attempted a tentative smile.

CHAPTER SIXTEEN_
ELI

She saved him. There was no appointment. And Liam knew it.

Holding out his hands, Eli knew better than to avoid the gaze of his sparing partner. While Cole began working Eli's gloves off, Liam stood beside him, staring intently into Eli's face.

Shelby was already leaving. He could feel the slap of her confident feet against the floor of the boxing ring. She'd done her part, and now she would wait for him outside.

Lifting his chin slightly, Eli forced a cocky grin.

"She's chasing you now?" Cole asked, yanking first one glove off and then the other.

Dropping his arms, Eli shrugged and turned away from them. At his back, he could feel two sets of eyes studying him.

The crowd around the boxing ring began to dissipate and his eyes locked onto the bounce of Shelby's red hair as she pushed her way to the double front doors and out into the sunshine.

She'd come at just the right time. He was lucky for once.

"You should've pinned him sooner," Cass stated, as Eli climbed out of the ring and jumped down beside her. "You let him work loose."

Giving his head a slight shake, Eli looped a sweaty arm around his sister's shoulders. Cass tried to shrink away but he held on tight and forced the two of them to walk towards the locker rooms together.

"Yuck." Cass made a face. "You're gross. Get off me."

"Ah, but Sis…" Eli huffed a laugh as his mind and body regained control of themselves. "I love you."

Coming to a dead stop, Cass rotated to face him. Eli's easy expression fell as he looked down into her searching eyes.

"You…" Cass stumbled over her words a bit. "You've never said that to me before."

"I haven't?" Eli frowned.

How could that be? He'd felt it so strongly in his memories. He loved his sister. She was the only family he had.

"No." Cass shook her head slowly. "I mean… I know you did, but it just wasn't something we ever said."

"I'm sorry." Eli reached out and grabbed her chin. "I should've said it before. Because you're my sister and I do."

"I do too." Cass sniffed and then gave him a shove. "But not now, 'cause you're trying to get your stink all over me."

Laughing, Eli let her step out of his reach.

"Where are you going?" He asked.

"To the shop," she answered easily. "You don't have to follow me everywhere I go. I don't need a babysitter here Eli, we're safe."

Fighting the pinch of worry that tickled in his gut, Eli nodded. From what he was remembering, he knew that to be true. Inside the Wall, she was safe.

"Alright," he relented and turned away from her.

Entering the men's locker room, Eli shucked off his gear and grabbed a quick shower. A million thoughts zoomed through his head but he worked to clear them all away.

He'd allowed a few snippets of memory through when he was hanging with Cass the other day, but they'd all been focused around their childhood together. He remembered high school and Garrett and football.

But today, grappling with Liam in that ring, a hundred other violent voices had rung in his ears.

They'd wanted to come forward. They'd wanted to take him over and plunge him into the past.

And for a good long time, he'd been able to resist. But in the end, when he'd had Liam on his back and Eli's hands had found the guy's neck... he'd almost come undone. The gray voices had been so loud.

So. Damn. Loud.

Rubbing soap all over his body now, Eli watched the bubbly suds cover up those fucking tattoos.

He wished like hell he didn't have them. He wished like hell he could peel them off and start over. He wanted a life here, a *real* life. But the truth was... he couldn't have one. The memories were just too demanding, they wouldn't let him be.

By the time he was done and dressed, Eli's stomach was growling.

Pushing out of the gym, he stepped into the bright sunlight and sighed. Shelby was just off to his left, leaning against the wall of the building, her body tucked into a sliver of shade.

"Doc," he said, and smiled. "You hungry?"

Those blue eyes studied him as she kicked off the side of the building. Her mouth parted slightly and, as always, it looked like she had about a hundred things to say.

Eli waited for her at the top of the stone steps, his body priming for her, even when he didn't want it to.

"Yes," she said finally and surprised him. "I could eat."

Lifting his brow, Eli was washed with relief and also a bit of interest. She wasn't going to grill him just yet *and* she was agreeing to lunch. This was new.

In his mind, that made the next few hours into a sort of date.

Offering her his arm, he grinned.

Rolling her eyes, Shelby placed her hand in the crook of his elbow and allowed him to lead her down the stairs. He fucking loved every single second she touched him.

When they got to the bottom and began to walk along the sidewalk, her hand dropped to her side. He felt the absence of her immediately. He didn't like it.

"So, what's our appointment about?" He asked, and shoved his hands into the pockets of his shorts.

Glancing up into his face briefly, Shelby nibbled at her bottom lip. Eli's eyes dropped to her mouth and his stomach tightened. Quickly, Shelby looked away.

"You and I both know we didn't have an appointment today," she admitted quietly.

"But you *were* looking for me," he pointed out. "You never come to the gym."

At this, Shelby merely nodded. They were walking slowly side by side. The cafeteria was a few minutes travel around rolling lawns and beneath overhanging trees.

. . .

Occasionally, Eli let the length of his arm brush lightly against hers. He noted the baby-pink flush that crept into Shelby's delicate neck whenever he did it. He wanted to kiss that neck. He wanted to bury his face there and breathe her in.

"I took an oath when I first became a doctor," she began finally. "I was very young, the youngest in my class and I didn't practice medicine in that sense for very long, but it meant something to me."

"Okay." Eli's brow furrowed.

"I ended up focusing exclusively on genetic research. I preferred the lab over real live patients and I excelled there."

"You're very smart," Eli confirmed. "I can see that."

"Eli, in a sense I see you as my patient," Shelby stated, turning her head to look up at him as they walked.

"I don't like that," Eli admitted, and sucked in a breath. "You know I don't like that."

"I know." Shelby nodded her head.

"You're saying that's all I am to you?" Eli stopped in the middle of the path and stared down at her. "That you want to keep this professional? That you feel nothing more?"

Stopping in front of him, Shelby's impossibly blue eyes bore into his. Her hands came out to wrap his wrists and he couldn't help the pinch in his heart when she did it. He wanted more with her, so much more. But if she didn't feel the same, then he could accept that. He would learn to deal with it, if that's what she truly wanted.

"That's not what I'm trying to tell you," she said.

Eli's face screwed up in confusion, his lips parted but he didn't know what to say.

"I'm trying to explain that I have a duty to put you first," she said. "That I will always protect you first, and help you first. Do you understand?"

"No." Eli gave his head a shake. "I don't."

"You can trust me." She squeezed his wrists with her hands. He could feel the warming of his skin, the desire for her seeping into his blood. "Anything you tell me, anything you share with me, will always stay between you and I... if that's what you want. I won't share any information you give to me, unless you allow me to do so."

"Ah." Eli nodded. She wanted his memories.

Removing his wrists from her grip, he turned away and resumed their slow walk. After a beat, Shelby fell into step beside him.

A crow flew overhead, first one then two. The pair of them landed in a nearby tree. Silent and watchful.

"You're remembering things," she spoke quietly and kept her gaze focused straight ahead. "I can help you."

Eli lifted his chin and let the slight breeze tickle his cheeks and the end of his nose. The cafeteria was coming into view now and with it, more people. She hadn't denied having feelings for him, he realized. She'd merely steered their conversation somewhere else.

"Does this count as a date?" He asked and glanced at her quickly.

"What?" Shelby's nose scrunched. "Eli..."

"Lunch in the cafeteria." He gestured to the building now looming in front of them. "You and me, eating food, no experiments. Is that what's happening?"

"Eli..."

"You saved me back there," he admitted and sighed. "You didn't have to do that. Thank you."

Nodding her head, Shelby twined her fingers together in front of her.

"You're welcome," she offered. "You were about to pass out. Your eyes got all glassy and far away, like you were seeing something. I remember what that's like."

"Oh yeah." Eli stopped at the base of the stone steps leading to the cafeteria and turned to face her. "You lost your memory too."

"I did," she acknowledged, and tapped a finger on the small scar located on the back of her hand near her right thumb. "And I got it all back too. There's no use fighting it, Eli. It all comes back eventually."

"Yeah?" Eli pursed his lips and started up the steps before mumbling, "We'll see about that."

CHAPTER SEVENTEEN_
SHELBY

FOLLOWING ELI UP THE STONE STEPS, SHELBY STUDIED HIS back. She noted the way his shoulders shifted beneath his gray t-shirt and how his arms moved at his sides. When he got to the glass door of the cafeteria, he pulled it open and stood aside, waiting for her to enter first.

Ducking her head, Shelby shifted the bag on her shoulder and passed through the threshold. It was blessedly cool inside. It was also incredibly loud.

People were everywhere, standing in line waiting to be served, seated at one of the hundreds of tables spread out around the expansive space.

Floor to ceiling windows lined the far wall and a few doors were propped open, leading to an outdoor garden.

"Thank you," Shelby said, and glanced at him as she passed.

"You're welcome." Eli smiled and picked up his feet to walk beside her.

The aroma of fresh baked bread hit her first, causing her to inhale deeply. There was a sandwich station at the far end of the room and a salad bar in between.

"What do you feel like?" Eli asked. "I'm buying."

Shoving one hand into the pocket of his shorts, Eli drew out some crumpled bills that served as money inside the Wall. Shelby's stomach rumbled and her eyes drifted over the different options.

"What do you like?" She asked.

"Whatever you want," he replied and placed his palm on the flat of her back.

Steering her expertly, he seemed to sense what she wanted. They arrived at the sandwich station and grabbed a pair of plastic trays.

Plastic. They couldn't manufacture it here. The substance that had once drowned the world in its quantity, was now a rare thing indeed.

Fresh sliced ham, turkey, bright red tomatoes and leafy green lettuce. Shelby licked at her lips as she pointed to each item. Sliced cheese, mayonnaise, mustard, chopped pieces of yellow bell pepper.

"I'll take the same." Eli trailed along beside her. "You're not afraid to eat."

"No." Shelby huffed a laugh and shook her head. "I'm not."

After Eli paid for their meal, they grabbed a couple of iced teas from the drink station and found a lone table. Sitting down across from one another, Shelby plopped her bag on the tabletop and took a large bite.

Eli hesitated a moment, his hands in his lap, his eyes on her face. Shelby held up her hand to cover her mouth and glanced down, but then Eli was picking up his sandwich and doing the same.

"It's good." He grunted the words so they came out more like... *Iffs gooh.*

Shelby swallowed her bite and laughed.

"Yes," she agreed. "It is. Thank you."

Eli nodded and took a sip of tea.

"How did you get here?" He asked and waved a hand vaguely in the air.

"Inside the Wall, you mean?" Shelby's hands gripped her sandwich.

"Yeah. Inside the Wall." Eli ducked his head. "Did you come by train?"

"No." Shelby sighed. "I was one of the first to be transported here and we came by bus. I'd already been working for the source for some years prior. I mean, I didn't know it was the source at the time. I'd been given grant money by a company called PL Growth Collaborative and they defined certain parameters for my research. I didn't look too much into it and to be honest I was thrilled by the project."

"And what project was that?" Eli took another bite and chewed slowly, his eyes on hers.

"Well it's sort of complicated."

"Dumb it down for me." Eli reached for his drink once more. "You're not eating."

Huffing a laugh, Shelby set her sandwich down on her plate. "I don't want to talk with my mouth full."

"I don't care about that," Eli countered and then shot her a wicked grin. "You're pretty cute with your mouth full."

"Alright." Shelby rolled her eyes. "My specialty is in genetics and my research was used to test and modify the microchip that was inserted into all of us here. In the end, the source was successful in developing a chip that prevented disease in a wide variety of recipients without major side effects."

"Side effects? Like the memory loss?" Eli tapped at his own temple.

"No." Shelby shook her head. "Your memory loss is because the chip was removed. There was also the mind control aspect, but that was outside my portion of the project. I wasn't aware of it until it was too late. The effects were… awful."

"Mind control?" Eli frowned.

"Right, you wouldn't remember that part." Shelby looked down at her plate briefly. "When the chip was inserted, the source could encourage you to do things, or prevent you from doing things. It controlled chemical releases from the brain that had a great physical affect on the body."

"It could make you feel pain," Eli offered.

"Yes," Shelby confirmed. "It could make you feel anxious, tired, happy, sad, afraid. The feelings were strange in that you knew logically you had no reason to feel them, but your body kept insisting that's what was happening. It's hard for the mind to overcome the body, almost impossible in most circumstances."

"And this *source*, it's gone? It's dead now?" Eli's eyes were intent.

Shelby's gaze dropped to the scar on the back of Eli's right hand. Her tongue snaked out to wet her lips and her heart tapped in her chest.

"Yes," she said quietly. "At least, we think it is. It's gone from here. It's gone from inside the Wall."

Nodding, Eli picked up his sandwich and took another bite. Shelby followed suit.

All around them, the sounds of the cafeteria at midday raged on. Chairs scraped across the floor as people sat down or pushed back to stand and leave. There was the clank of porcelain plates, the scrape and click of silverware, and so many voices raised in conversation.

"So you got here before the war," Eli put in. "Did you experience any of it? See any of it?"

"No." Shelby sucked in a long breath. "I didn't experience the war like most other people here. I was already working in my lab here when the first bombs dropped."

Pursing his lips, Eli seemed to consider. Shelby watched him. Her sandwich had been consumed already, his too. Their drinks were drained and they were pretty much done.

"That's a good thing," Eli stated finally, and leaned back.

"You remember some of it," Shelby kept her voice low, her eyes locked on Eli's handsome face.

A tightness came to his jawline then, and his nostrils flared ever so slightly. But Eli didn't say anything out loud. His glittery hazel eyes simply stared deeply into her blue ones. The look he gave her had her entire body springing to life.

"You can trust me," she breathed.

"I would like to take you out again," Eli countered. "We could go for a bike ride. It might be fun."

"Eli…"

"Or we could listen to some live music." Eli's mouth turned up on one side. "You seem to like to dance, from what I can recall."

"Eli…"

"Or dinner," Eli cut her off and leaned forward. "I could make reservations at one of the restaurants. You could order wine. Do you like wine?"

"Your memories will return one way or another." Shelby placed a palm flat on the table, urging him to listen. "Better that you do it with me, than with Commander Linfield present. And that's what's coming next, Eli. It's coming sooner than you think."

Eli's mouth snapped shut and his jaw ticked. Leaning back, he folded his arms over his chest and looked away.

Shelby watched the pulse jump angrily in his neck. Her heart hurt. Why did her heart hurt?

"Let me help you," she whispered.

Reaching an arm across the table, Shelby turned her palm up. Eli's eyes darted down to it.

"We need to continue our experiments together," she continued. "I'm being watched. We need to at least make it look like we're trying for as long as we can. I can skew the results. I can give you time to remember everything before reporting it."

"But you will report it," Eli qualified, his eyes bouncing up to lock on her face. "Am I right?"

Shelby held his gaze as an uncomfortable sort of tingling rippled through her body.

"No," she said. "I won't report any of it, not unless you let me. I swear."

"You swear?" Eli's brow raised and he leaned suddenly forward. "And I'm supposed to what... take your word on that? You don't give a crap about me. I'm just a thrilling project, like the microchip was before me. That's all I am to you."

"That's not true." Shelby's mouth twisted as if she'd sucked on something sour.

"Isn't it?" Eli huffed.

"No. It's not."

Reaching for her bag, Shelby dug out her hand written

reports and shoved the stack of papers at him. Eli's hands fumbled over the pages and he glanced from them to her.

"What's all this?"

"A copy of every report I've ever turned in about you," she stated. "Including the olfactory one. The one where you were clearly triggered into memory recurrence by the smell of smoke."

Blinking, Eli paled.

Shelby watched him swallow hard before he looked down.

For several minutes, he studied the reports. Licking his thumb, he turned page after page until finally he frowned.

Looking up at her, Eli's eyes narrowed.

"You lied," he whispered. "You didn't tell him I passed out."

Shutting her eyes briefly, Shelby nodded.

"You told him the smell test thing didn't work, that it failed," he continued.

Opening her eyes, Shelby tilted her head to one side. "That's right," she confirmed. "I lied to Commander Linfield and I will lie to him again."

"Why?"

"Because you are my patient Eli." Shelby reached for him, and this time he let her grab on. "And more importantly than that, I care about you. You are my friend. You can trust me."

Eli stared down at her hand as it curled around his own. His chest worked air in and out. His lips pursed. Then finally, he rotated his hand palm up, and grasped her back.

"You might change your mind about all that," he said lowly. "You might learn things you'll regret."

"No I won't," Shelby insisted. "I promise."

## CHAPTER EIGHTEEN_
## ELI

IT TOOK ELI ANOTHER WEEK TO THINK ABOUT IT. ANOTHER week of waking up in a cold sweat, shaking and alone. Another week of fighting the gray voices with every ounce of energy he had. Another week of avoiding a certain redhead and her searching blue eyes and candy-scented skin.

But in the end she was right. The memories were chugging along like a diesel locomotive, steady and insistent and strong. He spent his waking hours trying not to pass out and his sleeping hours trying to stay awake.

Cass kept feeding him chicken noodle soup and asking if he was okay. Eli tried to reassure her, but the bags under his eyes were only getting darker.

*Maybe I'm coming down with something, a bug. It's probably just a cold.*

Cass would blink at him quietly then, and nod her head. The worry lines at the corners of her eyes were deepening. Eli's heart was laced in guilt.

So on the morning of the seventh day, he relented.

After a cold shower and a shave, he donned simple blue

jeans and a white tank, and headed out into the sunshine. It surprised him to note that the air was cooler. Time was passing and summer was nearing its abrupt end.

This was the North and seasons here could be extreme and sometimes short. Fall was coming. Eli didn't know how exactly he knew that, but he did all the same.

Shoving his hands into his pockets, Eli kept his held tilted towards the ground. He still wasn't sure about this but the alternative seemed less appealing. He could continue to try to fight this battle alone, which meant hiding out in Cass's apartment until one of the guys stopped by to seek him out.

At which point Eli would be forced to fake it and hope like hell a memory didn't drag him under in front of anyone. Or he could work with Shelby. Maybe if she helped him to remember everything in private, then he could stop with the fainting and figure out his next move. Probably, he would have to leave.

His simple sneakers took him along cement sidewalks and over green lawns. The shadow of a few trees swaying in the breeze decorated his path.

Shelby's apartment building wasn't too far off and before he knew it, Eli was pulling the door wide and stepping onto the first floor.

At either end of the hall was a set of stairs. Turning to his right, Eli chose that side and started his ascent. It was four flights to Shelby's place and on his way up he passed a few other people coming down. They smiled at him and nodded their heads, men and women both.

Eli pursed his lips and kept moving.

By the time he reached the landing, his heart was pounding and his lungs were sucking in air, but it wasn't the climb that winded him. It was fear. Plain and simple. Eli was fucking scared.

But fear wasn't a new feeling to him. In fact, he felt it all the damn time.

He was living in it, entrenched in it, every single day. He was afraid of himself. He was afraid of what stepping back into his full past would be like.

But he was tired of running. He was tired of fighting. He was just plain tired.

Stepping up to apartment number 402, Eli didn't hesitate. He lifted his fist, rapped a knuckle against the white wood and waited. He didn't know if Shelby was even home, but it was early yet and this was as good a place to start as any. Her lab would be next.

"Eli?" Shelby's surprised voice floated to him from the other side of the door.

The sound of her alone had him exhaling. But it wasn't until she opened the door and he saw her face that he realized why.

She was like the eye of a hurricane, a center of complete calm in a sea of chaos. As soon Eli stepped into her presence, the wind rushing all around him stopped, the storm ceased, the voices quieted. He could breathe. Shelby made it so he could breathe.

"Are you okay?" She asked, her eyes darting over his face as she stepped back to let him in.

"I'm fine," he said.

Walking past her, Eli glanced around her apartment. She lived here alone. He knew because he'd asked. Cass had lived here too, before moving in with Garret, along with Mia, who was away on business outside the Wall.

"I haven't seen you in awhile," she said, and closed the door behind her. "Cass said you were sick."

"Yeah." Eli huffed.

Coming to a stop, he shoved his hands into the front pockets of his jeans once more and glanced around. All of the apartments inside the Wall were furnished in the same manner. Blue sofa. Wooden table. Overhead lighting.

There was no kitchen in this apartment, which had apparently been set aside for bachelors. The family apartments (like the one he lived in with Cass) were the only ones where you could cook.

"You know, people don't get sick here very often," Shelby commented. "The children do, of course, because they never had the microchip. But even that is rare.

Adults certainly don't catch colds, something about the chip has left a lasting effect in the blood. There are several doctors on site, anxious to monitor the eventual return of disease."

Shutting his eyes, Eli fought the tension that wanted to work into his shoulders and spine. He could hear Shelby padding along the carpet on her bare feet. She was moving closer to him, coming around him, peering into his face.

"Cass asked me not to mention your illness to anyone," Shelby spoke quietly. "She knows, Eli. I think she knows."

Eli's eyes popped open then and locked onto Shelby's face. Her unruly hair was pulled back from her face. Her nose boasted an irresistible smattering of freckles. Her intelligent blue eyes were awash with concern.

"I'm fighting it," he admitted. "But it's winning."

"Why fight it?" Shelby shook her head slowly side to side, her brows drawing down in concentration.

Holding out his tattoo covered arms, Eli showed her the backs of his hands, so clean and unmarked. Even now, it was hard not to envision them covered in blood.

"I don't want to know what I did," he whispered. "I wish you could make it all go away permanently instead. Isn't there a pill you could give me? A chip you could inject me with? Something that would make me forget forever?"

Shelby's face fell and she reached a hand out to rub at his upper arm.

"I'm sorry Eli," she answered. "But there's no such thing."

Taking a deep breath, Eli shut his eyes and dropped his head. The feel of her warm hands rubbing along his arms, dropping over his tattoos and down to his wrists was too good.

He leaned into her touch, he couldn't help it. She was like a liferaft in the middle of a tumultuous ocean. He could feel the spray in his face, the water and the wind, but then she was there beneath it all, steady and calm.

"Why don't you sit?" She asked, and gave his hands a quick squeeze.

Eli's eyes popped open and he grabbed her hands with his own. Shelby let him.

Her face tipped up and they regarded each other for several moments. Eli's heart tapped in his chest and his body coiled and heated like it always did when he was this close to her. His gaze dropped to her mouth, and he *wanted*.

In another life maybe, he could have had her. In another life, he wouldn't have hesitated.

"Alright," he conceded and let her lead him to the small sofa. Blue, they were always blue.

"What have you remembered so far?" Shelby asked.

Taking a seat, she tucked her legs beneath her.

Eli sat beside her, but kept his hands folded together in his lap. He leaned back against the cushions and spread his long legs out in front of him, knees bent, feet flat on the floor.

In this way, Shelby was looking at the side of his face.

"Things," he murmured finally. "Bits and pieces mostly."

"And what were they about?" Shelby prompted.

"Death," Eli exhaled the word like a long sigh. "I've killed people… multiple people."

"Okay." Shelby bobbed her head, he watched her in his peripheral vision. "You were a soldier during a war, that's to be expected. I can understand why you're fighting your memories, there's a lot of trauma involved."

"Trauma?" Eli scoffed and shifted uncomfortably on the couch. "What do you know about it?"

"Only what I've studied," Shelby admitted. "So I know with certainty that burying it, ignoring it, has deep and lasting repercussions. You will only continue to suffer."

Swinging his head to stare at her, Eli frowned.

"And what if I deserve to suffer?" He asked. "What then?"

"Eli…"

"I've killed people," he said, shifting slightly to face her. "*Innocent* people. *Defenseless* people. As in hundreds and hundreds of them."

"You've seen this in your memories?" Shelby's eyes darted over his face. "Specifically."

"I've seen the aftermath." Eli turned away from her and held out his arms in front of him. "I've buried their bodies. I've seen myself drenched in their blood. What other explanation is there?"

Shoving up from the couch, Shelby stared down at him.

Eli held her gaze, forcing himself to absorb her expression. What he saw there had his own brow furrowing. She wasn't repulsed by him. She wasn't afraid.

"There's only one way to find out for sure," she said and gestured to the couch. "Why don't you lie down and we'll get started."

Blowing out a breath, Eli leaned forward and braced his forearms on his thighs. His foot began tapping out a nervous beat against the floor and his stomach clenched tightly. He didn't want this. He didn't want any of this.

"What you think you've done and what you've actually done are two different things," Shelby coaxed. "It's time to find out the truth. It's time to face it."

Without raising his head, Eli spoke. His eyes stared down into the carpeted flooring, so clean and soft and simple. The apartment was quiet, save for the pounding of his heart like a drum in his throat.

"The first time I killed a man, I was fourteen years old," he stated flatly. "The guy wasn't innocent and he wasn't defenseless, but I murdered him just the same. I squeezed the life out of him with my bare hands."

"Eli…"

Lifting his head now, Eli eyed her.

"I would do it again," he announced. "I would kill him a thousand times over, I would watch the life bleed from his eyes every night if I had to."

"You must've had your reasons," Shelby's voice was low. "If you feel so strongly about it, maybe there are reasons for the rest of your memories, too."

"I am not a good person," Eli hissed. "You've got to understand that."

"Lie down," Shelby commanded and once more indicated the couch.

Eli's mouth dropped and he wanted to continue. He wanted to argue with her, prove to her, convince her to stay away from him, convince her not to do this.

But Shelby's eyes were so fierce, her cheeks flushed that perfect shade of pink, so he couldn't refuse. He might not ever get to have her in the way he longed for, but he could give her this, he could give her a successful experiment.

Jaw napping shut, Eli shifted around and laid out on the couch. It was standard sized but he was oversized and so his legs dangled well over the arm of one side. Folding his hands on his stomach, he leaned his head against the opposite arm of the couch and blinked angrily at the ceiling.

"Ready?" Shelby asked, and he gave a curt nod.

She wandered away from him then. He listened as she rummaged through a set of storage cabinets. When she came back over, she sat on the edge of the wooden coffee table by his head.

Eli refused to look directly at her. His heart was cracking open. He could feel it oozing inside his chest.

"This time…" Shelby stated calmly. "Don't fight it."

Producing a candle in one hand and a lighter in the other, Shelby flicked a flame into life. Eli's eyes slammed shut. As he inhaled the smell of smoke, he let go.

## CHAPTER NINETEEN_
### ELI

*T*HERE *WAS THE SOUND OF A TRAIN.* A *WHISTLE BLOWING ONCE, then twice. They were long, deafeningly loud blasts, and they turned his insides sick.*

*Looking down, Eli could see the wooden platform under his boots. His black rifle was clutched in his slick palms.*

*It was fucking hot. The sun was beyond intense here.*

*"Stand back!" Someone yelled. It was another solider, the guy's name escaped him.*

*Eli took a giant step back as the train came screeching and grinding and crackling to a stop. The cars banged and hit together, as the wheels slowed. Car, after car, after car. They should be filled with cattle, with livestock, with animals. But Eli knew they weren't.*

*They were filled with people.*

*"Hey," the soldier spoke again, walking over to stand beside him. "You worked these trains down in Arizona?"*

*Swallowing, Eli nodded. His stomach twisted and turned. He could taste vomit in the back of his throat, but he forced it to stay down.*

"How'd you get up here? In Cali?" The soldier again, watching as the cars came to a stop and the people inside started groaning.

My sister, Eli thought, I'm looking for my baby sister. And if I'm the luckiest man alive, then she's going to be riding in one of these awful trains. If I'm fast enough, I just might be able to save her.

"Man of few words." The soldier rocked onto his toes and rolled his eyes.

Eli released a controlled breath. He didn't give a fuck about conversing with this guy. Time was of the essence, and once those doors opened, then the clock of death started ticking.

"Alright!" A voice boomed over a loud speaker. "Face masks on! Remember, they're all sick, there's no saving them! Open the doors!"

Slipping his mask down over his face, Eli breathed in the hot stink of rubber as it mingled with his own breath.

Bracing himself, he watched as a dozen other soldiers stepped up to the doors of the cattle cars and began working the latches.

Inside, people shifted and moved. They called out. They were hungry and thirsty. Some, he knew from experience, had already died.

Gripping his rifle tighter, Eli blew out a quick breath before charging forward. His boots slapped against the wooden floorboards of the platform while his heart turned to stone.

When the door in front of him slid open, he jumped in without hesitation. He was the first one inside, but he was not the first one to fire a shot. But shoot he did.

Shoot. He. Did.

Turning on the soldier beside him, Eli lifted his rifle and pulled the trigger. The guy who'd been asking him all those pointless questions only moments before, gasped his last breath and collapsed to the floor.

The people in the train car cried out and cowered. Their bodies were covered in dirt and piss and shit. They'd been trapped inside for who knew how long, slowly starving and dying of thirst.

Eli's eyes swept them greedily. Even as a dozen other shots rang out all along the length of the train, he took the time to stare into each and every face in that train car.

Cass. Cass. Come on.

His lungs heaved and the sound of his harsh breathing through his mask filled his ears. She wasn't here. She wasn't fucking here.

"What's happening?!" A few people began to scream. "Why are you doing this?"

Eli's heart tapped at him, but the sound of gunfire continued and he knew he didn't have any time left. Without answering them, he retreated from the car and jumped back to the wooden platform. Jogging to the next car in line, Eli leapt inside.

Two soldiers were working systematically, standing shoulder to shoulder. With each sweep of their weapons, they sprayed the train car with bullets. Dead bodies were strewn across the floor, soaking in pools of their shared blood.

Men shouted. Women screamed. They were running into the sides of the train car and each other, clawing over top of one another to avoid being shot. A child blinked quietly against the far wall, utterly silent.

Eli stepped up behind the soldiers and shot them in the back. First one. Pop, pop. Then the other. Pop, pop.

Lowering his weapon, he scanned the space. Curly dark hair. Curly dark hair. Diving forward, he reached for a woman's body. She was lying face down. His stomach punched up into his throat.

The people all around him were still screaming. They ducked away from him, darted around him, tried to escape.

Eli's hand clasped the dead woman's shoulder and very carefully pulled her to one side. When he saw her face, he cried out.

*"Thank God," he exhaled. "Thank God."*

*It wasn't Cass. It wasn't his sister.*

*But in the background, guns continued to fire. Straightening, Eli fled the train car and entered another. Then another. Then another.*

*Systematically, just like the soldiers he was shooting in the back, Eli cleared each and every car on that track.*

*And to no avail. Cass wasn't inside.*

*Which meant she hadn't died here... but that didn't mean she was alive either.*

*Ripping off his gas mask, Eli stood still on the wooden train platform and sucked in the hot summer air. He was absolutely covered in blood. People all around him murmured and wept. They swiped at their eyes and staggered away from him, out into the barren fields.*

*There were no more guns firing. There were no more soldiers killing. He was the only one left, and he'd fired every bullet he had.*

*Swiping the back of his arm across his brow, Eli began walking away, along the wooden platform. People scattered quickly, ducking out of his way. His rifle hung down limply at his side, swaying lifelessly as he went.*

*Cass wasn't here, so he'd do what he did the last time and the time before that... he'd keep looking.*

*Jumping down off the platform, Eli's boots landed in the dirt. He walked along the tracks then, heading north. He'd find the next train station. He'd check every single one until he found her. What else could he do?*

*Nothing.*

*He could do nothing else.*

SETTING THE GLASS OF WATER DOWN ON THE WOODEN COFFEE table, Shelby resumed her seat just beside it. Her hands were trembling ever so slightly, and so she pressed them together in an effort to calm her nerves.

Eli was awake now, with perspiration beading on his brow and upper lip. He'd been out for a solid six minutes and thirty-eight seconds, throughout which Shelby swore she'd held her breath the entire time.

"Drink this," she urged and nodded her head towards the glass.

"I don't want anything," he murmured and continued to stare at the floor.

He was sitting up, his feet planted firmly on the floor between them, his forearms braced along his thighs.

"It will help," Shelby whispered.

"Nothing helps," he countered and shook his head.

Biting at her lower lip, Shelby held back the million questions she wanted to ask. Unlike the other times she'd witnessed Eli pass out, this time he'd been perfectly still. He hadn't thrashed around or called out.

When he came to, he didn't say anything. He'd just pushed up to sitting and failed to meet her gaze.

"You can tell me…" she ventured finally. "I won't judge you."

Huffing a laugh, Eli glanced up at her. His hazel eyes were bloodshot, his face worn as if it'd seen a thousand years instead of twenty-eight.

"I'm worried about you," Shelby blurted.

Her body jumped forward slightly with the admission. Her hands went to reach for his, but she hesitated.

Eli's eyes dropped to them, but he didn't breach the space. Instead, his palms curled in on themselves and he heaved a gigantic sigh.

"During the war I worked a train transport crew down in Arizona, or what was left of it," he began. "It was an awful assignment, and they couldn't keep enough soldiers on staff. It wasn't long before I figured out why."

Swallowing, Shelby lowered her hands. "Why?" She asked.

Looking up at her, Eli's face twisted before he leaned back against the blue sofa. His hands came to fold in his lap and he turned his head to stare out the sliding glass door that led to her small balcony.

"Because it was our job to bury the dead… or burn them," he stated, his voice was devoid of emotion. "Drag the bodies out. Load them in trucks. Drive them to a big hole in the ground. Light it all on fire. Cover it with dirt when it was over."

"I don't…" Shelby's stomach pitched. "Understand."

"The trains would roll up." Eli pursed his lips a moment

before continuing. "They would be filled with dead bodies. Women. Children. Old men. Anyone who'd ever been loaded up and told they were heading to safety, that's where they really ended up. They thought they were going to a place like the Wall, but they weren't."

"Eli..."

"But you see, down in Arizona they were already dead," Eli cut her off. "When the trains got to the stations, the people inside were already *fucking* dead."

"I... uh..." Shelby swallowed.

Turning to her abruptly, Eli leaned forward, his face flushed and his eyes damp. "You see that's what I didn't understand. That's what I didn't expect when..."

Eli's gaze darted over her face, as he trailed off.

Sucking in a sharp breath, Shelby waited. Her heart was twisting and her pulse skittering. But then Eli's jaw snapped shut and his eyes dropped to the ground. His shoulders shook and heaved.

"When what?" Shelby exhaled the question, unsure if she actually wanted the answer. "Tell me."

"When Garrett told me that he put my sister on a train to a refugee center, all I could see were the thousands of people I'd already burned and buried. So I fucking lost it. We fought, I tried to kill him, I *thought* I actually killed him... and then eventually, I went looking for her."

"For Cass," Shelby clarified.

"Yeah." Eli sniffed. "I knew it was probably pointless but I had to try. I had to see her body and bury it myself if I could. I figured if I got to a train quick enough, then maybe she'd still be alive. I didn't know how those people in Arizona died. None of us did. There was no trauma... no blood..."

"So the smell of burning…" Shelby murmured to herself. Her mind was clicking over with the information now, with what all this could mean.

"The transport trains in California were different, though." Eli's shoulders tightened and his forearms flexed as he made fists once more. "The soldiers working them all had the tattoos. I didn't have them yet, but no one seemed to care. I just walked along the tracks until I found a station with a bunch of soldiers hanging around and I waited."

"But you didn't find Cass," Shelby offered.

"No." Eli shook his head. "I didn't find Cass."

"She was already here," Shelby filled in the blanks.

Nodding, Eli pushed up to standing and slid away from her. Shelby tipped her face up and watched him go. He was like a tiger in a cage, prowling along the perimeter of the room, seeking a way out when there was none.

"When the first train pulled up, everyone got out their gas masks and put them on." Eli stopped at the sliding glass door and stared out. "I did it too, although I didn't know why. I still don't really understand why. The people weren't sick… I don't think."

"Who told you the people were sick?" Shelby watched Eli closely, but he didn't glance her way.

Lifting a hand, Eli pressed his wide palm to the sliding glass door and sighed.

"I don't remember that part, I don't have it all back yet," he said. "I just remember the trains. I can see it now in my head. It's playing on repeat like a horror movie."

"Eli…"

"It's a damn horror show Shelby!" Eli yelled at the glass, still not turning to face her.

Closing her eyes, Shelby straightened her spine. She remained seated on the coffee table and held perfectly still. Drawing in a calming breath, she listened. When Eli failed to speak, she opened her eyes.

He was staring at her. His hazel eyes were so wrecked it made her throat ache. His back was leaning up against the glass now, his face tipped up towards the ceiling.

"I hesitated… that first time," Eli rasped. "I didn't even have my rifle in my hands when they pulled open the doors. I was in shock. The people inside… I could hear them. They weren't all dead. They were still alive."

"Eli…"

"The other soldiers, they jumped inside and they started shooting," Eli choked out. "People were screaming and you could see the train cars rocking around as they ran into the sides and tried to get away.

I just fucking stood there with my mouth hanging open. I listened to it… I don't know for how long. But at some point I realized… Cass could be in there."

Eli's voice cracked and tears ran unchecked down his cheeks. "So I got my weapon out, and I went to go save her. I jumped up in those train cars and I shot those soldiers in the back, in the side, in the face. I did one right after the other until they were all dead. Then I checked the people to see if Cass was there."

"But she wasn't there." Shelby's chest tightened and her stomach rolled within her.

"No, she wasn't there." Eli shook his head. "So I just fucking left. I left those people in the train cars on the train tracks and I kept walking. I kept walking until I found the next station with soldiers waiting and the next one after that. So do you see?"

Eli shoved off the sliding glass door and stalked towards the sofa. His palms were outstretched and shaking. His eyes were wide and imploring.

"Do you see now that I am a *bad* man?!" He cried. "Do you see now what I've done? What I told you I didn't want to remember?"

"Eli, you are not a bad..." Shelby tried to cut in, but he waved her off.

"No," Eli insisted and slammed himself down on the couch across from her.

"You didn't shoot those innocent people," Shelby reasoned. "You tried to save them."

"I walked away!" Eli shouted. "I left them there to be finished off by someone else!"

"What else could you have done?" Shelby asked. "You can't save the whole world, you're only one person."

Holding up his arms in front of her face, Eli fisted his hands and sent his tattoos rippling across her vision.

"Look at these," he hissed. "At some point... I got these, just like those other soldiers. And do you know what I think?"

Shelby's mouth opened, but no sound came out.

"I think I killed innocent people then too."

CHAPTER TWENTY-ONE_
ELI

THE KNOCK ON HIS BEDROOM DOOR CAME AS A SURPRISE. HIS baby sister didn't knock. Usually, Cass just came storming in to plop on the edge of his bed and begin talking.

Lifting his head, Eli frowned at the white wooden door. He was lying on his back, still in bed.

Sure, it was sometime in the late afternoon, but at this point he didn't really care. He couldn't face it. He couldn't get up and face himself in the bathroom mirror. Not today.

"Go away," Eli sighed and dropped his head back to his pillow.

The gray memories had gone from him now. Ever since he'd told Shelby about the trains, he'd been given a reprieve. There were no new images trying to haunt him, only the fresh vibrant ones now bubbling at the surface.

He hadn't had a solid night's sleep in a week.

When the knock came again, Eli didn't bother to respond. He blinked at the blank ceiling above him and pursed his lips. His stomach was growling but he didn't care. Just as he was about to turn onto his side, the door swung open of its own accord.

"Hey." Liam stood in the doorframe, his head cocked to one side. "You alive?"

Frowning, Eli eyed him.

"Do you mind?" He asked and had Liam's mouth twitching.

"It's three in the afternoon," Liam stated, and tapped at an invisible watch on his wrist. "I think you've reached your moping quota for the week."

"Moping?" Eli's brow raised, but he did not make a move to get up.

"Yeah." Liam watched him a moment before clearing his throat. "Cass mentioned you and the Doc had a falling out or something. She said you've been pretty upset."

"Upset?" Eli pushed up onto one elbow and stared. "Is that why you're here? To check up on me?"

Eli's gut churned and his chest tightened. His sister had been covering for him, again.

Commander Linfield still wanted answers, and Liam was still an interrogator. But according to Shelby, no one was going to believe that he was sick with a cold.

Cass didn't know for sure what was going on, but Eli was almost certain she had an idea it was his memory. She didn't ask though, and he didn't offer. She just let him stay in his room and hide.

Shrugging now, Liam inched his way inside the room but not very far. He had to duck his head to fit under the doorframe, same as Eli.

"She's chasing you. She's not chasing you." Liam made a

so-so motion with one hand. "Your sister's worried, which makes all the other girls worry…"

"Ah." Eli smirked. "Hannah. You're only here because your wife made you come."

"A couple guys were gonna play baseball," Liam ignored him. "You're coming."

"I'm coming?" Eli's face twisted.

"You're coming," Liam repeated. "Now get up."

Flopping back down to the bed, Eli shut his eyes. He absolutely did not want to spend the rest of the day being watched by the world's foremost interrogator. Liam was anything but stupid and if given the slightest indication, he would know that Eli was hiding something. Hell, he probably already did.

"Get lost Liam," Eli breathed the words.

"Yeah, Liam," a female voice repeated. "Get lost."

*Shelby.*

Eli's eyes sprang open and he turned his face towards the door. She was standing just behind Liam, a canvas bag looped over her shoulder and a concerned expression on her face.

Eli's eyes drank her in. Flaming red hair, faded blue jeans and a simple white blouse. His tongue darted out to wet his lips but at the same time he frowned.

"Shelby," he said and looked to Liam.

Holding up both hands, Liam's mouth twitched at one corner.

"The lady has spoken," he announced and backed away. "But you should come play with us tomorrow," Liam added, before he disappeared down the hall.

"No thanks!" Eli called, but he knew it didn't matter what he said. Liam would be coming for him tomorrow just the same.

Standing quietly, Shelby waited for the front door to open and close before speaking.

Her eyes never left his face and Eli, too, found he was unable to look away. He'd rushed out of her apartment the other day, after he'd yelled at her, scared her, told her about things he hadn't wanted to be real.

She'd come to see him a few times since then, but he'd made Cass send her away.

Guess Cass was done sending people away, or maybe she was just out of the apartment right now. He was suddenly ashamed to say he didn't know which.

"You look like hell," Shelby said finally and made Eli laugh.

It was the first time he'd laughed or smiled in so long, he couldn't remember. And it was short lived. When he looked into her face, Eli couldn't maintain the fleeting feeling. Her eyes were just so deep and so blue and so intense. He'd watched a thousand women just like her die. He'd let them die.

Rubbing a hand roughly down his face, Eli slid his legs to the edge of the bed and planted his feet flat on the floor. The blankets fell to his waist. He wasn't wearing a shirt, only boxers and white socks.

"You can't live like this," Shelby murmured.

"Live like what?" Eli dropped his hands to his lap and blinked at her.

"Blaming yourself." Shelby stepped inside the room. "Torturing yourself."

"You know nothing about it," Eli countered, and watched her advance on him.

"Maybe not in the same way," she admitted. "But I've made mistakes that have cost lives. I've watched people die that I couldn't save, that a whole team of doctors couldn't save."

"That's different." Eli blew out a breath.

"In a way it is." Shelby nodded. "But there's still the guilt. There's still the pain and the wonder. Maybe if I did this better, faster, differently. Maybe that person would be going home to their children, to their husband or wife, to their mother."

"Shelby…"

"Eli," Shelby cut him off. "This world needs you to remember."

Pursing his lips, Eli glanced away. "I know…"

"But it doesn't have to be today," she offered, causing him to look back into her face.

"What?"

"You need a break," she explained and gestured around the room. "We both need a break from all of this. From the remembering and the experiments and the pressure."

"What are you saying?" Eli tilted his head to one side.

Shelby's eyes darted down over his bare chest, to his stomach, and then back up to his mouth. Eli's heart quickened in his chest and his muscles tensed automatically. Blood rushed through his system as he watched her look at him… like, *really* look at him.

But then her cheeks were tinging pink and she was glancing away.

"Cass says you haven't eaten," Shelby answered. "So I've packed us some food. Let's go for a walk."

"A walk?" Eli shifted his head, trying to get a better view of her face.

"You wanted a picnic," Shelby said finally and brushed her

palms quickly down her sides. "So let's go have one. You'll need clothes, though. The air is getting cooler."

Eli's mouth dropped, but then just as quickly he snapped it shut. Shelby was asking him out… sort of… maybe.

Standing from the bed, he kept his eyes glued to the little redhead. She snuck another glance at his body as he stalked her way. It made his insides coil. It made him forget.

Brushing by her on his way to the tiny closet, Eli couldn't help but smirk as she let loose a surprised squeak before backing a few steps away.

He relished the brush of his arm against her shoulder as she side-stepped and blinked at his closeness.

The hangers clicked and snapped together as he pulled out a long sleeve shirt and a pair of blue jeans. Stepping into them, he jumped in place as he zipped up and fastened the button. Shooting Shelby a look, Eli hid his grin. Her neck was completely red at this point and the flush crept all the way down her chest.

"It's working," he commented and gave her a little nod.

"What? What's working?" She asked and cleared her throat.

"You're making me forget about the bad," he admitted. "Thank you."

Pulling a black shirt on over his head, Eli held out a hand. Shelby blinked down at it, confused.

"Let me carry your bag," he said, and wiggled the fingers of his open palm. "You packed lunch. Let me carry it to wherever we're going."

"Oh." Shelby cleared her throat. "Of course. Thank you."

Shucking the bag off her shoulder, she handed it over. Their fingers brushed when he accepted it, because he made sure that they did. Shelby's hand sucked back to her side and her eyes widened, but then she was tipping her chin up and rolling her shoulders.

Bravado. How had he not noticed this about her before?

"Where are we going?" Eli asked and gestured for her to walk through the doorway first.

"Somewhere familiar," she answered, and gave him a small smile.

"You're not going to tell me?"

"Nope." Shelby shook her head and started walking. "You'll just have to see it for yourself."

CHAPTER TWENTY-TWO_
SHELBY

BY THE TIME THEY CLIMBED TO THE TOP OF THE PERIMETER
wall, Shelby thought her head was clear. Her chin was lifted,
her shoulders were relaxed and that awful blushing response
that seemed to go along with seeing Eli shirtless was gone.

This man... he was a ball of complication for her, in a way
she'd never experienced before. He was intelligent and
thoughtful, tortured and resilient, beautiful and tragic.

She wanted to save him. She wanted to make it all okay.

"Here we are," she announced.

Her voice echoed strangely in the metal interior of the
perimeter wall. They'd hiked up over ten stories to the very
top and now all that was left to do was open the door and step
outside.

Eli came up beside her and offered a tentative smile.

"You're afraid of heights," he pointed out.

"No," she denied the obvious, shaking her head.

At that Eli's brow rose and his smile turned up a few
notches. Without hesitation he pulled open the door and
stepped aside.

"After you then," he countered. "Doctor."

Rolling her shoulders, Shelby ignored the jump in her belly and stepped into the light.

Sunshine danced from the western sky. A cool breeze blew white clouds over the blue expanse. A few strands of her unruly hair tickled and danced along her cheeks and nose. Reaching up, she brushed them away, only for them to return with the wind.

"I can go first," Eli offered, coming out and closing the door behind them. "Unless you want to just sit down right here."

"No." Shelby willed her voice to be strong as she refused to look down. "You have a spot that you like. Let's go to that one."

Taking the lead, Eli shifted the bag on his shoulder and held out his hand behind him. After a beat, Shelby took it.

Warmth flooded her skin and flowed like magic up her arm. Her pounding heart intensified.

"The sunset is incredible from here," Eli said as they walked along the perimeter wall. "If you want to stay that late and watch it, of course."

"I don't know if I can walk back this way in the dark," Shelby admitted and kept her eyes fixed on Eli's back.

"We could take the other door back down." Eli gestured to the metal entrance still about fifty yards away from them. It was the one they'd sat in front of before. The one that had given them shade and something to rest against.

"Why didn't we just walk up from there in the first place?" Shelby huffed.

"I'm sorry," Eli chuckled. "I like walking across the top. I should've brought you that way before."

When they got to the platform with the door, Shelby pressed her back up against the metal and slid down quickly. Tipping her head back, she shut her eyes and exhaled.

"You okay?" Eli asked quietly.

She listened to him set the bag down at her feet and then slide down beside her. His arm ran the length of her arm. His leg against her leg. His side against her side. After a beat, he looped his arm around her shoulders and drew her in closer.

Shelby let him, and laid the side of her face on his chest.

"We didn't have to come up here," he murmured. "I didn't realize you'd be this freaked out."

"I'm not," Shelby denied the obvious. "I just need a minute."

Nodding, Eli ran his hand up and down her arm. Shelby breathed through her rush of adrenaline and focused on the steady tap of his heart beneath his shirt.

"You should eat something," he said finally. "Take your mind off of it."

"Alright." Shelby cleared her throat and opened her eyes, she was supposed to be helping him, not the other way around.

Shifting slightly, Eli grabbed for the bag with his right hand and dragged it onto his lap. Without letting go of her with his left arm, he began rummaging around.

"Apples," he commented. "Bread. Cheese. Salami. Are these olives?"

"Yes," Shelby exhaled and straightened a little.

Almost reluctantly, Eli let her.

"I can't remember the last time I had olives," Eli commented and offered her the glass jar. "Of course, that's not saying much since I can't remember a lot of things."

Giving her head a shake, Shelby pushed gently off of Eli's

chest and took the jar. This time, his arm snaked back to his side, allowing her room to move.

"Let's not talk about remembering," Shelby reminded him, and twisted open the lid.

Eli's hands stilled in the bag and his brow furrowed a moment. "Okay," he agreed finally and resumed his exploration.

Before long they were munching quietly and staring off at the horizon. Eli tore pieces of bread off the loaf and handed them to her. Shelby accepted them and in return sliced off thin bits of cheese with a small knife. They traded food back and forth that way, eating on top of the world, listening to nothing. Only the birds flew higher than them.

If she looked down, Shelby would be able to see the tops of the trees. But she didn't look down, not directly. She looked out.

Out at the mountains to the east, out at the valley to the west. Out at the empty train tracks that snaked and twisted towards them from somewhere far, far away.

"What's your favorite color?" Eli asked, and had Shelby smiling.

"Is that the best you can do?" She countered and lifted her face to look at him.

"Yes, Ma'am," he admitted and looped his arm back around her shoulders. "It is."

"Alright." Shelby averted her gaze from his square jaw and full lips. "My favorite color is blue."

"Like your eyes," he pointed out and she nodded.

"Yours?" Shelby cleared her throat. "What's yours?"

"Blue," Eli announced with a grin.

"You're lying," Shelby accused and stuck an elbow gently into his side.

Unfazed, Eli absorbed the blow and shrugged.

"So what if I am?" He asked. "If it was anything but blue before, that's gone now."

"Fair enough," Shelby murmured. "What's your favorite food?"

"Olives," Eli teased, grabbing for the jar, he shook it side to side, causing the leftovers to swish inside.

Laughing, Shelby pushed the jar away. Eli set it back in the bag and sighed.

"What's your favorite food?" He asked.

His hand was rubbing along her arm again, sending ripples through Shelby's system. Her feet were outstretched, her body tucked up into Eli's side. The breeze had gotten stronger, the air cooler. The sun was waning, sending the sky towards lavender and rose.

Biting at her lip a moment, Shelby said the first thing that came to her mind.

"Strawberries," she offered and couldn't fight the blush.

Eli's hand stilled on her arm. His head tilted and he looked down at her. Shelby kept her gaze straight ahead, focused out and not at him. Even so, she could feel him studying her. She could feel his eyes burning against the skin of her face, then settle on her mouth.

Her lips parted, and her core clenched. Drawing her legs up, Shelby shifted her body.

Eli let her move against him, let her seek comfort where there was none to be had. His gaze refused to leave her face though and his palm spread slowly out over her skin. She could feel his fingers moving, one by one and it had her heart pounding in her chest.

It was like he was waiting, and waiting. When she finally looked up at him, that was it.

Eli's hazel eyes locked on hers for a solid count of three, before he leaned down and took her mouth with his own.

He was slow and deliberate, causing her to gasp and then to sigh. His lips brushed softly against hers once, twice. His tongue flicked out to taste and test. Shelby's mouth parted to receive him, and he took the invitation for what it was.

Eli turned his body to her, engulfing her with his presence. His right hand came up to wrap the side of her neck, where his thumb soothed the skin of her throat. He kissed her then, long and deep, until her entire body was a melting, tingling ball of lust.

But just as surely as it had started, Eli pulled back and stopped.

His eyes bore into hers, darting across her face. His hand at her neck, stroked, then dropped away.

Leaning back fully against the closed door, Eli blew out a long breath.

"I'm sorry," he said finally. "I shouldn't have done that. I promise, it won't happen again."

Swallowing, Shelby's hand went to her own throat. It was like she had to do something to stop the tingling and burning that vibrated from where he touched.

He was sorry? He'd made a mistake? She'd heard those lines before.

Closing her eyes, she nodded her head.

"Alright," Shelby whispered. "Alright, Eli."

CHAPTER TWENTY-THREE_
ELI

ELI'S FINGERS GRIPPED THE FOOTBALL AS HE DROPPED BACK from the line of men in front of him. His eyes scanned the field. His chin tipped up.

A guy named Teddy was completely covered by two guys off to his left, which was a pity, since that's the play he'd wanted to run. Down the middle, Cole wasn't having much luck getting open either.

Shit. Eli didn't like to lose.

Dancing on the balls of his feet, Eli's arm cocked back and he swiveled to his right. The pressure was on all around him. He could sense the guys on the line of scrimmage shoving and grunting. He didn't have a lot of time left and so he did what he'd always done.

He looked to the tallest motherfucker on the right and sent one deep.

Releasing the ball in a perfect spiral, Eli held his breath. Liam's eyes widened just a touch and he took off running. Good thing he was fast and his arms were long because he had to dive full out for the ball. With a satisfying thump, it landed perfectly in his wide hands before he tumbled and skidded along the grass.

Sound erupted all around them.

People cheered. Men heckled one another as sides were taken. Women laughed and chased after screaming children.

A substantial crowd had gathered to watch this game. It was evening, and cool. A BBQ nearby sent the pleasant curls of cooking meat up into the air.

Eli's eyes snuck over to the sidelines as he walked forward with the rest of his team. Shelby was there observing him with her trusty pen and pad of paper in hand. Uriah Linfield was seated just beside her. As their eyes locked, Uriah gave Eli the slightest of nods.

Eli forced himself to grin cockily in return.

He was supposed to be enjoying this, not freaking the fuck out because a memory might drop him to his knees in front of hundreds of people at any moment.

"Shit, you've got an arm on you." Cole jogged up, out of breath and smiling. "What college did you play for again?"

Frowning, Eli's heart tapped at him guiltily in his chest. *UCLA on a full athletic scholarship, thank you very much.*

"I don't remember," he responded and motioned with his hand for everyone to huddle up.

That was a lifetime ago, and it didn't fucking matter anymore, did it? The lights. The roar of the crowd. The rush of adrenaline. The high. The promise of fame and fortune. It was all gone forever. It was all just gone.

Quickly, Eli explained the play he wanted to run. Some of these guys were familiar with football and the rest were just out for some fun.

It was fine with Eli both ways. He enjoyed the game, both

playing it and teaching it. Thankfully, doing so didn't bring any gray voices forward to stalk him. On the contrary, playing seemed to clear his head, soothing it from headaches and sharp hot demands.

The rest of the game went just as smoothly as the first half. Eli let his muscles remember their former purpose. He allowed himself to sink into old rhythms and it truly felt good down in his bones.

By the time it was all over, he was drenched in sweat and stinking to high heaven. Uriah Linfield had long since left the scene.

"Shower and dinner?" Cole asked, and slapped a hand on Eli's shoulder. "The wife's going to make some spaghetti. You're welcome to come."

The two of them headed to the sidelines, both still sucking wind.

Eli lifted his eyes to find Shelby. She was waiting for him on a nearby bench, like she had been every night for the past six or so days. He hadn't kissed her again, because he didn't deserve her and he'd made a promise. But that didn't mean he didn't want to. That didn't mean he didn't think about doing it all the damn time. Like right now.

"Or not..." Cole's voice faded into a chuckle. "Maybe you've already got plans."

"Maybe I do," Eli acknowledged.

Giving Eli's shoulder a tight squeeze, Cole let his hand drop away. "Don't fuck it up," he murmured, and shoved off.

Shelby stood up as Eli approached, and looped her ever present bag over her shoulder. Eli's eyes tracked the motion.

Uriah Linfield had been thumbing through her notes this time, Eli noticed him doing it between plays. The fact both unnerved and settled him at the same time.

Eli'd read through her books too. She was keeping up her end of the bargain, listing failed experiment after failed experiment, not exposing his memory recurrence just yet.

"Good game," she said as he came to a stop before her.

When her nose crinkled and her lip curled, Eli let out a laugh.

"I stink," he stated the obvious.

"No." Shelby shook her head and blew out a breath. "Of course not…"

His grin only grew wider as she tried to deny it, tried to be polite for him.

"We've still got plans though right?" Eli lifted his brow as sweat trickled from both temples. "I'll pick up some food to-go. Roast chicken, salad and breadsticks?"

Ducking her head, Shelby agreed. They'd been meeting every night now. It was the perfect time to try to jog his memory while not being watched by Liam, Cole or Uriah. Everyone around them thought Eli and Shelby were dating. In his heart, Eli wished it was true as well.

"I'll go get cleaned up," he amended. "Then meet you at your place?"

"Sounds good," Shelby agreed and stepped away. "See you in a few."

"Yeah." Eli swiped at his face, tasted the salt on his lips. "See you in a few."

It was quite possibly the fastest shower he'd ever taken.

Even Cass said she was impressed when he slipped into jeans and a long sleeve shirt and headed out the door. A part of him was ashamed that he had to take his baby sister's money to pay for this dinner, but the other half was consoled by the fact that Garrett was taking care of her, and in Eli's mind Garrett still owed him... big.

Outside, darkness had well and truly fallen. Tipping his head back, Eli took in the millions of glittering stars flung out among the blackness. It was sparkly and intricate and down right beautiful. He wished Shelby was here right now, to take it all in with him.

Dropping his head, he inhaled the fresh night air and picked up his feet. He would hit the cafeteria first, then he'd be off to see her.

Sidewalks and green grass passed beneath him without notice. He fetched their dinner and was climbing the stairs to her apartment in no time at all.

When she pulled open the door, Eli's chest expanded as his eyes devoured her. She was just so damn pretty. She didn't need fancy clothes or makeup or any of that stuff. If he could, he'd kiss every single freckle that dusted the bridge of her pixie nose.

"That was fast," Shelby commented and stepped aside.

"Hope you're hungry," he said and lifted the warm bag. "'Cause I'm starving."

With a chuckle, Shelby accepted the bag and turned towards the table. "I'll bet you are," she murmured. "I hope you got yourself seconds."

"I did," Eli confirmed.

Walking inside, he let the door click shut at his back. He loved the sound of it. He loved what it meant, that he was alone here with Shelby, in their own little world, one neither of them shared with anyone else. It was an intimacy he hadn't realized he craved. It was a mark on her he hadn't realized he so desperately needed to make.

Coming up behind her, Eli held himself back from brushing the hair off her neck and placing his lips against her skin. Instead, he pulled out her chair.

"Sit," he commanded, and had her glancing up over her shoulder at him. "I'll serve it."

"Oh." Shelby's face flushed. "Okay."

Holding his breath, Eli kept himself from inhaling the scent of her hair as she sat and he scooted her chair close to the table.

She'd already poured two glasses of water, and had an extra jug filled and ready as well. In a past life, he would've thought to bring wine. But here inside the Wall, alcohol was hard to come by. You could buy it with dinner at one of the restaurants, or at the Rec Center when the band was playing, but other than that, there was no where to get it.

Circling around, Eli brought out the carefully wrapped ceramic plates and sets of silverware. He would have to return them to the cafeteria tomorrow.

"Thank you," Shelby commented and gave him a smile.

Taking a seat beside her, Eli smiled back. This routine was becoming an addiction for him. He was living each day, looking forward to this moment at night, when they'd be alone, and he could pretend he was more to her than a pet project.

"You're welcome," he replied and the familiar dance began.

They fell into easy conversation. They talked about her upbringing, the fact that she was the only child born to a set of brilliant, older parents. Both had advanced degrees. Both taught at prestigious universities.

She couldn't remember a time when her life didn't center around education. She couldn't remember a speck of dirt in their two story conservative home.

It was a far cry from Eli's childhood spent in squalor. Even so, he didn't hold that back from her. When she asked him what he remembered, he told her everything. He told her about Neal. He told her about Wendy. He told her about hiding Cass in their bathtub and running out of food each month.

It was like a gift, he figured. The only thing she truly wanted from him were his memories, and so he gave up everything, even when it embarrassed him, even when it ripped at his ego to do so.

"I know the last few things we've tried haven't worked," Shelby said finally, and set down her fork with a clink against the plate. "And you haven't noticed any new triggers."

Easing back in his chair, Eli took a sip of water and sighed. The food had been delicious and was now completely gone. The guise of this being nothing more than a dinner date was quickly fading.

"No, I haven't," he stated honestly.

There had been no looming gray voices, no headaches, no fluttering memories trying to break through.

"Well, I have an idea," Shelby said carefully. "If you'd be willing. I'm a little concerned about it, but I think it just might work."

"Alright." Eli watched her face. Shelby was uncertain. She had no idea that he'd do anything for her at this point. "What is it?"

Shelby's eyes zeroed in on his arms. One was slung across the empty chair beside him. The other folded easily against his side, his hand resting in his lap.

"Physical pain is one of the human body's most effective ways of learning," Shelby stated. "Hold your hand over a flame, feel the burn, and never do it again."

"You want to hurt me?" Eli's brow rose and he tilted his head to one side.

"I want to simulate the experience of you getting those tattoos." Shelby nodded her head at his arms. "If you close your eyes and you feel the pain of a tattoo needle on your skin in the same location as before, it might trigger something for you."

"Ah." Eli ducked his head as his stomach clenched.

"But I won't do it without your consent," she rushed. "I don't want to pressure you. You can just say no and we can keep trying other things."

Drawing both hands to his lap, Eli pushed up his sleeves and stared down at his own skin. The tattoos were dark and heavy. A part of him twisted up at the sight. He didn't want to remember what he did after he got those tattoos. He didn't want to live with that person. It was hard enough living with what he knew so far.

"We'll try something else," Shelby announced, and had Eli's head snapping up.

"No, it's fine," he said suddenly. "Let's do it."

Frowning, Shelby nibbled on that bottom lip of hers. Eli's eyes dropped to the movement and his heart gave a jump in his chest. He wished he could kiss her again. He wished he had an excuse.

"If you're sure…" she trailed off.

"I'm sure," he cut in.

Standing from the table, Eli glanced around the room. It was tidy and sparse, with the exception of a stack of books piled haphazardly on the coffee table.

"Where do you want me?" He asked and couldn't help but notice her slight blush at his words.

When she responded to him like that, it gave him the tiniest slice of hope. Dangerous thing, hope. Very dangerous.

"On the couch." Shelby gestured and rose from her seat as well.

Eli strode over and laid full out, like the last half dozen times. His legs dangled over one side and he cushioned his head on a pillow wedged up against the other. Rolling up his sleeves even higher, Eli stared at the ceiling and exhaled.

Do good men do bad things? How many bad things can a good man do, before he loses his goodness?

Shelby arrived at his side and sat on the edge of the wooden coffee table. Her warm palm smoothed at the skin of his left forearm and he closed his eyes.

"Ready?" She whispered, and his chest began to tighten.

"Ready," he echoed.

Then came the pain.

CHAPTER TWENTY-FOUR_
ELI

THE PINCH IN HIS ARM IS WHAT BROUGHT HIM AROUND. GROANING, Eli rolled onto his side and grabbed for the crook of his elbow with his opposite hand. His eyes were closed tight, his head throbbing.

"Easy," a male voice soothed.

Cool hands covered in latex came down to block his reach. Eli's eyes shot open then, but the lighting in the room blinded him.

"Welcome back to the land of the living," the voice gave a soft chuckle. The hands held firm though, preventing Eli from clawing at the prickling sharp pain zinging from his inner arm.

"What?" Eli rasped, his throat was so dry.

"You took quite the blow to your head," the voice went on. "I'm gonna need you to lie still, that's an IV in your arm and you need the fluids."

Blinking stubbornly, Eli fought against the blurry tint to his vision. He turned his head to one side, towards the voice, and at the same time forced his own body to relax.

After several seconds, the hands pulled away.

Eli listened to the spin of wheels against smooth flooring,

watched the figure of a man move away. The overhead light flipped off then, and Eli exhaled.

The room was dim now, not too bright and not pitch black either. Eli's vision sharpened, and the man wearing a lab coat floated back over on what appeared to be a rolling stool.

"You're a doctor?" Eli asked.

The man nodded his head before adjusting a few pieces of medical equipment. The lights on them blinked and glowed green.

"Yes, I am," he spoke quietly before returning his focus to Eli. "And you've had surgery recently... major surgery to your lower left side and back."

Swallowing, Eli's brain zipped to the fight with Garrett, the stabbing and subsequent intervention by an anonymous neighbor at an abandoned hospital.

"It's excellent work," the doctor went on, his eyes more curious than anything else. "I'm sure the surgeon who did it instructed you to take it easy for awhile."

Eli blinked slowly, but did not answer.

"Doesn't look like you take advice well," the doctor commented. "Medical or otherwise."

At that, the doctor lifted his gaze to settle on the far corner of the room.

Shifting his head to follow the man's line of sight, Eli felt his belly twist. A pair of soldiers stood silently by the only door in the small space. One of them he recognized. It was Ricky/Ronnie. The soldier's eyes were serious, his face a mask of blankness.

"I don't remember," Eli whispered and turned his head back to the doctor.

"Ah, well..." The doctor straightened on his stool and smoothed at his white lab coat, his hands were covered with blue latex gloves.

"Between the knock to your head and your level of dehydration, I can safely say that's normal... for now."

Nodding, Eli's tongue snuck out to wet his chapped lips. They were cracked and painful. The doctor sighed.

"I've done a scan of your body and I don't see that you've had a microchip implanted," he said. "Can you tell me if that's true?"

Eli's heart began to dance in his chest, but he forced a slow inhale and willed himself to calm down. The monitors set up behind the doctor continued with their steady beeping, not giving away the fact he was scared as hell.

In that moment, Eli desperately wanted to turn back to Ricky/Ronnie and stare into his face. He wanted to ask a million questions about the microchip and what he should say or do, but it was too late.

"I don't know," Eli managed finally. "I don't remember."

Nodding, the doctor wheeled away and lifted a tablet from a nearby countertop. Eli's eyes tracked him as he swiped his finger across it and tapped a couple of times on the screen.

"I'm going to need to implant one," he said, not lifting his eyes from the tablet. "I'd prefer to wait a few more days, until your body is stronger, but that decision is not up to me."

Eli's eyes widened and his lips parted, but no words escaped him. He was confused. He didn't know what was going on.

"It looks like you've caught the attention of some people in high places." The doctor glanced up at Eli, then back down to the tablet. "You've got a skill set that's in high demand."

"Skill set?" Eli frowned.

"It says here that you took out an entire train transport team." The doctor's eyes narrowed on his screen. "No wait... three. Three entire teams, and apparently you did it all by yourself."

Lifting a hand in the air, the doctor made a motion to the

soldiers standing along the wall. Without a word, they advanced towards Eli, who scrambled back on the hospital bed.

"I don't..." he sputtered, as the IV yanked at his arm and his head swam with dizziness.

"We're just going to hold you tight for a second," the doctor explained. "Just until we get the chip implanted."

"I don't want the chip. I don't need the chip," Eli protested, but his body was weak.

Twisting on the bed, he ripped at the IV, causing it to spurt blood and the doctor to curse. The soldiers were on him in an instant. Their hands gripped his arms, then his legs as he continued to struggle.

"If you can't hold still then we'll have to sedate you," the doctor grunted, adding his hands to the mix. "We're running low on sedative and I really don't want to waste it."

"Then stop!" Eli cried.

His heart was trying to punch a hole in his chest and his breath came out short. Just then Ricky/Ronnie leaned down and spoke directly into his ear.

"You've got to do this," he insisted, as his grip on Eli tightened. "You've got to let us do this."

Eli's eyes widened and for just a split second his body stilled. Turning his head, he stared into Ricky/Ronnie's face. The guy's eyes were intent, his mouth pressed into a firm line.

"Okay," Eli relented.

His body was still taut, his muscles flexed against the idea of being held by so many, forced by so many to do something he did not want to do. His instinct was to fight. His instinct was to break free.

Quickly, the doctor left his side, then returned again. Eli swallowed, his eyes still locked on Ricky/Ronnie's face. The soldier *nodded ever so slightly, but his hands did not relent where they held Eli in place.*

*There was a sharp pinch in Eli's right hand and a clicking sound.*

*"There," the doctor announced.*

*As one, all of them took a giant step back. Eli's eyes danced from one face to the next as they silently observed him.*

*"We'll know in about ten minutes," the doctor spoke quietly. "If he gets sick or not."*

*Eli blanched. Ricky/Ronnie ducked his head.*

*"You've got your gas masks?" The doctor looked to the soldiers and in unison, they nodded.*

THE MOMENT SHE PRESSED THE TIP OF THE NEEDLE TO HIS ARM, Eli's face screwed up and he shoved her away.

Shelby's heart popped up into her throat and she let out a yelp. She hadn't been expecting that, so the tip of the needle left a long thin slice along his skin. Blood oozed immediately to the surface and trickled down to the couch.

"I'm so sorry," she rushed, and sucked her hands back to her lap.

Eli didn't respond. He didn't open his eyes.

Quickly, Shelby set the needle down beside her on the coffee table and picked up a square of gauze. Reaching for him, she held the gauze firmly against the fresh cut and glanced at his face.

He was still as a statute. Frozen. Unmoving.

"Eli?" She asked, as her brows drew together.

Holding her breath, Shelby slid a hand down to his wrist and took his pulse. It was steady and strong. He was out cold.

Memory recurrence.

The pain experiment worked.

. . .

For the next four and a half minutes, Shelby busied herself cleaning and bandaging Eli's arm. She scrubbed uselessly at the blood spots on her couch and threw the dirty rags into a laundry basket.

By the time he began to groan and stir, Shelby was more than ready for him to come back to reality. She sat perched on the edge of the coffee table, her hands pressed to her knees, her toes tapping against the carpet.

It wasn't until Eli's eyes fluttered open that she let her shoulders relax. Her lungs sucked in a fresh breath of air and it was all she could do to keep herself from reaching a hand to steady his arm.

"Hey," she spoke first. "You okay?"

Sucking in a breath, Eli's body tensed. His face titled over towards her and his eyes blinked open.

"Eli," Shelby tried again, and this time she did reach out and touch him. "I hurt you, I'm sorry."

The movement drew his eyes down to the bandage now wrapping around his forearm. Eli's brow furrowed a moment while he worked his hand. The muscles in his arms jumped and flexed before he relaxed his palm and looked back at her.

"A scratch," he commented. "I don't hardly feel anything."

Nodding, Shelby tried to stuff the guilt down inside of her. She could tell by the look on his face that the injury she'd inflicted on his body was secondary to the one she'd just inflicted on his mind. The doctor part of her wanted to ask him what he remembered during the four minutes he'd been unconscious, but the human part of her knew it wasn't right.

"Still, I'm sorry," she repeated. "You jumped and I wasn't

ready. The scratch is fairly deep."

With a grunt, Eli pushed up to sitting on the sofa. Shelby leaned back in an attempt to give him room, but the coffee table was positioned so close that they couldn't help brushing against one another.

Eli planted his feet on either side of hers, so that her knees were placed between his legs.

They were facing one another, so close that if Eli bent down, his forehead would be resting against hers.

Shelby's pulse spiked and her body flushed hot. His broad shoulders seemed to dwarf her as her eyes settled on his chest.

"I didn't remember about the tattoos," he said.

She could feel the exhale of his breath stir the hair on the top of her head. It tickled her face, causing her to reach up and tuck a chunk of hair behind one ear.

Eli's hand went to hers then, and intercepted. Before she could do it, his fingers were the ones brushing the red wisps back and sliding them into place.

"You're beautiful," he whispered and then looked away. "I remembered how I got my microchip."

Shelby's lips parted but she couldn't get any words to leave her mouth. Her brain was caught up, unsure as to which avenue to take.

Easing back, Eli decided for her.

"I was in a medical facility of some kind," he stated, and kept his gaze fixed on the sliding glass door.

Beyond it was the darkness of night and the smattering of a million glittering stars.

"After I took out that last train crew, I was picked up by a solider. He took me to a facility. I think it was in California, but I'm not sure."

"Was it an office building? A hospital?" Shelby prompted.

Shaking his head, Eli shrugged. "I wasn't awake for that part. I just know the guy was driving me somewhere in Cali and then I woke up in a room. It looked like a hospital room, but it didn't have any windows."

"Okay…"

"There was a man in a lab coat," Eli went on, his jaw ticking ever so slightly. "He said he was a doctor. He injected me with the microchip but…"

"But what?" Shelby leaned forward and placed her hands on Eli's.

Turning his head, Eli eyed her. His hazel eyes darted over her face and he frowned.

"When you guys were implanting the chip in people here," Eli began. "Did it make anyone sick?"

"There were some mild side effects," Shelby recalled. "Pain at the injection site, skin rash, headaches. But they all went away after forty-eight hours."

"No one got some awful contagious disease?" Eli asked. "No one died?"

Sitting up straight, Shelby kept hold of Eli's hands. She didn't know why, but she couldn't seem to let go.

"Unbeknownst to the general public, the source had been doing clinical trials with its microchip for several years before the start of the war. By the time the Wall was in place, the microchip was more than ready for human implantation."

Pursing his lips, Eli nodded silently a few times. His hands dropped away from hers then and he reclined back against the sofa. After awhile, his gaze drifted back to the sliding glass door, back to the night.

"The doctor in my memory, and the soldiers, they were

afraid I was going to get sick," Eli explained finally. "They were legit afraid of what would happen, but they injected me with it anyway."

"I…"

"The people on the train, Shelby," Eli cut her off, his eyes darting back over to focus on her. "The soldiers were afraid all of them were sick, too. Before they started shooting… they all put on gas masks. They said the people were sick."

Shelby's stomach dropped and her head tipped back as Eli rose to standing.

Making room for him, she watched as he scooted out from between the couch and the coffee table and strode away.

"Why was the chip that you all got injected with safe, while this other one wasn't?" Eli stopped in his tracks and pivoted to face her.

Closing her eyes briefly, Shelby had to inhale in an attempt to steady herself.

"Because it wasn't the same chip," she supplied, and opened her eyes.

Eli's face twisted as he tried to make sense of things. Shelby blurted the assumptions that leapt to her mind.

"If you were implanted with a microchip from someone other than the source, then it explains a lot," she offered. "It explains why you were still getting affected by the chip in Oregon, after the source had already been deleted here behind the Wall. It explains why you only lost your memory when your chip was removed from your hand."

Eli's eyes widened and his skin grew pale.

"It means…"

"There's another entity out there controlling people," Shelby whispered. "And it isn't the source."

TEETERING OVER TO THE COUCH, ELI SLAMMED HIS BODY DOWN onto it. His lungs squeezed in tight as he leaned forward and braced his arms on his knees.

"There are other locations throughout the world that have facilities like this one, facilities like the Wall," Shelby went on. "Were you ever close to one? Do you remember seeing one?"

Shaking his head, Eli's gaze locked inextricably on his tattoos and the white bandages that now covered some of them. He didn't have the full story back yet. He didn't remember what came next, and it unnerved him.

"There should be one somewhere in South America," Shelby offered. "And another in Europe. They were scattered throughout the globe. Is it possible you were at one of those? Were you ever in an airplane? Or on a ship?"

"No." Eli's face screwed up and he clenched his fists. "I think we were in California still. I can't explain why, but I got that impression. The doctor and the soldiers, they weren't that far from where I took the train."

"Alright," Shelby exhaled the word and bit her lower lip.

Eli glanced up into her face briefly and then back down to his arms. His heart was hammering at him and his throat was bobbing.

"We have to tell…"

"No," Eli cut her off, his voice low and hoarse.

"But…"

"I said *no*." Eli lifted his head and stared into Shelby's eyes. "I don't know enough yet. What could I possibly tell them?"

"That there's another threat."

"They already know that, am I right?" Eli's eyes swept across her pretty face. "That's why they want these answers so bad. That's why they're pushing so hard for me to remember."

"We could tell them where the threat is coming from," Shelby reasoned. "That it's probably based out of California."

"Probably?" Eli scoffed. "Do you think that will satisfy Uriah Linfield? Do you understand what will happen to me the moment they suspect that I'm remembering?"

"You have nothing to be afraid of," Shelby tried.

"This whole buddy-buddy act from Liam?" Eli's brow lifted. "That will end. And your scientific experiments to get me to remember? Those will be over too. The only thing that will matter is that the pain trigger works."

Reaching out for him, Shelby covered one of his clenched fists in her tiny warm hand.

Eli yanked his arm away and stood up, forcing her to lean back to give him space. He was off and pacing again, staring out into the night, but no longer seeing it, no longer appreciating its beauty.

"Just…" Eli sucked in a sharp breath and glanced at her over his shoulder. "Give me a little more time. Work with me to get all of my memories back first, then we can go to Linfield."

"What if I just put some feelers out?" Shelby rose from her seat on the coffee table and approached him. "I won't mention your memories, I'll try to find out what the next steps are."

Whirling to face her, Eli's shoulders broadened and his lungs expanded. He could feel the panic bubbling throughout his entire body. He could feel it just the same as when the soldiers had held him down, when he knew there was no way out, when he knew his body was too weak to stop the inevitable.

"When we first started doing this," Eli reminded her, his voice low. "You told me I was like a patient to you. You told me that you swore an oath and that you would protect me first."

Shelby gave him a quick nod and came to a stop just in front of him. Her head tipped back, her flaming red hair fell away from her face. Those pale-blue eyes of hers shot into him and his heart came to a sudden halt in his chest.

"I remember," she assured him, and once more her hand sought his own. This time he didn't yank away. "And I will hold true to my word. I won't say anything... until you're ready."

Stepping into her space, Eli took both of his hands and framed her delicate face. His bloodstream was coursing with so many things. With fear and relief. With uncertainty and desire.

Shelby's mouth parted, causing Eli's pulse to jump start again.

Slowly, he ran the pads of his thumbs along her cheeks. The freckles. They were calling to him.

"I don't think you have anything to fear though," she whispered.

Her throat bobbed as she swallowed. Eli felt the movement beneath his palms. Exhaling through his nostrils, Eli held himself back. His eyes drank her in, his mind raced in the direction he wished like hell he could go.

"Thank you," he whispered finally, and forced himself to let go.

Stepping back, Eli's arms dropped to his sides and his hands sunk themselves in his pockets. He looked towards the front door.

"I better go," he said. "Can we take a break for awhile?"

"A… a break?" Shelby's voice was low and thick.

It made him want to grab her again. It made him want to grab her with bruising hands and cover her with bruising lips.

The impulse became so strong, that he dropped his head and started stalking towards the door. He had to get some air. He had to breathe and think.

"Yeah," he managed. "With the memory stuff. Can we take a little break before we try again?"

Coming to a stop at the front door, Eli pulled it open without waiting for her answer. He stepped through the threshold and only then looked back.

Shelby was standing right where he'd left her, a stunned sort of expression on her face.

"Of course." She bobbed her head. "Let me know when you're ready to start again."

"I will," Eli promised, and then he left.

CHAPTER TWENTY-SEVEN_
SHELBY

WHEN THE DOOR TO HER LAB PUSHED OPEN, SHELBY'S HEAD instantly snapped up. Her body clenched and tingles shot to her fingers and toes.

But when her blue eyes landed on the woman standing in the threshold, Shelby's heart fell.

"Hey Shelby." Hannah offered a tentative wave. "Am I interrupting anything important?"

With a shake of her head, Shelby dismissed her disappointment and forced a smile.

"Come on in," she said.

Setting down the specimen she'd been analyzing, Shelby removed her rubber gloves. They came off with a familiar snap before she shoved them in the pocket of her lab coat.

She was wearing simple jeans beneath it today, instead of a dress. It had been two weeks since she'd last seen Eli, and so she'd stopped caring what she would look like if he walked in.

Apparently, her body hadn't received that message though, it still jumped and danced at the thought of him.

"What can I do for you?" Shelby asked finally.

Hannah moved through the door, letting it swing shut at her back. The other woman was alone, which was rare, now that Shelby thought about it. Usually one of her guys was with her. But not here. Not today.

"Well…" Hannah glanced over her shoulder, as if her thoughts were running along the same lines, making doubly sure there was no one behind her. "I've come for a little favor."

"A favor?" Shelby's brow rose in interest as Hannah slowly made her way down the aisle that ran between the two countertops in the room.

Glancing around, Hannah took in the space and remained silent. Shelby's eyes followed the other woman's gaze. Microscopes, Petri dishes, trays, utensils, note pads, pens, beakers. The place was an organized sort of mess. There was so much stuff… so much wonderful scientific stuff.

"I need to run a DNA test," Hannah admitted finally.

Coming to a stop a few feet from Shelby, the very pregnant woman placed a hand on her belly and heaved a sigh.

"I see," Shelby intoned, her eyes dropping to said belly.

"I know there's an electronics ban," Hannah continued. "But is there a way you can run one anyway? Maybe without the equipment or without anyone noticing?"

"You mean without your brother noticing?" Shelby arched a brow and folded her arms across her chest.

"Well yes, him too, but actually I meant… I don't want *anyone* to know," Hannah explained.

"Oh." Shelby frowned. "Ohhhhh. Yes, I believe that I can be discreet and run one without anyone being the wiser. All I need is a genetic sample from the two parties involved. I recommend you wait until the baby is born, however."

Hannah's mouth dropped then and she huffed a laugh. Her

hand stroked a quick circle on her belly before giving it a light tap.

"It's not for my baby," she corrected. "I don't need to know the biological father."

Now it was Shelby's turn to gape. Her face fell, then a few seconds later, screwed up as if she'd tasted a lemon.

"I don't..." she sputtered. "Get it."

"I want to run a DNA test on Liam and Eli," Hannah stated.

Bracing a hand on the counter and cocking a hip, the woman's brown eyes sparkled with interest. Her belly swayed heavily with the movement, and she let out a sigh.

"Don't tell me you don't see it." Hannah gestured with her hand vaguely in the air.

"See what?" Shelby gave her head a little shake.

"Same height, same build, same coloring," Hannah ticked off reasons with her fingers. "They even walk the same. There's been more than one time when I've seen Eli walking away across the grass or at the gym and I've had to do a double take."

"But..." Shelby considered. "It's not unheard of to have similarities such as that and not be biologically related."

Shrugging, Hannah smirked. "So, let's find out. Cass says they never knew their dad and Liam's awful father was a traveling salesman of some kind. It's entirely possible he cheated, more than once. The age range matches too."

"Have you discussed this with Cass?"

"No way." Hannah rolled her eyes. "She's so protective of her brother and won't do anything without his permission and from what I've seen of Eli, he would not agree to this willingly."

Shelby blinked.

"And neither would Liam... *if* he knew," Hannah offered. "But I'm pregnant and I have a lot of leeway right now to do pretty much whatever I want."

"I... uh..."

"Come on!" Hannah stepped forward and placed a hand on Shelby's forearm. "Aren't you even the least bit curious? If they aren't a match, then we can just pretend like it never happened."

"And if they are?" Shelby whispered, making Hannah smile.

"Then we'll deal with it then," Hannah offered with a shrug. "I'll take full responsibility."

"I don't... know." Shelby trailed off and nibbled on her lower lip. "Do you have the samples from both of them?"

Reaching into her back pocket, Hannah fished out a glass jar with a bunch of short dark hair inside of it.

"I've got Liam covered," she explained.

Holding the jar out between them, Hannah offered her specimen. When Shelby didn't take it, she set it quietly down on the countertop.

"And Eli?" Shelby asked. "What have you got from him?"

"Well..." Hannah offered Shelby a Cheshire Cat grin. "That's where you come in."

CHAPTER TWENTY-EIGHT_
ELI

ELI'S HANDS FLEXED AROUND THE WOODEN HANDLE AS HE pushed the tip of the shovel further into the rich earth. Blisters that had appeared and cracked a few days ago, were slowly turning to calluses now.

Overhead, the sun beat down against the impossibly high glass of the greenhouse. It gave everything a strange greenish tint, and heated the air considerably.

But that didn't matter to Eli. He just kept on digging.

Sweat collected and dripped from his temples, forehead and spine. He let the salty substance roll off, not bothering to swipe it away. His shoulders burned and his arm muscles protested. But it served to clear his mind, and he was grateful for that.

"What are you doing?" A familiar male voice broke the air.

Eli paused in his shoveling, but didn't bother to look up. He would recognize Liam's voice anywhere. The guy had a habit of creeping up when you least expected it.

"What's it look like?" Eli grumbled, before resuming his activity.

The shovel sliced through the dirt, making a delightful sort of gritty sound.

Somewhere in the back of Eli's mind, he knew this activity should trigger him. It should remind him of the thousands of dead bodies he'd buried in his short life. But for whatever reason, maybe it was the greenhouse air, the lack of smoke, the lack of burning, his mind remained settled and clear.

"You're digging," Liam answered. Along the ground, his giant shadow loomed.

Eli continued to dig, but watched the shadow's movement. Liam stalked along in that predatory way he had, until his boots were at the far edge of the hole Eli was working on.

"I'm working," Eli corrected.

"Why?" Liam asked.

Eli's jaw ticked and his hands clenched down harder on the handle. He pushed the shovel into the earth, filled it up to overflowing, then tossed the dirt aside.

"Maybe I'm tired of taking money from my little sister," Eli offered. "I'm trying to make my own way here."

"As a farm laborer," Liam put in, and the tone he used had Eli pausing in his effort.

Lifting a hand to his brow, Eli shaded his eyes and looked up. Liam's head was tilted to one side, his arms folded casually across his broad chest.

Eli heaved a sigh. "What do you care?" He asked and gave his head a little shake. "Fuck off."

Snorting, Liam suppressed a tiny smile and glanced to one side.

Eli's eyes narrowed beneath the shade of his hand. Liam's smiles were rare, apparently reserved for drinking, getting his ass handed to him in the boxing ring, and being told where to stick it. Regardless, Eli remained unamused.

"Not many people talk to me like that, you know," Liam commented and returned his gaze to Eli's face.

With an exaggerated shrug, Eli dropped his hand to his shovel and began to dig once more.

He knew that whatever sort of things Liam was capable of, they were currently being held in check. As long as Eli had the potential to remember, but hadn't remembered anything yet, Eli was safe.

Besides, he had bigger problems. Internal problems. Shelby problems.

For a few moments, the sound of Eli's shovel was all that could be heard. He could feel the brand of Liam's critical stare lingering against his skin, but he ignored it. Whatever the guy was here to do or say, he'd spit it out in his own time. Eli had no interest in begging for it.

In fact, he'd be a hell of a lot happier if Liam kept his mouth shut and walked away.

Instead, the static of a radio crackled.

Eli glanced up just as Liam reached for the handheld on his hip. Bringing it to his mouth, he depressed the button and spoke.

"Go ahead," he commanded and then adjusted a few of the tiny dials on the black walkie talkie.

"We've received contact from Officer Jameson," a voice reported. "The convoy is a few hours out. We expect them before sunset."

"Copy that," Liam replied and returned the handheld to his belt.

"Convoy?" Eli asked. "You've heard from Garrett?"

Liam narrowed his eyes. "That's Jameson's first name," he commented. "I keep forgetting."

Eli's gut pinched but he kept his face plain. "That's what my sister calls him," he explained. "I can't seem to think of him any other way."

Nodding, Liam seemed to accept the answer.

"Is he coming home?" Eli pressed.

Now that he remembered his friend, Eli truly longed to see him. He wanted to wrap the guy in a giant bear hug right after punching him in his stupid face for making a move on his litter sister. Even though Garrett clearly made Cass happy, like beyond happy and safe, which made Eli grateful.

"Yes, they're all heading here now," Liam informed him before adding, "Everyone appears to be in one piece."

Ducking his head, Eli tried to hide the instant flood of relief that washed over his face.

He hadn't realized until this moment that he'd been worried about his best friend. He hadn't stopped to acknowledge the nagging fear that Garrett wouldn't return from his mission outside the Wall, the fear that he would leave Cass alone and heartbroken.

Picking up the shovel, Eli slung it over one shoulder and hopped up out of the hole. Sweat stuck to his skin, causing his back to itch and his shirt to cling. Loose earth shifted and slid beneath his worn boots.

"Better go tell Cass," Eli commented, and began heading for the tool shed where the shovels were stored. "She'll be excited to see him."

"Yeah," Liam commented and fell into step beside him. "I'm sure she will."

Pursing his lips, Eli exhaled through his nostrils. It

would've been way too easy for Liam to just let him walk away. It would've been too simple for the guy to get side-tracked with the return of the convoy and let whatever he'd been meaning to talk to Eli about fade away.

For several silent minutes the two of them walked that way. Side by side. Equally silent.

Eli made it the storage shed and put his shovel back where he'd found it. Open door. Close door.

Liam said nothing, just waited and watched.

Making their way to one of the many exits in the massive greenhouse, the pair of them pushed outside. Eli forced himself to remain calm. He held back his desire to tell Liam to get lost. He held back the words that wanted to leap from his lips.

He figured this must be one of the many ways Liam got people to talk. As a rule, people don't like silence. If you leave uncomfortable gaps in the air space, then most people feel compelled to fill them.

Well... not Eli.

He knew better.

Whenever the cops would bring him in for questioning as a kid, he'd just wait them out. Let them talk. Let them question and threaten and pace around. As long as Eli kept his mouth shut, then eventually they'd let him go.

It had worked well enough after Neal's body was found in their apartment building's dumpster. Eli had said nothing. The neighborhood had said nothing. Eventually, the cops closed the case.

Magically, Eli hoped like hell the same thing would happen now.

Cool air from the outside hit Eli like a wave rolling in from the ocean. It was like stepping into a pool. Eli's hot, sweat-soaked body was engulfed in the fall breeze, causing goosebumps to rise and dance along his forearms.

The tattoos hid them though. The tattoos hid everything, even the long slice from the needle Shelby had inflicted on him not so many weeks ago.

He hadn't seen her since that night.

Well… maybe that was a lie. He'd watched her from a distance since then, across the cafeteria or over the rolling green lawns outside.

He hadn't approached her though, just let his greedy eyes track her body as she walked to and from work. It had been damn harder than he'd imagined, staying away from her. Somewhere over the past several months, Eli had become well and truly addicted to the fiery redhead.

He missed her. His entire being missed her, and it only served to complicate things for him. She wanted one thing. He wanted another.

"There's nothing wrong with farm work," Liam offered finally. "As a rule."

Eli's brow furrowed but he kept his gaze straight ahead. They were crossing an expanse of grass now, weaving their way between buildings, heading towards Cass's apartment. Occasionally, their boots slapped against cement sidewalks. Once, they had to wait for a pair of bicyclists to glide by before crossing.

"I'm glad you approve," Eli mocked quietly.

At this, Liam huffed a breath and glanced his way.

"You're a real dick, you know that?" He commented, and had Eli's mouth parting.

On a laugh, Eli shot him a bit of side eye. "*I'm* the dick?"

"Yeah." Liam rolled his shoulders and smirked. "You are."

Giving his head a slight shake, Eli stuffed his hands in his pockets and kept walking. Liam kept pace beside him and the two of them were lulled into silence for a bit longer.

"Look, I know the memory thing has you a bit messed up," Liam spoke finally. "But you've got the skill set of a soldier, not a day laborer. You can do more with what you've got, is all I'm trying to say."

Walking up to the entrance of Cass's apartment building, Eli let his hand rest on the long metal handle of one of the double glass front doors. Before pulling it open, he turned to Liam and tilted his head to one side.

"What do you want from me Liam?" Eli asked. "Aside from the obvious memory shit."

Liam's dark eyes bored into Eli's questioning hazel ones.

"Commander Linfield is putting together a Strike Team," Liam stated. "I'd like you to be on it."

Of all the things Eli was expecting to hear come out of Liam's mouth, that was definitely not one of them. His brow raised and his mouth dropped slightly. In that instant, he was unable to cover his shock.

Liam seemed to warm to this expression, and gave an approving nod.

"I'll be running it," he explained. "And we could really use a guy like you... attitude and all."

"Attitude," Eli repeated and huffed an uncertain breath.

Backing a step, Liam held up both palms and delivered yet another smirk.

"It pays well," he added. "You could afford to take the Good Doc to a nice dinner. Maybe fix whatever shit you've screwed up between the two of you."

"Fuck off," Eli spat the words automatically and yanked open the front door.

"Think about it!" Liam called, as Eli pushed his way inside and headed down the hall.

CHAPTER TWENTY-NINE_
ELI


"GET OUT!" CASS'S MIGHTY FIST POUNDED AGAINST THE LOCKED bathroom door, causing Eli to grin.

"Almost done!" He called and rotated around in the shower.

Reaching up, he angled the shower head as high as it would go. Even still, the water refused to spray above the dead center of his chest.

As the soap suds flowed in rivulets down his body, Eli wondered about the design of this place. If he'd of had anything to do with it, he would've made sure the showers accommodated people taller than five foot three.

"Seriously Elijah!" Cass called through the wood. "You've been in there forever!"

"Alright! Alright!" Eli suppressed a chuckle.

Rotating quickly, he rinsed the rest of his body before twisting the faucet off. The patter of water stopped abruptly and he pulled the shower curtain to one side. The rings made a satisfying scraping sound against the metal bar and he stepped out onto the bathroom rug.

Water dripped from his body, causing him to leave several soaking wet footprints, before he grabbed a fluffy white towel from the nearby rack and wrapped it around his waist.

Steam fogged the bathroom mirror and clung heavily in the air. Crossing to the bathroom door, he flipped the lock and sucked his hand back as Cass yanked the door wide.

Her glaring green eyes locked on him and only caused the delight he felt to increase. Look how far we've come, he wanted to say. Hot water. Electricity. A rug in the bathroom for Godsakes. It's a miracle.

Instead, he ducked his head sheepishly and did his best to scoot out around her. Cass fisted a hand on her hip and sniffed.

"You used my shampoo," she commented.

Eli shrugged. "So?"

"There's a limited supply of that," she began, then pushed her way into the bathroom. "Never mind," she announced before slamming the door. "You have no idea what it's like to manage this type of curly hair." Her voice came out muffled through the door.

Sticking his tongue in his cheek, Eli strolled into his bedroom. With a sigh, he pulled his own door shut.

Whipping his towel off, he rubbed it roughly over his body before spending less than three seconds scrubbing at his own hair. Now damp and heavy, he tossed the towel haphazardly over his dresser before digging around in his tiny closet for some clean clothes. There was a central laundromat for each building, but he hadn't had a chance to hit theirs in awhile. Too busy working.

Stepping into his last pair of clean boxers, Eli yanked on some simple blue jeans that rode just a bit too low on his hips.

He was about to reach for a belt when he heard a distant knock on the front door.

Frowning, Eli forgot about a belt and a shirt and wandered the length of their narrow hall. After crossing through the living room, he looked through the peephole of the front door and paused.

"Shelby," he stated, as an electric current shot from his heart straight to his dick.

"Yeah," the redhead answered. He could see her nibbling on that damn lower lip of hers. It made his own mouth water.

Flipping the lock, he twisted the handle and pulled the door wide.

Shelby's mouth dropped and her eyes widened as she took him in.

Eli stood there with one long arm braced against the door, absorbing the sight of her like a greedy sponge. Her cheeks flushed pink and her gaze held fast to his chest before dipping slightly to his stomach. When she swallowed, he noted the slight bob in her creamy white throat. That's when he remembered he was half naked and for once he was glad of it.

Every male inch of him recognized that look in her eyes. His body tensed and primed, even when maybe he didn't mean for it to. There was something about watching a woman react to you in this way that had a man itching to claim what was so obviously his. On the surface anyway, Shelby was attracted to him. It was the first time he'd known it for sure.

Instead of following the impulse of his body, Eli sucked in a sharp breath and stood aside.

"Come on in," he said and gestured to the living room. "What's up?"

"Oh, um, thanks," Shelby murmured.

Tucking a hair behind one ear, she pushed past him and into the room. Eli inhaled. The smell of cotton candy hit him full force, making his teeth ache as he clenched them together. Swinging the door shut, he rotated around and watched her walk away from him.

She didn't have her bag with her this time, which meant no notebook and no pen. His eyes swept her delicate shoulders and trim waist, which were covered in some flowy long sleeve blouse, before settling on her round ass, stuffed perfectly into a pair of tight jeans.

Briefly, he wondered how hard it would be to pull those useless pants over her hips and down her thighs.

Down boy, he thought and blew out a silent breath.

"Can I get you anything?" He asked, as she picked a spot on the couch and sat down.

"Oh... ah..." Shelby looked flustered, and it had him smiling.

He was still shirtless. She was still noticing. And yet, this was the exact reason he'd been avoiding her.

When he was in her presence for any amount of time, he folded like a damn lawn chair. Shelby wasn't the only one noticing. And even if she wasn't, she remained irresistible to him. In the end, he'd give her anything she wanted. And although his heart tapped at him dangerously, and he knew he should be wary, Eli couldn't seem to help himself.

"You want a glass of wine?" He prompted. "I think Cass has an open bottle in the fridge."

"Ah, no." Shelby shook her head and glanced away. "No wine. Thank you."

"Alright." Eli nodded.

Walking over to the couch, he picked a spot directly beside

Shelby and sat down. Turning slightly to face her, he slung a long arm over the back of the sofa and stared at the side of her face. Was it his imagination, or was she turning an even deeper shade of pink right now?

"I haven't seen you in awhile," Shelby announced suddenly.

Eli bobbed his head in agreement, but he made no verbal reply.

Shelby was watching him out of the corner of her eye, refusing to look at him directly. For some reason, it made him lean in closer.

"I was ah…" Shelby jumped a little and rubbed her palms along her thighs. "In my lab the other day."

"Uh-huh," he intoned, not really caring so much what she was saying.

Reaching out, Eli tucked a strand of her amazing red hair behind her ear. When her eyes darted over to him, his breath caught in his throat. She wasn't the only one having a reaction. She wasn't the only one flushing with heat.

Eli was playing with fire.

Subconsciously, he knew that. In the back of his mind… hell in the front of his mind… he knew he should keep his damn hands to himself.

But he was a moth and she was the flame. He wanted her. He always had, and the self-imposed separation he'd implemented the last two weeks had officially backfired on him. Instead of gaining space and control, he'd only served to make himself more desperate.

"You were in your lab," he prompted.

Shelby's eyes grew wider, as his fingers left her hair and traced along her throat.

"You know I do genetic…" she whispered. "Work."

"Yes." His eyes flicked from the skin he was touching, up to her face, trying to gauge if he was pushing this too far, doing too much.

"Elijah…" Shelby trailed off.

Those big blue eyes of hers flicked up to lock on his. Her mouth was parted but no more words came out.

Eli licked his lips as his fingers slowly, carefully danced along the skin of her throat. His heart was pounding like a drum in his chest, insistent, demanding, strong.

Still, what came next surprised him.

Shelby closed the gap between them and pressed her lips to his. *She* kissed him. *She* wanted him.

Eli's eyes widened just a touch at the initial contact, but in the next second they slammed shut. She was so fucking sweet. He wanted to taste every single bit of her.

Angling her head to one side, Shelby deepened the kiss. Her lips brushed against his, her tongue snaked out to flick against his.

A groan rumbled somewhere down low in Eli's chest as his entire body flooded with sensation.

Shelby's hands swept up his stomach, to his chest. Her fingertips flitted over his skin, causing his muscles to tense and jump.

Eli slid his hands down the length of her back, before circling around to her sides and gripping hard at her hips. In one swift motion, he yanked her closer to him, brought her up against him, just as her fingers snaked up to tangle in his damp hair.

Her hands curled into tiny fists, pulling and clawing, sending a brief spike of pain along his scalp, which shot immediately down into his dick.

Eli just about lost it then. A growl curled itself in his throat and he nipped at her lower lip.

Shelby gasped… then moaned. Eli swallowed the irresistible little sound she made down his throat.

Tipping backwards onto the couch, he pulled her down on top of him.

Shelby let out a soft cry as her chest crushed against his chest, but the kissing didn't stop, the grabbing didn't stop. Her hands threaded and yanked at his hair, so hard he felt another pinch of pain, but then she released. It sent a jolt straight down his spine this time, making his dick throb and his hips jump.

Shelby's hands left his hair to brace on either side of the couch. Eli's mouth never left hers as she straddled him and shifted her hips. He was so hard it fucking hurt, and the more she moved, the more he wanted her.

His hands flew everywhere, sneaking beneath her top to feel the perfect soft skin of her belly. His fingertips brushed along her sides, traced up her ribcage and then back down her spine.

He wanted her bra off and her shirt off and her pants off. It was only then that he remembered where they were, in the middle of his sister's living room, with her due out of the shower any minute.

Eli's eyes flew open.

Pushing up to sitting, he snaked both arms around Shelby's waist and hoisted them both off the couch. Shelby's legs wrapped instantly around him, but she gasped in surprise.

"Bedroom," Eli managed, before he slammed his mouth back to hers.

He had just enough time to witness Shelby's eyes flutter closed as she gave into his kiss.

Staggering along the hall, he made it to his bedroom and through the threshold. He kicked the door shut with a decided slam and they were both down on his bed seconds later. He was on top this time, with Shelby wriggling and arching beneath him.

"That top's got to go," he announced and tugged it off over her head.

Her bra was next. She arched up as he pulled back to fumble with the straps. Her blue eyes almost seemed darker now, as they swept over his bare chest and stomach. Eli let her look.

His heart was pounding a million miles an hour in his chest but he held still a moment and took the time to absorb her too.

She was everything his imagination had thought she'd be… and so much more.

Reaching out, his finger traced the delicate line of her throat, watching her pulse skitter and jump.

He swallowed and licked his lips, but held himself back as he continued to trace a line down her beautiful body. His finger played along her collar bone, and down the center of her chest to her belly button.

When he got to the snap of her jeans, she was already arching up for him again. Helping him. Encouraging him.

He worked her pants off of her hips, down and away. When he came back up to her, she scooted back a bit on his bed, making room for him. His eyes danced along her breasts, and his mouth went where he looked.

When he pulled that first nipple into his mouth, Shelby

cried out. It sent a shockwave of need crashing through him. His hips jumped forward and he ground himself shamelessly between her legs. She was hot, he could feel her through the fabric still between them.

"You're so beautiful," he murmured against the skin of her breast. "I've wanted you for so long."

Shelby's eyes rolled back in her head and she groaned.

Switching from one breast to the other, he licked and tasted and sucked. His hand pushed down between them and he rubbed her through her little pink panties. She gasped, and he could feel her hands snake back through his hair.

His mouth kept exploring her breasts, switching back and forth between them as his fingers worked carefully over her panties. He did it until her thighs were shaking, and he could feel her wetness through the fabric.

Shelby was panting and moaning, making the most delicious sounds that had his dick leaking and his chest expanding. When he pulled his hand away from her, she let out a little cry of protest. When his mouth left her breasts entirely, she outright growled.

"Please," she gasped.

When he pushed all the way up to look at her face, her hooded eyes found his. "Please," she repeated and reached for his pants.

"You're begging me now?" He whispered, and something inside of him coiled.

Biting at her lower lip, Shelby's eyes continued to plead with him. After a heartbeat, she gave a him a little nod.

That was it.

Something inside of Eli snapped. All that careful reserve from moments before? His plans to show her how good, how slow, how long he could go? What he could do to her, if she only let him? Gone.

His body crashed down to hers, on top of hers, pressing her hard into the mattress. Eli's mouth covered Shelby's, swallowing her moans as his hands turned bruising and rough.

He gripped her hips, then squeezed her ass.

He bit at her lip, then dragged his tongue along her neck where he stopped and sucked her skin into his mouth.

His hands tore at her panties, causing the fabric to rip and Shelby to pant.

When she arched up between them and rolled her hips, he yanked down on the waistband of his own pants and boxers. He couldn't hardly get them to his thighs, he was so fucking crazy. She drove him crazy.

His tip found her entrance then, and where his mind told him to slow the fuck down, his body refused to listen. He buried his face in her neck, held his breath, and pushed inside of her in one swift motion.

*Fuuuuuuuck.* His mind exploded. She was so wet and so hot.

His eyes squeezed shut and he whimpered like a little bitch into her neck.

Shelby's hands wrapped his back, her palms were flat against his shoulders as her nails dug into his flesh. She was groaning and rolling her hips beneath him.

That only made him more frantic.

Eli worked himself inside of her. In and out. In and out. His hands came up to tangle in her hair. His face remained buried in her neck, inhaling the intoxicating smell of her skin.

Shelby was pushing back against him, matching his

rhythm. He could hear her breath coming out in short pants as his weight continued to smash her down into the mattress.

Eli wanted to slow down, he knew he should prop himself up, give her some more room to breathe. But everything inside of him was building, coiling, demanding.

"Don't stop," Shelby bit out the words. "Don't stop."

Her fingers tightened on his back and her thighs came up to squeeze his hips.

Eli was the one to gasp this time, and went harder. His eyes squeezed shut and he could feel his own release coming. He pushed back on it, he held himself back as best he could. But she felt so fucking good. She felt so fucking amazing.

"I've gotta stop," he panted. "I'm gonna come."

"Don't. Stop." Shelby moaned the words, sending a tingle straight down Eli's spine.

He held his breath and didn't stop. Every inch of him was wired, every piece of him wanted to come apart. But then she was squeezing him, pulsing and crying out.

Shelby's release engulfed him, overtook him, and in his next breath, Eli followed her over the edge.

CHAPTER THIRTY_
SHELBY

*GUILT, THY NAME IS SHELBY.*

Running the pads of her fingertips over her lips, Shelby swore she could still feel the tingling from Eli.

She'd gone to his apartment, just like she and Hannah had planned. She'd distracted him, kissed him, pulled his hair out by the roots without him even noticing. All of that had been according to plan.

But what happened next?

Not part of the plan.

Shoving off one of the long countertops in her lab, Shelby stalked towards the Bioanalyzer in the corner. The computer sitting beside it hummed quietly, although its screen was dark.

Even still, the almost imperceptible sound had her pulse spiking. She was breaking all the rules right now. All of them.

It had been a solid week since she'd completely lost herself and crossed every line imaginable with Eli. She hadn't meant to do it. She was only going to kiss him, steal his DNA and walk away. But that man. The things he made her feel. The things he made her want.

She hadn't been able to stop. Her heart had been pounding and her entire body yearning for everything he was giving her.

And each night since then? When he came to her door and whispered her name? Instead of confessing, instead of telling him the truth of what she'd done… she let him in. She wrapped her arms around his body, pressed her cheek to his chest and stole more of his love.

*Guilt, thy name is most definitely Shelby.*

Outside now, the cold wind blew. Night had fallen.

Glancing around her lab, Shelby tried to push the worry from her mind. It wasn't unusual for her to be working this late, and by now her assistant and any other coworkers had long since gone home. The DNA results comparing Liam Byrne and Elijah Roe were processing. The hair Shelby had yanked by the root from Eli's head had given her more than sufficient material to work with, and likewise the hair Hannah had taken from Liam was viable too.

All of which made Shelby feel as if she'd swallowed a bumble bee. Because she'd felt *everything* with Eli that first time. And every single time they'd been together since? Shelby only felt *more*. More lips pressed against lips. More heartbeats thundering in chests. More skin sliding against skin.

And more of what happened in the morning too. Quiet conversation. Shared coffee. Eli stroking her hair.

"You're a terrible person," she murmured to herself.

Drumming her fingers on the countertop, Shelby waited, wondering what exactly she would do with the results when they were ready… Tell him? Not tell him?

A soft knock on the door had her jumping.

Turning wide eyes in the direction of the sound, Shelby held her breath as the door pulled open a crack.

"Hannah," Shelby hissed as her heart jumpstarted in her chest. "What are you doing?"

"Is it ready?" Hannah hissed back and slid her bulky body in as best she could without opening the door all the way.

"No, not yet," Shelby whispered, then placed a palm on her chest. "You're trying to scare me to death."

"Why are we whispering?" Hannah asked, and waddled over to stand beside her.

Rolling her shoulders, Shelby shot her a sardonic look. "You may not be afraid of what your brother will do if he finds out about all this, but I sure am."

With a shrug, Hannah made a pfft sound and smiled. Apparently she was feeling none of the guilt that cruised like wildfire through Shelby's system. Her chocolate-brown eyes danced with amusement and her cheeks flushed with a healthy glow. She was well and truly pregnant, filled out in every way and yet beyond lovely. Liam wouldn't disown her for this, Shelby realized. Hannah was secure in her knowledge of that.

"How's the pregnancy?" Shelby asked, trying to focus her thoughts elsewhere. "Everything good with the baby?"

"Yep." Hannah sighed contentedly and patted a hand on her belly. "Baby is on track to destroy me shortly."

Huffing a nervous laugh now, Shelby rocked onto her tiptoes and then back to her heels. There was a giddy part of her that actually wanted these test results. But still, with everything going on, she was finding it hard to settle. If word of her violating the electronics ban got back to Uriah Linfield, she might lose her job here, in addition to losing whatever she currently had going with Eli.

"Have you seen Mia since she's been back?" Hannah began.

Frowning, Shelby glanced over. "She moved across the hall," she answered. "I haven't had a chance to talk with her yet."

"Did you hear she was kidnapped?" Hannah rotated to face her and propped a hip against the cabinets.

"What?" Shelby's throat constricted.

Hannah nodded as her hand came up to stroke steady circles against her own stomach. "Yes, she was only gone a few hours and she didn't get hurt, thankfully. Cole was talking about it to Liam the other night. I guess they also found some more men with tattoos down in Utah. Has Eli remembered anything yet?"

Shelby's heart plummeted and she glanced back to the machine. "No," she lied. "He hasn't."

"The weird thing is…" Hannah glanced over her shoulder, as if making sure the two of them were still alone in the large room. "The guy that snatched Mia didn't have the tattoos."

"What?" Shelby frowned, her eyes whipping over to Hannah.

"The guy was from some stronghold in California," Hannah offered. "Supposedly there are troops there and other people too, maybe."

"That's…" Shelby's mind whirled. "Crazy."

"I know, right?" Hannah waved a hand vaguely in the air. "But we've witnessed crazier, right? We know what can happen."

Nodding, Shelby blew out a slow breath.

"Yes," she agreed. "We do."

For a moment, both women turned their focus to the machines before them. They breathed quietly and listened to the subtle whirring. When the computer let out a sudden *ding*, it had them both jumping.

The two women looked at each other with wide eyes and leaping hearts. The results were in.

But then the door to the lab swung open wide, and Eli stepped into the room.

"Hey Shell... oh." Stopping short, he gave his head a little shake. "Hannah. How are you?"

Hannah gaped openly at him. Her hand stilled on her belly.

Shelby let out a nervous chuckle as her face flushed pink. Holy. Crap.

"We're just..." Shelby stammered, and then glanced at Hannah. "She's..."

"Good! I'm so, so good," Hannah cut in and forced a laugh. "We were just catching up. It's been a long time."

Letting the door swing shut behind him, Eli stalked into the space in that entirely male way he had. Shelby's insides curled in response, so she cleared her throat and looked away.

"I didn't know you two were buddies," Eli commented.

"Yes, of course." Hannah stepped away from the machine and waddled towards him. "We worked together back when we both lived here."

"You did?" Eli cocked his head to one side.

*Lies. All lies.*

Shelby shoved off the counter abruptly and came up behind Hannah. She rubbed her palms together, then shoved them in the big pockets of her lab coat. Firming her lips, she gathered her nerve and tipped her chin up to look Eli directly in the face.

He was already watching her critically. His intelligent hazel eyes didn't miss a thing.

"Yes, we did," Shelby lied.

"Cool." Eli ducked his head a moment before flashing the two women a smile. Raising a hand he pointed a finger and wagged it between them. "It's sort of late. You ladies up to something?"

"What are you now, the new curfew officer?" Hannah fisted a hand on her ample hip. "Are you going to report back to your little friends?"

"Little friends?" Eli's brow rose and he huffed a laugh.

"Did Liam send you?" Hannah accused, mustering some much needed female sass. "Or Cole?"

"No, Ma'am." Eli held up both palms in surrender. "Sorry I mentioned it. I was just saying it's pretty late, that's all. I was hoping to catch Shelby alone."

"I see." Hannah's sass turned to a purr in an instant, causing Shelby's cheeks to transition from pink to cherry.

"It's not…" Shelby stammered, causing Eli's grin to widen. "We don't…"

"I'll just be going then," Hannah announced and glanced quickly at Shelby. Her eyes flitted briefly to the machine. "We can finish up later. Come find me?"

"Of course…" Shelby sighed, her gut twisting unhappily.

"She'll come find you *much* later," Eli cut in. "But do you want me to walk you home? It's pretty dark out."

"I'm fine, thank you." Hannah waved him off before waddling past him towards the door.

Eli turned to track her, making sure to open the door for her as she passed through.

Shelby took the opportunity to scurry to the computer in

the corner. With her heart in her throat, she quickly tapped her fingers against the keyboard, and before Eli could stride back over to her, she managed to shut the whole thing down.

"I want to talk to you," Eli spoke quietly at her back.

She could feel him looming just inches behind her. His breath was an exhale she felt in her bones.

Lifting her head, Shelby refused to turn around. Her insides were at war between what she wanted, and what she'd done.

"Look…" Eli heaved a long sigh. Shelby could imagine him running a hand back through his tousle of brown hair. "I know I've been putting off more of the memory recovery stuff and… I'm sorry."

Letting out a tiny groan, Shelby rotated around and leaned her back against the counter. Her arms came to fold in front of her chest. Her blue eyes locked on Eli's face.

"You don't need to apologize," she stated.

"But…" Eli cocked his head to one side, and as always, he stepped closer into her space.

She could feel his energy like a touch. She could feel his body like it was pressed up against hers, instead of where it actually was, hovering just six inches away.

"I'm the one that needs to apologize," she breathed the words, her insides quaking.

Pressing his lips together, Eli gave a little hum. His hands came to settle on her upper arms, where he squeezed lightly then slid his fingers down to her elbows.

Shelby's mouth parted and her insides ached. She needed to spit it out already. She needed to confess before the desires of her body overrode the demands of her conscience.

"Did you hear about the man from California?" Eli asked.

His fingers pulsed around her elbows now and his eyes darted over her face.

"Yes." Shelby nodded, before qualifying, "A little."

"He didn't have any tattoos," Eli stated. Stepping back, he held out his arms as if she could see the marks beneath his long sleeve shirt. "So maybe I was wrong."

"Eli," Shelby cautioned, her lungs were squeezing in on her now. "Mia was abductwed, and there's been some talk about California. Supposedly there's a military force there. You were there too. We both know that."

Dropping his hands abruptly, Eli tipped his face to the ceiling and blinked. Shelby watched him, her chest puffing and her stomach twisting angrily.

"You want more memories from me now," he stated finally. "Don't you?"

"Eli…" Shelby reached out, but he was already pacing away.

"You can have them," he said flatly. "Whatever you can get, you can have. Okay? Whatever experiment you want to try, then fine. I'll just do it."

Mouth parting, Shelby lost the confession she was about to make. The words she should have said to him, dried up entirely in her already clogged throat.

The words she did end up speaking were that of a scientist about to get access to new technology.

"You will?" She asked.

And when he nodded his acceptance, she felt ill.

CHAPTER THIRTY-ONE_
ELI

"You're alive," Ricky/Ronnie said. "That's good."

Nodding, Eli looked down for the IV in his arm, but this time, it wasn't there.

His heart let loose one solid thud as his brows drew sharply together. He was still in the little room with the medical equipment. He was still lying in the bed, still wearing the same light-blue hospital gown.

"It's been four days," Ricky/Ronnie offered. "It was touch and go with you. Half the time, it's like that."

He was the one sitting on the rolling stool this time, wearing a clean camouflage uniform. There was no doctor in sight, no other soldier either. They were decidedly alone, and the medical equipment had all been switched off.

"What's your name?" Eli asked.

His eyes lifted to settle on the other man's face. He was youngish, maybe early twenties, same as Eli. He had bland dark eyes set in a broad white face. His hair, sort of a mousy-brown, was cropped short and stuffed beneath a military style cap. He seemed amused by the question.

"Rene," he answered.

"Oh," Eli murmured. "I was way off."

Rene's lips twitched and he glanced to the side briefly.

"What did you think it was?"

"Ricky," Eli offered. "Or Ronnie."

Nodding, Rene huffed a quiet breath and braced his hands on his thighs.

"Those would be easier," he agreed. "But they're not me."

"Yeah." Eli thought about that for a moment, or he tried to. His mind was moving slower than usual.

"It's time for you to move out of here." Rene gestured around them. "You'll get a few more weeks to bulk up, then they'll put you through your paces and you'll get assigned to a unit."

"A unit?" Eli's brow rose in question.

Bringing his hand up to the side of his head, Rene tapped a pointer finger against his temple. His brown eyes scoured Eli's face, making Eli's pulse skitter and sink.

"Better to be in one, than at the mercy of one," he commented quietly and lowered his hand. "Besides, with the chip, things should be easier for you to handle. It helps you not to feel it."

"Not to feel it?" Eli's face screwed up.

"Yeah." Rene blew out a slow breath. "You'll see."

Pushing up to standing, Rene sent the stool rolling backwards a few feet. He stalked to one of the white cabinets attached to the far wall and pulled it open. Inside was a neatly folded uniform and a pair of brown lace up boots. White socks. Fresh underwear. Hat. No weapon.

"You need help out of bed?" Rene asked.

Eli shook his head.

"Alright then, I'll wait outside." Rene walked to the door and pulled it open. "If I hear a body drop, then I'll come back in," he said, before stepping out.

Eli watched the door swing quickly shut.

Where in the twilight zone of hell had he ended up?

Glancing down to his right hand, he opened it and closed it slowly. Rotating his palm down, he eyed the location where they'd injected the microchip. There wasn't even a scar.

Blinking dumbly, he wondered if he'd imagined the entire thing.

"We don't have all day!" Rene's voice rose from the other side of the door, jolting Eli back to reality.

Pulling aside the bedsheet, Eli swung his too long legs over the side of the bed. The linoleum floor was cold but clean beneath his bare feet; someone swept it regularly.

Taking a look around, Eli frowned. There were no windows in the space, he couldn't tell what time of day it was.

Gingerly then, he pushed up to standing. A wave of dizziness hit him first, followed by a hot flush of nausea.

Bracing one hand on the bed, Eli closed his eyes and breathed through it. He fought against the impulse to pass the fuck out and throw up all over the place. He fought and he won.

With a stubborn swallow, he made his way over to the cabinet indicated and exchanged his hospital garb for soldier gear. It took him longer than he would have liked, but in the end, he did manage to dress himself. By the time he opened the door and stepped a booted foot out into the narrow hallway, Rene was fidgeting.

"All good?" The guy asked and shoved off the blank, cream-colored wall that he'd been leaning up against.

"Yeah." Eli ducked his head. What else could he say?

Together the two of them started walking down the corridor. It was lined with doors, some were open and some were closed. The ones that were open revealed almost pitch dark rooms, but with the dim lighting from the hall, Eli could see they were just more hospital rooms with empty beds.

It was quiet here, almost too quiet.

Sucking in a breath, Eli turned his face towards Rene and opened his mouth to speak. Before he could utter a word, however, Rene cleared his throat.

"This is a restricted space," Rene announced and gestured to the end of the hall. "You won't be allowed back in here without permission."

Nodding, Eli's eyes shot to the area indicated. There was a small red light glowing in the upper corner near the ceiling. It took Eli's brain a few moments to register what it was. A video camera. They were being recorded.

Taking the hint, Eli kept this mouth shut. When they reached the end of the hall, Rene pushed the door open easily and walked through. Eli followed.

They were in a rather large room now, more brightly lit than the corridor from which they had just come, but still not bright by any means.

Overhead, fluorescent lights shone down from a ceiling not more than eight feet high. Being tall, Eli felt the need to hunch immediately. Again, there were no windows.

Off to their immediate right was a built in reception area with a high countertop the same as you'd see in any traditional hospital. There were a few men tucked behind it, one seated at a wooden desk, one standing at a filing cabinet, and one poised behind the counter itself.

They all said nothing.

And as Rene and Eli stalked past, only the one standing behind the counter followed them with his eyes.

The room had several doors positioned along the walls, each with *a label over it. Surgery. Supplies. Lounge. Office.*

*Rene disregarded them all and instead led Eli to the one door that was not labeled. Over the top of it instead, was another camera. Its beady red light was steady and unblinking. Eli couldn't help but look directly at it and wonder.*

*His heart rate increased as his stomach rolled. Sweat broke out on his upper lip and forehead. Swiping at it, Eli's lips parted.*

*"Where are we?" He hissed, and glanced quickly around. "Why aren't there any windows?"*

*With a sigh, Rene placed a palm on Eli's shoulder and gave him a hard squeeze. The tips of his fat fingers dug into Eli's flesh, causing a spike of pain, forcing him to pay attention.*

*"Try to calm down," he murmured. "They'll sense you're upset."*

*"What?" Eli's head whipped to look at Rene. "What do you mean they?"*

*A flood of warmth hit him then, instant and complete. A calming, permeating sensation cruised through his body.*

*It was like a sedative, it was like a drug, leaving you aware of why you should be panicking, but overriding that impulse with the overwhelming ability not to care.*

*Giving his head a slow shake, Eli's breathing slowed, his heart rate leveled off.*

*"Oh well." Rene's hand left Eli's shoulder and reached for the handle of the door. "You'll get used to it eventually."*

*"Used to what?" Eli tried to frown, but his face remained relaxed.*

*"Staying level," Rene offered as he moved forward.*

*Automatically, Eli followed Rene through the doorway and into another corridor.*

*There were still no windows, but this area was busier. Other soldiers walked the space. The hall was wider, brighter, with more* lights. About halfway along it, Rene ducked into a room and came to a stop.

Eli blinked dumbly and came to a stop beside him.

There were half a dozen bunk beds built into the space, each with a tiny metal dresser. In the corner, there was a single desk accompanied by one sparse metal chair.

A solider sat in it, his back was to them, and Eli could see that he was reading a book. Two other soldiers were sitting facing each other on one of the low beds, playing cards.

They looked up curiously at Rene, then critically at Eli.

"These are all new guys too," Rene announced and gestured around. "They haven't been assigned to duty yet. You'll be taking your meals together and going through some initial testing at the same time, although we already have a good idea of what you're capable of. Guys... this is Eli."

"Hey man," one of the soldiers on the bed nodded.

The man sitting opposite him looked down at the cards clutched in his hand. He did not say a word. The third guy, the one at the desk, didn't bother to turn around at all. Quietly, his hand flipped a single page in his book.

Eli cleared his throat then, and bobbed his head. Rene seemed unfazed.

"Look, just try to get some rest the next few weeks." Rene turned to Eli and lowered his voice. "You'll more than likely be assigned to a sweeper unit, so you'll see the sun again before you know it."

"The sun?" Eli frowned.

Rene stuck out his thumb and jerked it towards the ceiling. Even in here, it felt low and heavy.

"Yeah," he said. "Topside."

Eli glanced around, noted the lack of windows and shuddered.

"You mean..." he trailed off.

"We're underground," Rene supplied and then slapped his palm hard against Eli's upper arm. "It's cozy, but we can survive a hundred years down here if we have to."

Eli blanched. "How deep are we?"

Rene rolled his eyes at Eli's expression, and without bothering to answer, he strolled out the door. Making sure to shut it behind him, the latch snicked into place, all metallic and final.

Impulsively, Eli reached for the handle and twisted it. His heart rate skyrocketed when it refused to budge in his hand. Frowning, he tried the handle again, sure he'd made some mistake. But no... it didn't move... it was locked.

Mouth parting, Eli stumbled back. His breath caught in his throat. He couldn't breathe.

"Relax man," one of the soldiers said.

Whirling around, Eli's eyes darted over the tiny space. It seemed to grow smaller the longer he looked. Overwhelming bunk beds. Three other human bodies. Too low concrete ceilings. Barely enough light. And in the upper corner of the ceiling, a beam of familiar, steady red.

They were being recorded.

Eli tried to swallow, but he couldn't get any saliva past the giant lump in his throat.

"He doesn't need to relax," another said. "They'll drop him soon enough."

Eli's eyes darted to his own hand, to the place where the microchip now lay hidden.

"Chill bro," the first soldier said, and set down his playing cards. "No sense getting worked up. Besides, if you're set for a sweeper unit, you'll be able to open that door soon enough. You'll be out in the sun and the rain, so just take a seat."

"If he hits his head when he falls," the guy at the desk murmured, still not bothering to turn around. "Then they'll be back here to clean him up."

The two soldiers sitting on the bed looked at each briefly before one sighed.

"Go lay down over there," one said, and gestured to one of the other beds. "Before they hit you with the good shit and you pass out."

Eli's chest cinched down tighter, until his ribs felt as if they would crack. He hunched forward suddenly and his palms came to grasp at his own chest.

"When..." he managed. "When can I open the door?"

Staggering forward, Eli made his way to the bunk indicated and crashed down onto it. And it was a good thing too, because when his body impacted the mattress, a huge flood of sedative released into his system. Within seconds he felt his arms grow lax and his legs turn to jelly.

"When you get the tattoos man," the guy answered, although his voice was growing distant now. "The tattoos will open almost any door."

Eli's lips opened and closed, open and closed, like that of a fish. Nothing came out.

"Dude, if he's set up for a sweeper unit, then he must be one heartless motherfucker," someone commented.

"Doesn't look so badass right now though," another voice replied. "Does he?"

## CHAPTER THIRTY-TWO_
SHELBY

THIS TIME HE WOKE UP GASPING.

Eli's arms flailed wildly and his body rotated on the couch before tumbling off and landing hard on the floor.

Shelby jumped back, knocking into the coffee table with the backs of her legs and slamming down to her butt. He hadn't been out all that long. Seconds instead of minutes.

"Eli!" Shelby bent to reach for him as his body writhed on the floor. He was on top of her feet, and she couldn't move. "Hey! It's okay. You're okay."

"No," Eli bit out the word.

Rotating to his stomach, he shoved up to standing. With wide eyes, he turned away from her and staggered towards the sliding glass door.

Shelby's heart leapt to her throat and she pushed up after him.

"Eli!" She said his name with force, willing him back to reality. "What are you doing?"

He didn't respond. He didn't glance over his shoulder at her or acknowledge that he'd heard her in any way.

Instead, he plowed forward, grasping at the door handle and yanking it wide.

Cold air whipped into the room, flooding the space. On the dining room table, loose papers rustled and fluttered in the air.

Shelby's eyes darted across Eli's back as he stepped out onto the small balcony. His ribs were heaving. His fists clenched.

They were four stories up off the ground.

Was he going to jump?

"Eli! Stop!" Shelby ran for him, grabbing at his arms and his shirt. "Wake up!"

Bracing his hands on the metal railing, Eli dropped his head and sucked in air. His feet were set wide apart on the cold surface of the balcony and only now could she see how hard he was shaking.

"I'm awake," he murmured.

Clearing his throat, Eli spit saliva over the railing and into the night. Overhead, a million glittering stars winked and blinked at them. There were no clouds in the sky tonight. The wind had blown them all away.

"Just…" Shelby stuttered. "Step back from there, okay?"

Despite herself, Shelby was unable to let go of him. Her fingers threaded themselves in the material of his shirt. Tugging, she urged him away from the edge.

Eli gave his head a slow shake before clearing his throat and spitting over the railing once more.

"Are you going to throw up?" She asked, her own stomach clenching.

"Maybe," Eli muttered.

His head was still hanging, his shoulders were hunched.

"Come inside," Shelby tried again. "Let me get you some water, you should sit down."

"Don't need water," Eli said, his voice low and gravely. "Need air."

He rotated around then, forcing Shelby to let go of him. Eli's body melted to sitting on the balcony. His broad back was pressed against the railings, with one knee bent up and the other leg stretching out straight.

Closing his eyes, he tipped his head skyward and blew out a long breath.

Shelby sank down too, first to a crouching position. After a beat, she rocked forward onto her knees, and tucked her feet beneath her before sitting. She was positioned just inside the sliding glass door, with Eli taking up practically all of the space on the other side of it. It was a small balcony, and he was a big guy.

"Can I get you anything?" She asked quietly.

Her eyes dropped to his arm where she'd pierced his skin with the needle again. He hadn't jerked this time and so the injury was tiny, without the giant slice or leaking blood from before.

Even still, it made her feel twisted and sick. She hurt him on purpose in a physical way to get him to hurt even more in a mental way.

Squeezing her eyes shut, Shelby exhaled through her nostrils. She didn't want to do this anymore. She didn't want to witness this anymore.

"No," Eli replied finally. "I just needed to see the sky. I just needed to breathe the air."

Shelby's eyes popped back open and she shoved back on her flood of guilt. The color was just now returning to Eli's face. Picking up a hand, he swiped the perspiration from his upper lip and sucked in a controlled breath.

"The place in California," he stated a few seconds later. "It's underground."

Swallowing, Shelby nodded.

"There aren't any windows down there, just tunnels," he explained. "And cameras that record everything you do, and soldiers who lock you in tiny rooms. It's like a tomb."

"That's what you remember?" Shelby whispered.

Shutting his eyes, Eli braced an arm over his propped up knee. His hand dangled loosely as his breathing evened out. Shelby's eyes were drawn to his wrist, where the dark geometric code tattoos reminded her of their existence.

"I don't have everything back yet," Eli qualified. "But there are impressions, bits and pieces. There are things I just seem to know."

*Which are?*

Shelby held back the question that wanted to burst from her lips. Her heart beat faster and she leaned forward slightly. The cold wind continued to blow, and at her back, the heater inside her apartment clicked on.

"The place in California is a military installation," he stated, and opened his eyes. "It's large, but not nearly the same size as here." He gestured around them, indicating the Wall. "There are soldiers living there, well trained and with plenty of good equipment. They can hide underground and never come out for decades if needed."

Shelby swallowed. But didn't interrupt his confession.

"They are all controlled by…" he raised his right hand and tapped at the place where his microchip had been removed. "Someone."

"The source," Shelby breathed.

Frowning, Eli shook his head. "No, I don't think so," he corrected. "It's a person, or people. Rene said *they*, not it."

"Rene?" Shelby asked.

Pursing his lips, Eli exhaled through his nostrils. For a moment, he dropped his head down. His hand closed into a loose fist, but then just as easily opened again. When he looked back up, Eli's hazel eyes were almost mournful.

"Another good man," he offered. "Doing terrible things."

"I see," Shelby said and glanced away.

She couldn't maintain eye contact when he was like that. Not anymore. She understood it better now. She understood the pain of doing bad things, but still wanting to be good. The conflict. The weight that settled on your chest.

"The tattoos," he continued and brought her attention back over to him. "Are like a key."

"A key?" Shelby repeated.

Eli nodded. "When you have them, you can open doors that others can't. You can go places that others can't. I'm not exactly sure how it works, I don't remember that part yet."

"They're a key," Shelby whispered again, her eyes darting to his wrists. "Of course. You get scanned and they open a lock. Did you place your entire arms into something? Beneath something?"

"I don't know," Eli cautioned. "I don't remember that part. I just know they open doors. And I know you have to be in some sort of special classification to get them.

The classification they used was called a sweeper unit, and they said you had to be *brutal* to be on one. But if you had the tattoos, then you got to go outside. You got to leave the underground."

Shelby's brain lit with the new information. Her eyes darted over the space around them, but she was focused elsewhere, on the possibilities, on the pieces of a puzzle coming together.

"The men with the tattoos," she said. "They were soldiers, sent out in small groups with weapons and radios, but no uniforms. They were sent to different areas, where they would bait in survivors, kill them and take their possessions.

But at some point they would need a place to deliver everything they collected. And they would need a place to resupply on ammunition and fresh battery packs for the radios.

They must all return to the underground base. They must all go back there eventually, to California. And to get inside... they are all *wearing* their key."

"Shelby," Eli interrupted. "I don't know for sure that's how it works."

"But it makes sense, doesn't it?" Shelby's eyes darted to Eli's face and held.

"Well yeah, but..."

Shoving off the ground, Shelby paced away. Her hands came up to her forehead, brushing at her unruly hair.

"We solved it," she stated, and walked a few feet in one direction before turning around. "There's a military base in California and we have a key."

Eli's eyes widened and his head jerked as if he'd been slapped.

"Shelby," he huffed her name before pushing up to standing. "I don't remember if that's how it works and California is a pretty damn big place..."

"We have to tell them." Shelby's glittering eyes locked on

Eli's wary ones. "We have to tell Commander Linfield what we know, this could mean…"

"No." Eli swiped at the air with a flat hand and stalked back into the apartment.

"No?" Shelby's brow lifted and her mouth parted in shock. "But why…"

"Because it's dangerous and I don't remember everything," Eli cut her off.

His furious eyes locked on her face as he closed the distance between them.

"I'm never going back there, Shelby," he said. "I'm never going underground like that again. Whoever is running that, whatever is running that, is fucking dangerous. We're safe here. We just need to stay here."

"But there's an exposure," Shelby explained. "Mia was kidnapped by some man who talked about California. There was a data breach from an outside entity. They know we are here. We have an obligation, Eli."

Looming over her now, Eli's hands came up to wrap Shelby's upper arms.

Her head tipped back and she stared into his face. Those eyes of his were dark and sharp, in a way she hadn't witnessed before.

"This place…" he hissed, and drew her in tighter against him. "With its warehouse of fighter jets and surface to air missile system, and its insane perimeter wall, was built to withstand any sort of attack, even one from another refugee center, even one from that base in California. We don't have to leave. We don't have to go starting something."

"And yet it fell in just a matter of hours to a group of rebel soldiers with nothing more than homemade bombs," Shelby countered, remembering the night raid by Commander Linfield, and the explosions rocking the perimeter wall.

"It is my understanding," Eli gritted. "That the only reason this place fell was because there was an inside man pulling a job. When you cut the head off the snake, the body is useless. Without that inside man shutting down the source and causing every soldier in here to pass out, Commander Linfield would still be stuck on the other side of that fucking wall."

"It was a woman."

"Excuse me?" Eli frowned.

"The inside man…" Shelby breathed the words, his face was so close. "Was a woman."

Cocking his head to one side, Eli's gaze dipped from her eyes to her lips. For just a moment she thought he might kiss her, but then instead, he continued talking.

"If the base in California is still viable, then why haven't they bombed us yet? If they're leaving us well enough alone, then why go and poke the bear? Leave it, Shelby."

He gave her a little shake.

"Eli…"

"*Damn it…* I just want to be happy here." Eli sucked in a ragged breath. "Don't you want to be happy? Can't you just be happy with me?

I could be good for you Shelby. From now on, I could only do good things. It's hell out there. It's hell on the other side of that wall."

"Eli…" Shelby tried again.

"You made me a promise," he reminded her.

Stepping back then, he dropped his hands from her arms. The space between them felt immediately cold and vast. Automatically, Shelby folded her arms across her chest, seeking to replicate the sensation that Eli always left her with.

Her gut sank and her conscience protested.

"You remember enough now," she attempted. "The threat to you is practically non-existent. This is important, Eli. It's for the greater good."

"*Fuck...*" Eli spat. "The greater good. If you think for one second that I'm going to bring hell down on this place by marching back to California and opening doors in some underground bunker from which I will never escape... then you are gravely mistaken."

Turning away from her, he headed for the door.

"Eli!" Shelby called after him. "Eli, just wait!"

But it was too late. He couldn't be stopped. Storming to the door, Eli flipped the lock and jerked it open.

"Goodnight Shelby," he murmured, before shoving his way out.

CHAPTER THIRTY-THREE_
ELI

"Wake up," Garrett's voice next to his ear had Eli groaning.

"Fuck off," Eli murmured and rolled over in bed.

It was the middle of the damn night… it had to be. They'd had dinner hours ago, and with nowhere else to go anymore, Eli had stomped back to his bedroom and crashed.

Sleeping was the only way he could prevent himself from stalking Shelby. It was the only way he could keep from seeking her out and begging for forgiveness.

Suddenly, Garrett's fat hand came down to shake him, then shove him hard.

"Get up," Garrett spoke again, his voice low and urgent. "I need you."

The guy had been back with them for a whole month now, and yet this was his first midnight visit.

Eli picked his head up off the pillow and glanced blearily over his shoulder at his old friend. The guy was shirtless, still stepping clumsily into a pair of pants.

"What the hell?" Eli asked, his brow drawing down with concern. "Where's my sister?"

"She's fine," Garrett hissed. "Keep your fucking voice down and get dressed."

Pulling his pants up, Garrett padded silently away on bare feet. His broad back disappeared through Eli's open bedroom door. The hallway was dark. There were no lights on in the apartment.

A quick glance out his window had Eli verifying the time. It was the dead of night and socked in with fog.

Throwing back the covers, Eli stumbled to his tiny closet and rifled through it. Cass had taken pity on him just last week and did his laundry. He selected a pair of jeans and a long sleeve shirt. By the time he was pulling on his socks, Garrett was back and fully dressed.

"Grab your weapon," he instructed. "I'll meet you at the front door."

"Weapon?" Eli's question was lost in the night as Garrett quickly disappeared once more.

Eli's pulse spiked as a course of adrenaline shot through his system.

Hurrying into his boots, he pulled on a light jacket and grabbed his rifle. He was at the door with Garrett before he could even think about it.

"What the hell is going on?" Eli hissed.

Garrett held a single finger up to his lips in a shushing motion before opening the front door. The two men slipped silently out into the hall.

A soldier was waiting there in full uniform. He came to attention when he saw Garrett.

Ignoring him, Garrett shut the door behind them, pulled a

key from his pocket and locked it. Eli's eyes narrowed and his chest tightened.

"Cass…" He hissed.

"Is safe," Garrett cut him off. "And I need you to help me keep it that way."

Without further explanation, the guy shoved the key back into the pocket of his pants and moved off down the hallway. Eli kept step beside him and when he glanced back at the other soldier, he was surprised to see the man hadn't moved.

"Who's that?" Eli whispered. "What the fuck Garrett?"

"He's been assigned to guard the hall," Garrett spoke finally as they stormed out into the night. "Uriah's wife and baby live just across the hall, and Hannah's apartment is at the end. Two more soldiers are headed over now."

Picking up to a jog, Garrett took off over the dew-covered grass. Fog was hanging everywhere, misty and cold and white. It was impossible to see more than ten yards in any direction, so Eli was forced to follow suit.

Breath puffing, heart pounding, his mind whirled.

"Shelby," he stated. "I have to…"

"No time," Garrett hissed. "If you stick with me now, then no one will breach the perimeter wall. Stay with me. Trust me for once in your fucking life."

"Breach the Wall?" Eli gaped and his mind flashed back.

He remembered another time, only a few months ago, running with Garrett, rifles clutched in their hands. He remembered following his best friend through an abandoned town, out to a field where his sister was being attacked.

Fighting the bile that wanted to leap suddenly into his throat, Eli did now what he'd done all those months ago. He followed Garrett blindly, and trusted that it was the right thing to do.

The fog turned into a heavy mist as they ran. Buildings came up and disappeared as they passed. Eli's limbs were warm and his teeth clenched down tight.

When they approached the perimeter wall, voices and the pounding of metal erupted in the night air.

"What's going on?" Eli panted, as they came to a stop at one of the blown out entrances in the perimeter wall.

It was frantically being closed up. Men shouted. Hammers pinged. Sparks from more than one welder flew through the air.

A few armored Jeeps sat just inside the wall. The heavy guns mounted on their roofs pointed out, into the misty night.

"You're up top," Garrett instructed, and gestured to an interior metal door in the wall. "Grab some gear."

"What about you?" Eli asked, his shoulders heaving.

"I've got to make sure all four holes get closed up," he spat. "Now go."

Without protest, Eli turned away from his friend. He jogged to the door indicated and yanked it open.

Just inside, there was a stack of crates. He stuffed ammunition into his pockets until they were overflowing, then grabbed a helmet. An open box of thermal scopes caught his eye, and at the last moment he took one of those as well.

The climb up the interior of the metal wall was pulse pounding. He didn't know what he would encounter at the top. Was he in this alone?

When he got near the top, Eli's lungs were heaving in his

chest. One more level up, and he'd be on the very top of the wall itself, like all those times he'd come with Shelby.

Cresting the final landing, he looked to his right and saw the silent figures of other men. They were spaced out along a narrow corridor of sorts, standing sentry in the dark.

There were no overhead lights illuminating the space, like there had been on the stairs. Instead, each man's figure was revealed in silhouette, as they stood before tiny openings in the wall itself that let in the night sky.

They were above the fog here, and so the moon shone down. Even still, it was dim.

"All the way down," the first man whispered, and gestured to his right.

Eli didn't recognize him, but then again the guy barely lifted his head. His weapon was pointed out the little window in front of him and his body was set up behind it. Whatever he was looking at, he didn't peel his focus away, not even for a second.

Pursing his lips, Eli did as he was told. He made his way along the narrow passage, careful about the stomp of his boots now, so they didn't echo and pound. His ascent up the stairs, only moments ago, must have been unGodly loud.

The windows in the wall were long and narrow, with a sort of wedge type shape like you'd see in old castles from medieval times. The design, just like hundreds of years ago, allowed for an archer to swivel and pivot his shot in the widest range possible. Only now, instead of archers, it served the same function for a rifle.

Beneath each opening was a small metal seat bolted to the wall. You could pull it out and sit down on it or kneel on it and keep shooting. Alternatively, you could leave it flipped up, and maneuver around on your feet without it getting in the way.

A few of the men were seated on theirs, and a few weren't. There were eight bodies in all, and none of them breathed a word as he passed.

On the opposite wall from the openings were shelves inset into the metal. They contained more ammunition. Boxes and boxes of the stuff, and even a few spare rifles.

Eli adjusted the weapon slung over his own shoulder, and came to the last man in line. Unlike the others, Eli recognized him instantly. Mainly because he was so damn tall, but also because Liam stepped away from his post and turned to face him.

"Elijah," Liam spoke his name in that quiet way he had.

"Liam," Eli echoed the address.

"How good are you with a rifle?" Liam asked.

Eli could barely make out the other man's eyes assessing him in the dark, but he didn't have to, he could feel them.

In response, Eli shrugged.

"I don't suck," he admitted, then added belatedly, "I don't think."

Huffing a breath, Liam stepped aside and gestured to the opening he'd just been occupying.

"Take a look," he said.

Bringing his weapon in front of him, Eli affixed the thermal scope to it methodically. When finished, he stepped to the opening, slid his rifle into place and looked.

Directly below them, in the open stretch between the wall and the woods, the fog was fairly thin. There were no light signatures from heat there, not a bunny rabbit, not a fox, nothing.

Eli's heart kept a steady beat as he shifted his focus. Lifting his sight to the tree line, he blanched.

The fog was thicker there, weaving around the trunks of a thousand trees. It was difficult to see past the first few rows of trunks, but even so… the bodies. There were people here, men here, a lot of men.

"How did this happen?" Eli exhaled the words, but kept his rifle in place.

He watched the men in the tree line. They were waiting. Some were standing, some were sitting. They were leaning against trees, and crouched behind bushes. They weren't doing a lot of moving. They had Eli's throat closing.

"We have sentry posts," Liam explained quietly. "They're about five miles out on all sides. We had some notice, not much, but some."

"Have they made any moves?" Eli asked. "Do we know what they want?"

"They're soldiers," Liam answered. "And they've moved into position to surround us. They haven't made any contact yet. They haven't fired a single shot, or stepped foot into the open."

"Fuck," Eli spat.

"If they do," Liam added. "Then you mow them down. Understand? Any one of those fuckers that moves towards the wall without permission gets iced. Got it?"

"Got it," Eli gritted.

Shelby was right. He'd been a fool to think they were safe here. He'd been a fool not to say something about California, been a fool to think he could have a good life, that he could start over and forget.

"Hey." Liam grabbed Eli's shoulder and gave a single hard squeeze.

The unexpected contact had Eli glancing over at him, though he didn't pull his weapon from the slot. Liam's dark eyes bored into his face, as if searching for something.

"We have a drone doing a fly over now," Liam said. "We'll know what we're up against soon enough. I've been on the other side of this same fight. Uriah may be a complete jackass at times, but he knows his shit. We know the weaknesses, we know the strengths."

"The holes in the wall," Eli hissed.

"Are being fortified right now," Liam reminded him. "But I want you to stick with me, understand? Anywhere I go, I don't want to have to ask, I just want you to track me. Yeah?"

Frowning, Eli looked from the guy's face to his hand still poised on Eli's shoulder. Liam didn't budge.

"Yeah," Eli agreed finally. "I'll track you."

"Good." Liam's hand fell away then and without another word, he stalked over to the next opening in the wall.

CHAPTER THIRTY-FOUR_
SHELBY

THE SIRENS WERE LOUD, WAKING HER INSTANTLY FROM A DEEP
sleep.

Sitting up ramrod straight in bed, Shelby's heart zinged in
her chest as adrenaline shot to her fingertips. She hadn't
heard this particular sound in months.

After the source had been extinguished, Commander
Linfield insisted on routine fire drills, but they hadn't run one
in awhile. That's what this was, she told herself, and pushed
aside the blankets in her twin-sized bed.

She'd been sleeping alone for a few weeks now. After Eli
had stormed out, he hadn't been back.

She couldn't say it didn't hurt... badly. She missed him.
She ached for him. She was sorry they'd fought. She was sorry
she'd hurt him and kept things from him, important things.

But all around her now, the alarm continued to blare.
Bringing her hands up to cover both ears, Shelby tottered
groggily over to her small bedroom window and looked out.
It was nearing dawn she guessed, but still fairly dark. There

was a low fog covering everything, making it difficult to judge properly.

Walking over to her small closet, Shelby yanked out a long black coat and shrugged it on. She was wearing one of Eli's shirts he'd left at her apartment, along with a pair of comfy gray sweat pants. Stepping into some fuzzy slippers, Shelby walked to her front door and pulled it open.

Mia was standing there in the hallway, eyes wide, her hands pressed to her ears. The sound was unbearable and people were everywhere. Apartments were emptying and people were moving towards either end of the hall and then down the stairs.

Shelby could hear the raised voices and slamming of doors in between blasts from the alarm system.

Mia blinked at her, her short blonde hair all a tussle, before mouthing the word: *attack*.

Shelby's stomach dipped and she frowned. Mia crossed to her then and grabbed at her elbow.

"Come on!" She shouted and tugged. "Underground!"

Nodding, Shelby let down one arm and grabbed for Mia's hand. The two women flowed with the crowd down the stairs and out into the night.

Outside, the alarm was no less loud. Its signal continued to blast, over and over, as they made their way to the Rec Center along with everyone else. There were soldiers striding along the sidewalks and over the grass now, directing the crowd.

Shelby ducked her head as Mia pulled her in close against her side. The two women walked as quickly as they could, given the press of thousands of other people all converging on one building.

"Remain calm!" The soldiers were yelling. "Walk this way!"

Shelby's heart thumped like a bass drum in her chest. It was tuned in time to the alarm blasts now. Slow and insistent and painful.

Entering the Rec Center itself was a jostle of elbows and shuffled feet. People pressing into each other, stepping on each other accidentally.

Once inside, they were separated into three lines by the soldiers who were waiting there. Women with children were in one, women without children in another, and men in a third. The lines led to doors that were set into the floor, all of which were now thrown wide.

Shelby and Mia veered into the correct line but only stood there for a few seconds. A soldier walked briskly up to them and grabbed Mia's arm.

"Miss!" He had to shout to be heard over the alarm, his eyes darting over her face. "Come with me!"

Glancing at Shelby, Mia grabbed her palm tight and then nodded her head.

The two women broke from the line and followed the soldier. He led them out of the main room and down a short hall. Behind the stage, there were a dozen more soldiers and another open trapdoor.

The soldier didn't hesitate but continued to walk ahead of them, down the stone steps. Mia followed, her hand still closed tightly around Shelby's.

It took two flights and another narrow hall before the blaring alarm faded. Shelby's ears were still ringing from the residual sound and she had to squint due to the dim lighting.

Holding his walkie talkie up to his mouth the soldier spoke into it while he walked. He didn't turn to look at the women, as they went further and further underground.

"I've got her," he stated. "She's secure."

A voice crackled back, saying something unintelligible to Shelby's ears. Whatever the man said though, the soldier seemed to understand. He replaced his radio at his side and finally came to a stop at a closed metal door.

"Just wait here," he said to them and pushed down on the handle.

The door swung open and he gestured them inside. Mia went first, followed by Shelby. They had to hold up their hands at the brightness of the light.

After a few beats, the door swung shut at their backs and arms were wrapping their bodies.

"Oh thank God!" Cass was saying.

"We were so worried!" Hannah put in.

Stepping back, Shelby's eyes came into focus. They were in a giant living room of sorts, with leather sofas, ornate area rugs, carved wooden coffee tables and stained glass lamps.

Paintings adorned the walls, depicting wildflowers and crystal-clear lakes. The ceiling was painted the faintest shade of blue.

"*What* is going on?" Shelby demanded and glanced around.

There were several open doorways leading out of the room, but they were unlit. Shelby couldn't see where they went.

On one of the whisky-brown couches, little Ian was fast asleep, a silky soft blanket covering him. Lena sat beside her baby, rubbing his back.

"You guys should sit," Hannah commented. She was still holding Shelby's hands, and gave them a quick squeeze before dropping away.

Cass kept her arms around Mia and the two of them swayed slightly, not quite done with their reunion hug.

"This is about me," Mia spoke quietly before pulling back to arm's length. "Isn't it?"

Shelby's brow furrowed and she bit at her lower lip. Cass nodded.

"Come sit," Hannah urged again, and this time they all complied.

Taking a seat in one over-stuffed armchair, Shelby braced her hands along the cool leather. The alarm was nonexistent down here. It made her wonder if it was still blaring at all. It made her wonder what the hell was going on.

"Can I get anyone something to drink?" Lena asked, her pixie perfect face was tinged gray.

Mia shook her head no and looked down at the floor. Cass wedged down beside her blonde friend, and kept an arm slung over her shoulders.

Shelby's stomach sank.

"He's come for me," Mia whispered. "Hasn't he?"

"It's not your fault," Cass cut in, and Hannah nodded her agreement.

Lena looked away, her lips pressed together in a thin line.

Leaning forward in her chair now, Shelby's hands gripped the leather.

"What the hell is going on?" She asked.

Mia's face tipped up. Her cheeks had lost their color and she rocked slightly in place.

"My father," she said, and sucked in a ragged breath. "Is a very powerful man. He's been looking for me for a long time, and now... he's found me."

Shelby gave her head a little shake. Lifting one hand, she pointed at the ceiling and made a slow circle.

"The alarm... the evacuation..." she stated, hoping someone would fill in the blanks.

Cass gave Mia's shoulder a squeeze and then looked to Lena, who blew out a slow breath. After a few silent seconds of eye communication, Lena took over.

"Tonight an army of men was spotted in the woods," she explained. "Our spotters first sighted them at one of the five mile markers to the west. All of our soldiers were called to duty at that time."

Shelby gaped, but kept her eyes fixed on Lena, who swallowed thickly before continuing.

"We took emergency measures to shore up the holes in the perimeter wall, and posted snipers to prevent anyone from breaching. Thankfully, it seems all the enemy force has been instructed to do so far is take up position in the surrounding woods and wait."

"We're surrounded," Shelby clarified. "Right now."

Nodding, Lena cleared her throat.

"We estimate the force to be about five thousand men, but with the fog and the forest, it's difficult to tell. We have drones flying over, but thermal technology can only do so much."

"And what does this have to do with her?" Shelby gestured to Mia.

"About thirty minutes ago, a call came in over the radio," Lena stated. "It was a demand from the leader of the army, Edward Vanpell."

"The Vice President?" Shelby's face screwed up.

"Apparently he survived the war," Lena offered, her eyes flitting briefly to Mia and then back to Shelby. "He's the President now. We think he may have a military base of some kind in California."

Shelby's gut twisted, but she said nothing.

"And he found out I'm here," Mia whispered. "I brought this on everyone. It's my fault."

"Because you're..." Shelby trailed off.

Turning to stare hard at Mia, she let a million childhood memories zing through her head. The kidnapping of Marie Vanpell had been headline news for decades. They never found a trace of her. They never found a body. There was no ransom demand. Nothing.

"Marie Vanpell," Mia answered, and swiped at the tears dripping down her cheeks. "My mother, she hid me. She gave me away to protect me because he's a... he's a..."

"He's a monster," Cass finished and held her friend tight. "And we aren't going to give you to him."

Bursting into sobs, Mia covered her face with both hands. Cass cradled her close. Hannah and Lena exchanged a long look.

"Right?" Cass glanced around the room. "We aren't going to give her up."

Hannah exhaled and Lena looked at the floor.

Silence filled the underground space as Shelby's own conscience began to sit even more heavily than before. She knew something about this military base in California. She knew a lot more than anyone in this room.

## CHAPTER THIRTY-FIVE_
### LIAM

He had a brother.

Liam blinked through the scope of his rifle and tried to relax. The evacuation alarms were blaring on the other side of the perimeter wall.

Inside this corridor though, the sound wasn't overbearing, just insistent and ominous. On his immediate left, stood Eli, completely focused on his job and completely unaware of the war waging inside Liam's body.

He had a brother.

He had a bold as shit pregnant wife too.

Miss Hannah *I Can Get Away With Anything* Mae had gone behind his back and ran a DNA comparison, knowing perfectly well that Liam wouldn't have consented to it in the first place.

Why spread his evil father's genetic information around? Why bring that down on some other poor fucker's head?

But still. She'd done it. Then she'd announced it to him with that perfectly round belly growing happily in front of her and Cole looking shocked as shit leaning up against the wall of their living room.

Liam had wanted to be mad. He'd wanted to ask her what the hell she'd been thinking, but then she'd hit him with those big brown eyes and nibbled on that damn bottom lip of hers and he'd crumbled like the little bitch he was.

*No, I'm not mad. No, you can't tell anyone else. Yeah... I guess that means Cass might be my half sister too.*

That last admission had rocked him. He had a brother *and* he might just have a baby sister too. Holy. Shit.

Liam's eyes danced to his left now, and he couldn't help but stare. Eli was just a bit younger than him, by a year or so. And according to Jameson, Eli had never known his father, or any father.

*Well... lucky him.*

Liam figured that was a way better start to life than he himself had gotten. At least he'd taken that burden away from his siblings. At least their piece of shit sperm donor had left the two of them well enough alone, and their mom too, whoever she was.

At his hip now, Liam's radio crackled.

His focus swiveled back to his weapon and he swept the woods for the millionth time with his eyes. The enemy soldiers were there, and holding. The holes in the perimeter wall had been shored up.

About a half hour ago, Commander Linfield had received a radio communication from the other side. Apparently, they made a series of demands which caused him to pull an evacuation of the entire interior of the Wall. Hence the alarm system which for sure could be heard in the forest.

Even still, the soldiers in the woods had remained steady.

No one ventured out into the open space between the tree line and the wall. No one stepped out to get their head shot off.

At least… not yet.

It was quiet out there and it was quiet in here, too. The men now ranged out on either side of him weren't even whispering to one another, not even after hours of holding this position.

Sometimes, the view on the other side of the scope is just too fucking scary. It tends to cut the bullshit and replace it with something else entirely. Tension. Resolve.

Not a year ago, ninety percent of the men surrounding him had been the enemy force sitting amongst those trees, waiting to get lit up by those inside the Wall. Now the roles were reversed and the threat was all too real.

At his hip, Liam's radio let out a single plaintive beep. It pierced the air and increased his heart rate by double.

Frowning, he removed his hand from his weapon and retrieved the black walkie talkie. As previously agreed, he switched the channel to a private one with Uriah Linfield. After the count of five, he depressed the call button.

"Go ahead," he said.

"He's demanding confirmation," Uriah stated. "That she's here."

"And?" Liam's brows drew further together. He knew they still had to be cautious about what they said, in case the enemy was somehow listening.

"She's the only reason he hasn't leveled this place," Uriah gave Liam the information that had his heart squeezing hard in his chest.

The words they exchanged echoed down the length of the

corridor. Every soldier with a gun in his hands was listening intently.

Davey didn't move, he didn't shift, but he sure as shit did speak.

"Tell me he isn't going to fucking do, what I think he's going to fucking do," Davey growled.

At that, Eli glanced over into Liam's face. His hazel eyes locked on Liam's dark ones. He was confused. He didn't know what the hell was going on.

Liam pressed his lips into a firm line and exhaled through his nostrils.

"Go ahead," Liam prompted into the radio. Might as well get it over with.

"I'm giving him confirmation," Uriah stated. "We have Marie Vanpell in our possession."

"Fuck!" Davey spat. His body shifted nervously around his weapon now, but he continued to hold true to his position. "That son of a bitch!"

"Calm down," Liam commanded, making sure not to depress the radio's call button while Davey lost it. "He said confirmation, not that he was going to hand her over. As long we have her, then we're safe. It's going to be the world's longest stalemate."

"Fuck!" Davey released a string of curses then, clearly trying to shake the fear and jitters from his body.

Liam let him rage. His eyes darted from Davey back over to his own scope, and then back up and over to Eli... back to his brother. The guy's face had grown pale, his eyes glassy. Liam frowned.

"Eli," he stated.

No response.

"Eli!" Liam raised his voice.

In that moment, his little brother (who had no idea that they were related) tilted his head and looked him dead in the face. Eli's mouth parted and he exhaled a few quiet words. Liam had to strain to hear them.

"Marie Vanpell?" Eli whispered, and Liam nodded.

"Yes, Vanpell," Liam confirmed, his eyes darting over Eli's face. "As in Edward Vanpell's daughter."

Eli's eyes widened then and whatever color he had left in his face, drained completely away.

Before Liam could so much as blink, the guy's eyes were rolling up in the back of his head and he was dropping like a stone to the floor. The sound of his limp body impacting the metal was nothing compared to his rifle, which came crashing down after him.

Liam wanted to jump. He wanted to drop his own weapon and race to his brother's side. It took everything in him to stay steady. It took everything in him to stay true.

Forcing himself to look back outside, Liam focused on the enemy force lurking in the woods, and made certain they hadn't moved. His heart was pounding in his chest. Eli was having memory recurrence. Eli had been lying. The realization hit Liam full force.

Bringing the walkie talkie back up to his mouth, Liam depressed the call button.

"Copy that," Liam said. "We need to set up shift rotations."

CHAPTER THIRTY-SIX_
ELI

"YOU DID WELL," RENE SAID, AND CLAPPED ELI ONCE ON THE
shoulder. "I mean, I know your team always does well, but still."

Gritting his teeth and giving a single nod, Eli accepted the
compliment. Of course they did well, it's not like they had any other
choice.

Looking down at his right hand, Eli stared hard at the place
where the microchip lived beneath his skin. Rage. Guilt. Disappointment. Fear.

Whatever emotions he had about it were quickly and carefully
brushed from his mind. He kept his heart rate level and his
breathing even. It might have taken him years to learn how to avoid
being dosed, but he had learned eventually. Oh... how he'd learned.

"President Vanpell called this meeting," Rene spoke again as he
began walking along the underground corridor. "I'm sure it's all
good things."

Their boots stomped against concrete. Dim lights flickered
overhead.

"I'm sure," Eli echoed the words and kept pace beside his friend.

They didn't see each other much anymore. Rene had been

promoted and moved underground. Eli had been given a sweeper team to run and spent most of his time outside, hunting people.

Over the years, the type of people he hunted had changed. At first it had been women and children. He'd find them in groups and clusters barely clinging to survival, and he'd bring them back to the base with the promise of food, shelter and protection.

What happened to them once they went inside, Eli didn't know. Although, he figured he could venture a fairly educated guess, based on the talk of his fellow soldiers.

The women and children were injected with a microchip, same as everyone else. The ones that survived the implant, were stashed somewhere underground. The ones that got sick however, were sent away in trains.

And the trains had stopped running a long, long time ago. Just as the women and children above ground became scarce, then rare, then non-existent.

Now Eli hunted a different type of person, for a different sort of reason.

Men. Loners. Survivors.

President Vanpell needed whatever supplies they had on them, and more than that, he needed them gone.

So Eli had given up on ever finding his sister. He'd given up on finding Cass. She was dead. She had to be. Because she hadn't been any of the places that he'd been sent to search.

There were times...many times... where he seriously considered putting an end to it all.

Mostly, the thoughts came to him at night. When he was trying to sleep in some abandoned house, on some dead person's old mattress, he would lie awake and stare at the useless ceiling fans.

He would remember there had been a time when whoever lived here would flip a switch on the wall and turn it on. He would fantasize about what that person had done for work, what complaints they had about their spouse, what they did when their baby cried at night.

In the rest of the house, Eli's men would be snoring in the other bedrooms, or in the living room, sprawled on couches thick with dust and ash.

The thoughts would settle on him then, like a thick heavy blanket draped over his chest, and right before he fell asleep he would pray he didn't have to wake up.

But there was something inherent in the microchip itself that prevented such thoughts from going further. There was something about it, that made it impossible to remove, that made it impossible to fight, that made it impossible to stop.

So each morning, Eli found himself waking up, sometimes in a king-sized bed, and sometimes on the cold hard ground, blinking blearily at the harsh reality of his existence. He wasn't sure how long he would go on this way, but he also knew for certain that it wasn't his choice anymore, and it never would be again.

"It's going to be just here," Rene said, pushing through a door and into a wide room.

Eli frowned.

This wasn't the conference room that the President typically used, and it wasn't his personal residence either (of which Eli had taken dinner at on more than one occasion). Vanpell's wife was lovely, in a timid sort of way, and the only woman Eli had seen alive in over two years. She was one of the main reasons he held out hope that the rest of the women he'd delivered to this place were still here... somewhere.

Walking inside, Rene by-passed a few soldiers seated at wooden desks. The room was in the shape of an octagon and had a door set in each wall. Rene strode up to one and stopped.

*Coming up behind him, Eli read the white painted lettering on the metal door. BROADCAST.*

*"You gonna clue me in?" Eli asked quietly.*

*Rene offered him a knowing smile, which meant no.*

*Rolling up the sleeves of his shirt, the guy revealed the giant code tattoos covering all of the skin on his forearms. A laser light came out to do a scan before the lock on the door clicked.*

*Eli rolled his shoulders uncomfortably. He didn't like anything new, especially down here. But then Rene was reaching for the handle and pushing inside. Eli had no choice but to follow.*

*It was like walking into a giant computer.*

*Eli's mouth parted and his heart stilled a moment in his chest. He hadn't seen such blinking lights and flickering screens in so unforgivably long. There were soldiers stationed at various desks, clicking and typing and focused on their separate tasks.*

*"Blast from the past," Rene whispered. "But we have to keep walking."*

*Ducking his head, Eli's jaw snapped shut and he followed Rene's weaving steps. They left the large room and entered a smaller one. This one had a single desk, an array of computer equipment and a giant screen taking up the entirety of one wall.*

*President Edward Vanpell was already standing in the corner, his arms folded over his chest, with an assistant speaking quietly to him. When Rene and Eli entered the room, the conversation stopped. The President smiled.*

*"Mr. Roe," he said, and extended his hand for a shake.*

*"Mr. President." Eli crossed the space and clasped hands. "What can I do for you?"*

*"Please, Mr. Roe." The President released his hand and gestured to a single empty chair. "Have a seat."*

*Ducking his head, Eli fought the pinch of worry in his heart and did as he was told.*

*Rene remained in the room, but went to stand back against the wall by the door. The President's assistant began adjusting equipment. His hands worked busily, twisting knobs and tapping at buttons.*

*"Up until this point," President Vanpell began. "Our strategy has been to sweep through an area, locate any survivors and process them accordingly."*

*With a nod, Eli agreed. Although, the word "process" was actually a euphemism for systematically collecting or exterminating said survivors, based on their age and gender.*

*Eli may have thought it in his mind, but he didn't dare say it out loud. No one defied the President. No one spoke plainly here.*

*"We've worked through California, Arizona, New Mexico and Nevada." President Vanpell ticked off the states with his fingers. "And while you're doing a great job, your retrieval numbers are getting lower."*

*"Yes Sir," Eli answered. "There are no women left, Sir. No children either. I haven't seen any in years. Even the surviving men are few and far between. If the war and starvation didn't get them, then I think we have."*

*With a tight smile, the President tucked his arms behind his back. He looked down the length of his nose at Eli and blinked slowly.*

*Eli's gut twisted inside of him. He was now dangerously close to triggering a dose from the microchip.*

*"We have reason to believe that there are women still out there," Vanpell stated. "And so we've developed a new strategy."*

*Swallowing, Eli stopped himself from clearing his throat. His hands* remained still in his lap, his shoulders straight. He wasn't about to show weakness here, and so instead he latched onto the ray of hope the President had just offered him... there are women survivors still out there.

Maybe Cass. Maybe it was Cass.

With a glance to his assistant, the President took a single step back.

Eli's eyes zipped to the soldier now standing before him. The guy was thin and a bit pale, too much time without the benefit of sun had sallowed his skin. Even his eyes, once blue, seemed faded and gray.

"You will be making a distress call," the assistant explained.

His long fingers flew over the equipment and adjusted a small microphone. Words popped up on the computer screen and Eli squinted to read them.

"You will record this call for help," the assistant elaborated. "And then we will customize it for each region. Once your team arrives, you are to broadcast the call for no more than thirty days. Collect all women and children that you find, then return them directly here. Dispose of all men, retrieve their possessions and return whatever items you deem valuable here. Any questions?"

Eli's brow furrowed as he read the words. His heart squeezed in his chest and his throat bobbed. He didn't want to do this. He didn't want to bait these poor fuckers in and kill them. But the promise of women. The potential for finding Cass again (if indeed she was still out there) was too damn compelling to pass up.

"No." Eli shook his head. "No questions."

"Great." The assistant adjusted a few more things and then sighed. "Let's begin."

. . .

*A few hours later and Rene was walking him back up to the surface. Eli's back ached and his conscience ached, but he kept his arms swinging calmly at his sides.*

*"Stay a few days," Rene was saying. "We'll get your team all geared up, and then you can go."*

*Eli pursed his lips and gave a curt nod. The steady red lights of a hundred video cameras tracked their progress throughout the maze of underground tunnels. Another right turn, another metal door, and they'd be out.*

*Even now, the air seemed cleaner. The closer Eli got to the surface, the better he felt.*

*When they pushed through the final door and stepped into the cool shade of a warehouse, Eli exhaled.*

*Reaching for the cuffs of his sleeves, he undid them and roughly pushed the material up to his elbows. The dark code tattoos taunted him, but they were old news now and he didn't pay them much attention.*

*"You want to see the sun?" Eli asked.*

*This time, he was the one walking a little ahead of Rene. This time, he was the one taking the lead.*

*"'Course I do," Rene spoke quietly and shoved his hands into his pockets.*

*Together, the men wove through the massive warehouse, with its heavy metal shelving and old empty containers. It had once been a distribution center for a furniture company, but everything that had been stored here was officially used up and gone.*

*Coming to an emergency exit door, Eli shoved through it without ceremony. The thing popped open with no blaring alarm to speak of, and the fading sunlight hit him full in the face.*

*Behind him, Rene sighed.*

*"You're a lucky fucker," he commented.*

*Glancing around, the two of them took in the view.*

*The I-5 freeway was empty and gaping about a mile to the east. Past that, acres of flat farmland could be seen.*

*In the fields, hundreds of soldiers were working. They had to in order to supply the underground base with enough food to eat. And even with all that work the truth was, things were getting sparse down below. Meals were being rationed, guys were growing thinner.*

*Rene was right when he said Eli was lucky. At least the sweeper teams got to hunt for their own food. At least the sweeper teams got to breathe the beautiful oxygen in the clean air.*

*"Where are you guys holing up?" Rene asked, rocking forward on his toes.*

*Eli shot him a sardonic look. "Like you all don't know," he countered and huffed a breath.*

*The microchips were used for more than dosing, they could be used for tracking too. The base knew where they were located all times, what their heart rates were, what their oxygen levels were, when they were awake, when they were asleep.*

*"Just making conversation," Rene commented. "Like back in the day."*

*"Right," Eli muttered. "Back in the day."*

*"We know your team spent an extra day at Tejon Ranch," Rene spoke quietly. "No one said anything."*

*Pursing his lips, Eli exhaled through his nose. The ranch was vast and just too damn beautiful to hurry through, plus it was just south of here, tucked into the mountains in an area the people of LA used to call the grapevine.*

*"We're sleeping at the old Starbucks now." Eli nodded his head just up the road. "We'll be back in a few days to get everything."*

*"Alright," Rene agreed. "Good."*

*For several silent moments the two men just stood there in the daylight, letting the warmth of the sunshine flicker over their faces.*

*In the background, Eli could hear the rush of water in the old aqueduct that ran behind the warehouse. At least they had plenty of fresh water, or relatively fresh water.*

*"You know what to do then," Rene said finally and slapped his own palm down on his code tattoos.*

*"I do," Eli replied and glanced down to the marks covering his own flesh. "I do."*

## CHAPTER THIRTY-SEVEN_
## ELI

Letting out a low groan, Eli squeezed his eyes shut. His body was rocking rhythmically. The familiar sound of an engine was a steady purr in the background of his thick mind.

He remembered. He remembered it all.

"I hate that about people," Liam was saying. "That they lie."

Eli's brow furrowed then and he sucked in a sharp breath. His eyes flew open and he glanced around.

"What the...?" He spat the words quickly, as he took in his surroundings.

He was wedged into the rear of a Jeep, with Liam crouched just beside him. Someone else was driving.

"Calm down," Liam commanded, his wide hand coming to press on Eli's shoulder. "You passed out."

"Where the fuck?" Eli angled his head and peered up to the front seat.

The driver chanced a look over his shoulder then, before returning his attention to what was in front of him.

Low lying fog, just barely starting to lift. Green rolling

lawns. Buildings looming like shadowy figures all around them. They were inside the Wall. They were driving.

"We had to carry your heavy ass down," Davey grumbled, his fingers cinching down on the steering wheel. "Should've left you up there. Lee's getting soft in his old age."

Struggling to sit up, Eli braced himself against the rough flooring and rear passenger window. The seats in the back had been removed entirely.

"Where are we going?" Eli managed, his eyes finding Liam once more.

The other man pursed his lips and sat quietly for a few seconds. The vehicle hopped slightly as Davey's foot hammered down on the gas pedal and they tore over sidewalks and grass.

Eventually, Liam's gaze became so intense, that Eli was forced to look away. His heart hammered dangerously in his chest.

"Women can be the worst of all," Liam commented finally. "Because they have a habit of lying *to* you, and *for* you. Most men don't lie *for* anybody but themselves."

"I don't know what the fuck you're talking about," Eli hissed, and tried to fight the tightening in his chest.

"Don't you?" Liam's brow rose and he tilted his head to one side.

Eli fought back the panic bubbling in his body. "Whatever you think I've done," he said. "I've done it alone."

Something flickered across Liam's face then. Relief? Approval? The emotion was there and gone so fast, Eli couldn't quite place it.

But then Liam was ducking his head and sucking in a

breath. It was rare sight indeed. He'd been the first to look away.

"I wasn't sure there for a second," Liam whispered. "What side you'd come out on."

"I don't know…"

"I didn't know if you'd protect her," Liam cut him off, and lifted his head. "Or sell her out."

"There is no her," Eli gritted. *Shelby.*

He wanted to scream the words, but knew he couldn't. Inside, his body was racing and writhing and spoiling for a fight. He wanted to run. He had nowhere to go.

"Of course there isn't." Liam nodded his head in agreement. "And that's why you're going to tell me everything right here, right now. You're not going to wait to do it in front of Uriah.

You're not going to do it with Shelby standing in that room, where he can watch her reaction, where he'll find out she's been lying for you. Do you understand? You're having memory recurrence Eli, that much is obvious, and Shelby's been helping you."

Swallowing, Eli's eyes darted from Liam up to Davey and then back again. Liam pursed his lips and gave his head a quick shake.

"He'd put a bullet in Linfield's back before he'd sell out your girl," Liam stated. "But we better do this quick, because we're almost there."

"Almost where?" Eli hissed.

"Almost to Uriah," Liam explained lowly. "Almost to the girls."

CHAPTER THIRTY-EIGHT_
SHELBY

She was lying down in one of the back bedrooms when she heard them come in. Slamming doors and raised male voices would have anyone jolting awake.

And sure, it was technically sometime in the late morning, but she'd been woken up before dawn by that alarm. And after the evacuation, and worrying with all the girls, Shelby was exhausted. They'd all been exhausted. Except for Ian, who had woken up and cried for two hours straight.

It felt like he just drifted off to sleep. It felt like only seconds ago.

Springing out of bed now, Shelby stumbled to the open door and poked her head into the hallway. It was lit only by the bright lights from the living room. Somewhere in a bedroom nearby, Ian began to wail.

Rubbing a hand over her face, Shelby's senses sharpened when she heard Eli's voice.

"It's not going to be that easy," he protested.

The rest of his words were swallowed up in a symphony of other voices. Uriah's bark, Liam's low tones, Davey's growl.

Shelby's brain picked them out one by one and caused her heart to leap to life in her chest.

Across the hall, a closed door swung open and Hannah stepped out. Her hand went instantly to her belly and she frowned.

"What's going on?" She hissed.

"I don't know," Shelby answered.

Stepping out into the hall, Shelby wandered to the living room and watched from the open threshold. Hannah came up behind her and peered over her shoulder, placing a tentative palm on Shelby's back.

"You know the location," Uriah was saying. "*And* you can gain access."

The men were standing around the long mahogany dining room table. Its eight chairs had been pushed and pulled aside, to make room for their hovering bodies. Uriah was unrolling what appeared to be a map on the flat surface, with Liam helping him to hold it down flat.

Davey was standing beside Eli on the opposite side, his arms folded over his chest and his blue eyes shooting daggers at Uriah, who seemed either not to notice or not to care.

"The place is an underground fortress," Eli explained, and gave his head a little shake. "You can't bomb it, you can't storm it. There's only one way in and one way out that I know of, and the last time I checked it's all run by computer security."

"Yeah, well..." Uriah gestured across the space between them. "You've got the key. We might not be able to attack in the traditional sense, but we can't just sit here and do nothing."

"Why the hell not?" Eli spread out his arms. "We don't

need to leave the Wall for anything, and if what you say is true and we have Vanpell's daughter here, then he won't attack and risk killing her. We could live like this until the end of time."

"That's not usually how it works," Uriah growled.

"What about this is usual?" Eli countered.

"You're not going to hand her over," Davey put in. "I'll…"

"Of course not!" Uriah threw up his hands, causing half of the map to roll back up. "Why would I hand over our only piece of leverage?"

"Leverage?" Davey leaned in and hissed. "That's my fucking fiancé you're talking about…"

"Fiancé?" Uriah's brow rose. "When you left the Wall she didn't even like you."

"Hey. Fuck. You." Davey growled.

"Enough!" Liam raised his voice and had everyone sucking back. "This isn't getting us anywhere. We need Jameson and Cole. We need Malik and the rest of the officers. Let's get a real strategy put together, not try to slam some half-baked shit off last minute."

Pushing Shelby to one side, Hannah stepped around her and into the living room. Her hands went to her belly and she attempted to straighten her spine.

"Lee?" Hannah asked, and had all the men turning to stare. "What's going on?"

Liam's eyes darted between the two women and he sucked in a quick breath.

"Nothing," he said quickly. "Go back and lie down, Han. I'll be there when I can."

"He's right Hannah Mae." Uriah gestured vaguely at his sister. "We're handling it."

"Is that so?" Hannah huffed a breath, causing her shoulders to bounce. "Like you boys handled it last time?"

The two men exchanged a look. Uriah's face darkened but Liam's remained plain.

Before either of them could respond, Davey was nodding in Hannah's direction.

"Is Mia here?" He asked.

"Yeah," Hannah answered. "She's sleeping, we were all trying to sleep."

"So go back to sleep," Uriah spat, but by then it was too late.

Behind Shelby, another door opened, letting the sounds of a wailing child enter the space. Ian's cries grew louder as Lena carried him down the hall, balanced precariously on one hip. Uriah's face scrunched up and Liam spun away.

"I'm making the call," he said and stalked towards the front door.

All the while, Shelby's eyes absorbed Eli. She hadn't seen him since their fight. She hadn't seen him in way too long. Her chest ached and her cheeks flushed. He was looking down at the map. His fingers smoothed and traced along its surface as he tried to hold it open all by himself.

*Look up.*

She wanted to say it out loud, but Shelby couldn't bring herself to do it in front of all these people. The underground apartment that had seemed fairly large only hours before was quickly shrinking.

Pulling open the front door, Liam stuck his head out into the hall. A pair of soldiers that had been waiting, shifted closer to him.

"Go get Officers Tanner, Jameson and Malik," he

instructed. "I want it done in person, no radio contact. Got it?"

"Yes Sir," one of the men said.

Nodding, Liam stepped back into the apartment and swung the door shut. When he turned to face the room, he simply leaned back against a nearby wall and folded his long arms over his chest. His eyes zipped to Shelby and seemed to burn a hole right through her.

All around them, an argument ensued. It was Lena and Hannah against Uriah, with Davey rolling his eyes and muttering occasional comments under his breath.

Eli's figure remained hunched over the map, his shoulders tense, his jaw tight.

"You're pregnant Hannah Mae," Uriah pointed out. "And this is nothing like the last time. You have no idea what we're up against."

"I still have a brain Uri!" Hannah protested. "If you fill me in, then I could probably help."

"We don't need your help," Uriah countered. "You're just a distraction."

At that comment both Lena and Hannah jumped all over him. Their voices tangled with Ian's screaming and Uriah's exasperated groans.

Shelby met Liam's eyes across the room once more and he tipped his chin at Eli. Go to him, he seemed to say, and so Shelby did.

Circling around the women in the living room, Shelby walked up beside Eli at the dining room table. Her shoulder was inches from his arm. Her hip was inches from his leg. Bending forward over the map, she tried to follow his fingers as they traced and tapped over California.

"I remember everything," Eli spoke quietly. "And I told them. They know."

Swallowing, Shelby's heart pulsed in her chest and she nodded her head.

"But not about you," Eli whispered. "Because I never told you anything, because you never knew that I was remembering."

"Okay," Shelby whispered back. Bracing her hands flat on the table top, she sighed. "Alright Eli."

"I'm sorry," he said.

His hand traveled over to her hand then. His fingers brushed against her fingers. Tilting his head to one side, Eli eyed her.

She felt his look in every inch of her body.

"Me too," Shelby breathed the words. "I'm sorry too."

"You have nothing to be sorry for," Eli said.

"I…" Shelby hesitated.

Glancing over her shoulder, she looked at Liam and then back down to Eli. She did have something to be sorry for. She knew something he didn't know. She'd done something to betray his trust.

"Enough!" Uriah roared and threw up his hands. "If you two can't take a back seat here then I'm moving this somewhere else!"

Stomping over to the table, Uriah shoved one of the chairs aside and slammed his hands down on the wooden surface. Shelby rocked back slightly but Eli didn't budge. His focus dropped back down to the map and he exhaled through his nose.

"I'm going to check on Mia," Davey announced and strode out of the room.

Glaring, Lena scooped up her son and followed suit. Hannah shook her head. Liam frowned.

"Where is the location of this base?" Uriah asked calmly, nodding his head towards the map. "Could you find it again?"

"Without a doubt," Eli answered and tapped his pointer finger against the paper. "It's right here, just off the freeway. The entire place is underground, but they have a farm crew that works the fields located over here. Guys are coming and going all day long, every single day."

"Guys covered in tattoos?" Uriah asked. "Do they each have a key?"

Frowning, Eli shook his head.

"No," he said and shot Uriah a quick glance. "They go out with a foreman, and he has the code tattoos to gain access."

"Every man on your team had them," Liam commented from his position against the far wall. "Why is that?"

Glancing over his shoulder at Liam, Eli blinked a few times before answering.

"Because sweeper teams die on the job," he offered finally. "They put a lot of training and resources into us, so they want each and every straggler to be able to return. If they lose a farm hand or two, it's not a big deal. Plus, the farm guys work so close, they can just sleep overnight outside and then gain access in the morning, when the foreman comes back out."

"Did they have trouble keeping sweeper teams alive?" Liam asked.

Returning his focus back to the map in front of him, Eli pursed his lips.

Shelby watched him think, watched him remember. He had no idea he was talking with his brother. He had no idea that he and Liam were related by blood.

But Liam knew.

"It's violent work," Eli stated. "You have to be a certain kind of fucked up to do it over and over again, year after year."

"But the chip should've helped with that, right?" Liam again, pushing. "You had a helluva time when I was cutting it out."

Rocking forward, Eli stared hard at the map. His shoulders tightened and his jaw ticked. Silence filled the space for several moments and all Shelby could hear was the thud of her own heart.

Sliding closer to him, Shelby couldn't help but cover Eli's hand with her own. She had to touch him. She had to offer comfort where she could.

Eyes widening, Eli glanced up into her face. He searched her then, and she gave him a little nod.

"The chip only helps with so much," Eli spoke finally and eased back from the table, leaving Shelby's hand behind.

His gaze slid up to Uriah then, who was staring hard at the pair of them. Slowly, Shelby sucked her hand back to her side and then retreated to find a seat. She wasn't going anywhere. She didn't care what anyone thought.

"What is the extent of the chip's control?" Uriah asked, and shifted his questioning to Shelby. "Do we think it's the same one used here by the source, or is Vanpell's different somehow?"

Shelby's lips parted and she was about to speak but then Liam was shoving off the wall and striding over.

"Have a seat," Liam instructed and gestured at Eli, who'd been standing the entire time. "Right there's fine."

Uriah's brow furrowed, but he didn't say anything. Eli

glanced at the chair next to Shelby and lowered himself into it.

"Why not just cut the thing out yourself?" Liam asked, and strode around the edge of the table. "If you knew it was controlling you, and you had to be that fucked up to get the job done, then why not remove it?"

Huffing a laugh, Eli gave his head a little shake.

"I wanted to," he stated and watched as Liam took the seat directly opposite him. "I thought about it a million times."

"So?" Liam shrugged his shoulders.

"So, it's not that simple."

"Isn't it?"

"You've never had one, have you?" Eli stated it more than asked, before swiveling his gaze to Uriah. "You either."

The men glanced at one another but made no verbal reply.

"It's like it can sense when you focus on it." Eli leaned forward a bit. "It's like it somehow knows when you want to cut it out, and it stops you."

"How?" Liam's eyes were steady, dark.

"I don't know," Eli looked down at the table, at the map that had rolled back in on itself. "You think about removing it, or you open your mouth to ask your buddy, or even your enemy to remove it... but then it doses you and you stop."

"Do you need the chip and the tattoos to go underground?" Uriah asked. "Does it only work with both?"

Blowing out a long breath, Eli shifted in his seat. His hand came up to rest on the tabletop and he glanced sideways at Shelby.

"I don't know for certain," he said finally. "But it keeps track of everything. They know where you're located at all times. They know when you're sleeping and when you take a piss. I'm sure it probably sent up some signal when I gained access."

Shelby's heart beat hard in her chest and she pursed her lips. Uriah blinked a few times and then looked Liam's way. The other man cleared his throat before giving his head a quick shake no.

"I don't think it's a good idea…"

"I don't care," Uriah cut him off.

Turning his attention to Shelby, the Commander of the Linfield Army stared hard into her face.

"Do you think we can use one of the source microchips instead?" He asked. "If Malik was able to do his magical computer shit to it… do you think we could inject it in Eli and fake Vanpell's system?"

Shelby's mouth dropped and her heart came to a sudden stop in her chest.

"You want to inject Eli with another chip?" She looked nervously at Eli, who refused to meet her gaze.

"I don't think it's a good idea," Liam bit out the words for a second time.

"And I don't care," Uriah countered. "I'm not asking you, I'm asking her. Doctor? Can it be done?"

CHAPTER THIRTY-NINE_
ELI

SHELBY HESITATED, WHICH HE DID NOT WANT HER TO DO.

She shifted in the seat beside him and glanced his way. Eli kept his focus on the table in front of him but he could feel her conflict.

She didn't want to give an answer.

She wanted to protect him.

If it was that obvious to Eli, then it was more than obvious to the men seated across the table from them.

"I would need time to study it," Shelby offered finally. "I can't say for certain what the effect of inserting a second microchip after having one removed would be."

"But we could try," Uriah pressed, leaning forward now. "We have the means and the ability. We have the equipment."

Eli lifted his head then and eyed the man who held his life in the palm of his hand.

Uriah Linfield looked like any other man born to command armies of men. He was intelligent, calculating and somewhat detached. It took a man like him to win, Eli knew.

It took a man like him, willing to sacrifice the lives of a few in order to secure the future of many, to protect the Wall.

In that moment, Eli didn't fault him. After all, he'd done terrible things himself in his life. He'd done things without blinking, without thinking twice about them, all in the name of saving his sister. He was the reverse of Uriah, in a way. He'd been willing to sacrifice the lives of many, in order to save just one.

Easing back now in his seat, Eli let himself look at Shelby. He let his eyes scour her from head to toe, greedy for the time that he'd missed. He wished he hadn't wasted the past few weeks. He wished now that he'd spent them in her bed.

But he hadn't.

Because he'd still been running. He'd still been frantically trying to figure out a way to make this whole thing disappear. He'd been desperate to discover a life in which he and Shelby could be together, at peace, like normal people, like before the war.

But they were surrounded by enemy troops now. That life of peace just wasn't meant to be.

Reaching out, he trailed a single finger down her arm. She looked at him with pleading eyes, beautiful, intense and blue. He no longer cared what Liam thought he knew, or what Uriah thought he knew about what was going on between Eli and Shelby.

Eli had lived his entire life on borrowed time, trying to save his baby sister. He'd lived his entire life sacrificing many, in order to benefit one.

So now, that one person had changed for him. Instead of trying to save Cass, he was trying to save Shelby... that was the only difference.

And he could do this for both of them maybe, he could give Shelby *and* his sister a chance at a good life someday.

"You think sending me back in there..." Eli gestured to the map. "Would protect everyone in here?"

Uriah's face lit. Liam's face darkened. The taller man shifted in his seat uncomfortably and let loose a short breath.

Bobbing his head, Uriah's eyes were intent, focused. "Absolutely," he said. "I have a plan."

"We need time to discuss all this," Liam cut in, his eyes darting to Eli. "We shouldn't rush into anything."

Whirling on him, Uriah scowled.

"Officer Byrne," he gritted. "Do we need a word in private?"

Liam sucked in a breath, but before he could answer, the front door banged open.

Eli twisted to look over his shoulder as Garrett strode in, followed by Cole and another man, apparently Malik. Their hair was disheveled, their eyes tired, their faces set with deep lines.

"Any change?" Uriah asked, his attention momentarily diverted.

"None." Garrett shook his head as the three men made their way inside. "They want proof of life for Mia. They want to send in a delegation to take a DNA sample."

"Not happening," Uriah huffed. "Has the fog lifted?"

"It has," Garrett confirmed with a sigh.

Pulling out the chair next to Eli, the guy sat heavily. His broad shoulder knocked into Eli's shoulder and he slapped Eli on the chest once with his open palm.

Somehow, the presence of his best friend made what Eli was about to agree to all that more certain. Garrett would stay here and protect the girls. He would be their last line of defense.

"How many are there?" Uriah asked.

"Over five thousand, by my estimate," Garrett answered.

"Supply chain? How long are they looking to stay out there?" Uriah again.

Frowning, Garrett cleared his throat and looked at Cole. The other man had not taken a seat. He was leaning against the wall just behind Liam. His face looked grave.

"Not long," Cole offered. "They've packed enough with them for maybe a month. I don't think they're here to wait us out."

"Fuck," Liam swore and dropped his head.

"That's what I thought," Uriah commented. "No siege. They know they can't wait us out, they've got to attack."

"What do you think their plan is?" Eli asked, his knee jumping beneath the table. "How long do you think we have?"

Beside him, Garrett frowned.

"Long enough to deliver them a Trojan horse," Uriah offered. "Maybe we can take down Vanpell's army the same way we took down the source."

"Wait, what?" Garrett's face screwed up as he voiced his confusion.

A murmur rippled around the room. Liam shoved up to standing and paced away. Cole's eyes narrowed as he watched.

"Malik," Uriah continued. "It is my understanding that Vanpell is using microchip implants in all of his men, much like the source did here. Is there a way you can hack into the system he's using?"

Swallowing, Eli's heart tapped in his chest as he forced

down the lump now wedged in his throat. He would be that Trojan horse. His arms were the key.

His eyes went to Shelby briefly, but she wouldn't meet his gaze so Eli reached out and took her hand. She let him.

In silence, Malik appeared to think for a few moments. Walking the length of the room, he took a seat at the far end of the table, and propped one leg out to the side.

"I already did a cursory search and verified that they have a heavy use of electronics going," Malik stated finally. "Their system is well protected though. I'm not saying I couldn't hack it, I'm just saying it won't be easy. As usual, it would be better to have physical access to a server."

"What if I could get you access?" Uriah asked, his eyes traveling to Eli and holding firm. "Could you hack it then? Could you get us control of Vanpell's troops?"

Huffing, Malik glanced around. The room was frozen. All eyes were on him and he cleared his throat.

"He didn't bring a server with him," Malik offered. "If that's what you're implying."

"That's not what I'm implying," Uriah stated. "But I know where it is, and I can send someone in to compromise it. They could get you whatever remote access you need."

Mouth dropping, Malik's eyes narrowed on Uriah.

"I'd need to be within a mile of the location," he stated. "And the person with access to the server would have to physically touch it. They'd have to be able to plug in a data port for me and make sure it stayed in while I worked."

"Done," Uriah announced.

"I don't..." Malik's brow furrowed. "Understand. Who..."

"I'm doing it," Liam spat.

"What?" Eli's head jerked as if he'd been slapped.

Ceasing his endless pacing, Liam strode to his former seat at the table and plopped back down next to Uriah. For once, the Commander was caught off guard. Uriah's mouth opened and closed like a fish underwater and all he could do was sputter.

Behind him, Cole outright swore.

"I'll deliver the port," Liam stated, and stared straight into Eli's eyes. "I'm doing it, not you."

Beside him, Shelby's hand cinched down tight over Eli's. Slowly, he leaned forward in his chair. His face was still twisting, as if he'd eaten something sour, and his mind was drawing a blank.

"What?" Eli asked again, and gave his head a little shake. "How in the hell do you think that *you* could do this?"

"The tattoos are all the same, right?" Liam scooted his chair forward and laid his bare forearms on the table. "So, all I have to do is get the same pattern as you. I've never had a microchip, so they can inject me with one. You point me to the place on the map, talk me through it. I'll get access."

Stepping forward now, Cole's hand landed heavily on his buddy's shoulder. His face was red, his lips pursed.

"Lee, no," he said and gave a hard shake. "You can't do this."

Attempting to shrug his friend off, Liam kept his eyes on Eli.

"Yeah," he said simply. "I can."

"You have a baby on the way," Eli pointed out. "*Why* would you do this? I don't get it."

Clearing his throat, Liam looked away.

"You need to tell him," Cole hissed, and gave Liam's shoulder a tight squeeze. "Lee, you've got to…"

"No," Liam cut him off, his jaw ticking. Reaching up, he

shoved Cole's hand off of him and swung his gaze back to Eli. "This is who I am. This is what I do. Hannah still has Cole, and so I get to go to work. Simple as that."

Eli's gut churned as his eyes flitted about the room. Cole had his back turned now, pacing away. Uriah looked confused, but calculating. Shelby was positively pale.

"Eli," she whispered, but then Liam was shooting her this look. A warning.

Frowning, Eli sucked in a giant breath.

"What the fuck is going on?" He demanded. "Don't fucking look at her like that."

"He's your brother," Shelby bit out, and had everyone in the room sucking back.

"What?" Eli's heart pounded and his breath hitched in his lungs.

"I ran your DNA," she hurried. "You and Liam share a father. Cass too."

All around him, Eli heard the room explode. Garrett was hissing and Cole was groaning and Uriah was pushing up to standing. Shelby kept hold of his hand through it all, and Eli didn't have the strength to let go. He was winded. His chest heaved and it felt like he'd just run five miles.

Lifting his gaze, his eyes locked onto Liam's as the other man continued to stare him down.

A million questions flew through Eli's mind then, and he felt a weird sort of sinking sensation.

"Remember how I told you women lie?" Liam said quietly. "Seems like they're pretty damn good at sneaking around behind your back too. Looks like mine and yours teamed up this time."

Eli's lips parted. He tried to inhale, then exhale but he had no air.

"I had to forgive her though," Liam continued as the room pulsed with sound. "Because this time, Hannah found me a brother."

"I'M SORRY," SHELBY SAID.

Giving Eli's hand a hard squeeze, she tried to bring his attention over to her, but he wouldn't budge. He hadn't said anything yet. He was clearly in shock.

Across the table, Liam was leaning forward with his forearms braced on the tabletop. He hadn't said anything more. He was just staring at Eli, blinking those impossibly dark eyes of his and waiting.

All around them though, chaos ensued. Malik fled to the kitchen, where Uriah quickly followed. Jameson shoved out of his seat and stalked after Cole. They were standing face to face now, with Jameson alternating between swearing and whispering. He was concerned about Cass and what having Liam as a half-brother might mean.

"I don't understand..." Eli gave his head a little shake before looking to Shelby. "Are you sure?"

Nodding, Shelby bit at her lower lip a moment before answering.

"I'm sure," she said finally and gave his hand an extra squeeze.

To her surprise, he held on tighter. Bringing his focus back to Liam, Eli shifted a bit in his chair.

"Are you older… or…?" He asked.

"I am." Liam bobbed his head. "By about a year."

"So your dad…" Eli licked his lips, hesitating.

"Was a piece of shit," Liam offered. "You're lucky you never knew him. You're lucky he left your mom alone."

Pursing his lips, Eli exhaled through his nostrils a moment. Shelby felt her gut twisting for him. She wished she could take it all away.

"My mom was an addict," Eli stated.

"I'm sorry," Liam again, looking sincere for the first time since Shelby had met him.

"What was he like?" Eli asked, his voice dropping low. "Your… *our* dad."

Liam gave his head a brisk shake. Leaning back in his chair now, he rubbed a hand roughly over his face.

"You don't want to know," he answered finally and cleared his throat. "From what I can tell though…" Liam gestured between Eli and Shelby. "You're nothing like him."

"Alright." Eli frowned, then scooted to the edge of his seat. "Okay. Do we have any more siblings?"

"None that I'm aware of," Liam said, but then the corner of his mouth twitched. "I suppose now it's possible though. Maybe that's the only good thing the old man did in his life."

"He was *that* bad?" Eli asked, tentative, hopeful in a painful sort of way. Shelby's heart ached in her chest.

"He murdered my mother," Liam's voice was detached, as if he were speaking about someone else. "After years of beating the shit out of her and me. Like I said, you're lucky he left you and Cass alone."

Shelby's heart plummeted and her lips pressed into a thin line. Glancing into Eli's face, she watched the horror and disappointment collide.

"I see," he said said finally, and let go of her hand.

"You're not like him," Liam put in. "And I said you didn't want to know."

"Yeah, you said that." Eli swallowed and then looked up at something, someone, past Liam's shoulder.

"Cass?" He whispered.

Shelby followed his gaze and so did Liam, twisting around abruptly in his chair. Cass was standing in the open threshold of the hallway that led to the back bedrooms. Her brows were furrowed as she looked around the room.

"We woke you," Jameson announced and strode over to where she was standing. "Go back to bed."

"What time is it?" Cass asked and let Jameson wrap her up in a hug. "What's going on?"

"We're just having a little meeting," Uriah stated, and brushed back into the room. "Nothing to worry about."

All eyes swiveled to track him as Uriah strode down the length of the table and resumed his former seat. Malik sat slowly at the far end of the table, his eyes bouncing to Jameson, who frowned.

"Come on," Jameson coaxed, but Cass was having none of it. Her eyes landed on her brother first and then narrowed on Shelby.

"I'm just gonna hang here, if that's okay," she said, and without waiting for an answer, she pushed her way to the living room and sat in one of the arm chairs.

Pursing his lips, Jameson had no choice but to follow suit. Carefully, he balanced his oversized body on the armrest of her chair and gave Uriah a single nod.

"I've conferred with Malik and we've worked out a viable strategy," Uriah began. "The quicker we move on this, the better."

"What exactly is *this*?" Eli asked.

Standing up, Uriah spread the map back out on the table. Eli reached to brace one side and Liam another. Cole stalked up behind him, looking somber and a touch pale.

"There's an underground tunnel," Uriah explained. "That leads out from under the Wall and dumps you in the forest about three miles west of here."

Uriah's finger tapped at the location on the map. Shelby's eyes followed his movement, frowning.

"We'll need a small team," Uriah continued. "Liam can run point. You'll exit approximately here, and then you'll need to hike an additional five miles to this location."

"What's at that location?" Eli asked.

At that, Uriah glanced up and smiled. It was full, it was bright, and it shot a warning spike straight down Shelby's spine.

"A Jeep," Uriah stated. "And fuel reserves. Enough to take you to California."

"Enough to get us back?" Liam put in and Uriah shook his head.

"No," he admitted. "We'll figure something out at that time, or you'll have to walk until I can send someone to get you. If you manage to drop Vanpell's army, then I can send air support."

"Whoa, whoa, whoa." Eli held up both hands and the map

rolled in on itself. "You think it's going to be that easy? You think you'll just be able to waltz up to the door and scan your way in?"

"Why not?" Uriah asked, arching a brow.

"First of all," Eli stated and gestured towards Liam. "Sweeper teams do not return empty handed. They give notice when they're on their way, and the GPS in their microchips track them the entire time."

"Alright." Uriah eased back in his seat. "What happens when an entire sweeper team is taken out? Or partially taken out? According to your microchip, your crew was annihilated five months ago. Can't you swagger back to base with a buddy in tow? In fact, that would explain your lack of a microchip. You were attacked. It got sliced out, but you survived. You've been walking back ever since, the pair of you."

"No," Liam cut in with a swipe of his hand. "I'm going in solo. I don't need Eli."

Jerking his head as if he'd been slapped, Eli scoffed.

"You don't need me?" He asked, incredulous. "What the hell do you think you're going to do once you get inside? Where the hell are you going to go? What happens when someone asks you a fucking question?"

Shrugging, Liam glanced away. "It's gotta be a skeleton crew left down there, Vanpell's got all hands on deck here."

"You'll both go," Uriah put in and gestured between them. "And Malik will be posted up about a mile out with his equipment. We'll need to have another two guys to watch his back while he does his work. Simple."

Shelby's heart hopped in her chest. Her lungs pinched and her throat closed up on her. She didn't want Eli to go back.

She didn't want him to get hurt. So many things could go wrong.

"Simple?" Eli's brow shot to his hairline and he leaned forward suddenly.

"There is not a sweeper team in the country that would willingly return to that base without a microchip compelling them. There is absolutely no reason to go back. None."

"Food? Shelter?" Uriah offered.

"No." Eli shook his head.

"Women?" Uriah again.

When Eli hesitated, Uriah's eyes lit.

Shelby's gaze jumped to the side of Eli's face. His jaw ticked and his tongue snuck out to wet his lips.

"What is it?" Liam asked. "Are their women underground?"

Clearing his throat, Eli rocked a bit in his chair. His fingers came up to drum on the tabletop and he sighed.

"We brought women back," he offered finally. "Year after year, until there weren't any left to be found, until they were all dead."

"So what happened to them?" Liam this time, insistent.

"I don't know." Eli looked up, glanced around the table. "We delivered them down inside and someone else took them from that point. We never heard from them, never saw them after that. But there were rumors."

"What rumors?" Uriah prompted.

"That some of them made it," Eli explained. "That some of them survived the microchip implantation and that they're alive, that they're living there."

"In the last seven years..." Uriah shifted in his seat. "You've never seen a woman living inside that bunker?"

"Well…" Eli's eyes snapped to Uriah then, and held. "I saw one. Vanpell's wife. I saw her a few times, but that was it."

"Holy. Shit." Cole let loose a low whistle from his position leaning against the far wall. "Mia's mother."

"So even if we get you underground," Uriah clarified. "And you locate a computer, and we wipe Vanpell's army clean… then it's possible you won't be able to find the area with the women."

"Yeah." Eli blew out a breath. "That's right."

"And no one else there will be able to either," Liam added. "Because we're going to wipe their memories."

"Shit," Jameson spat. "By the time they remember, those women could be dead. Suffocated, or starved, or God knows what."

The room fell to silence.

Shelby's eyes dropped to the map, still half spread out on the table.

"But what if you took a woman down there with you?" Cass asked, her voice coming from the living room had all eyes turning to look.

"If you brought a woman inside with you, then wouldn't they take her to be with the other women? Then she would know where they were. She wouldn't have the chip yet, and so she'd remember how to get back out, right? She could call for help."

Leaning slowly back in his chair, Uriah stared hard at Cass.

"No," Jameson announced, and rose from his perch on the armrest of her chair. "Absolutely not. It's too risky. There's too much that could go wrong. No way."

Eli's face twisted. "You can hardly walk Cass," he pointed

out. "And Garrett's right, there's too much that could go wrong..."

"But it could work!" Cass insisted. "Wouldn't it? You said there's no reason a sweeper team would return to base without the microchip, but what if they found a woman? What if they brought her back to keep her safe? Wouldn't they? Isn't that what you'd do? You'd want her to be with the other women, the ones everyone talked about, but nobody saw."

"Cass..." Eli huffed an impatient breath, and Jameson looked like his head was about to explode.

"I'll go," Shelby cut in. Her eyes popped over to Uriah and she gave a tight nod. "I'll do it. I'll be the woman to go."

## CHAPTER FORTY-ONE_
## ELI

"THE HELL YOU WILL!" ELI PUSHED UP TO STANDING AND rounded on Shelby.

She rocked back in her chair, tilting her head up to take him in. Her pale-blue eyes widened and her cheeks flushed with color. She'd just made the most idiotic offer of her life, and there was no way Eli was going to let it go unchecked.

Swooping in, Eli grabbed her right up off of her chair and flipped her over his shoulder. Her body landed on his with a thump and the room exploded with sound.

Shelby let out a squeak. Her tiny hands braced themselves against his back as he rotated on his feet and began stomping away from the table.

Everyone was standing now. Liam was shouting and Uriah was stepping back. Garrett ran his hands up through his hair and let loose a groan.

Eli processed all of these things in an instant, but he didn't have time to care about any of it. Not really. He was sweeping aside dining room chairs with one hand and balancing Shelby's body with his other. Chairs clattered and crashed against to the floor.

"Elijah!" Shelby used his full name as her hands scrambled for purchase in the material of his shirt.

"Nope." Eli gave his head a brisk shake and kept plowing forward.

Stomping into the living room, he tipped his chin at his sister, who stood still and stared. Her mouth was gaping, her eyes were wide.

"Where's Shelby's bedroom?" He demanded and Cass frowned.

"Eli." Garrett stepped into his path then, but held up both hands. "Come on. You need to chill out."

Narrowing his eyes, Eli's shoulders bunched and his jaw ticked.

"*Where* is her bedroom Cass?" He asked again, all the while staring straight into Garrett's soul. "I think we all know there's not a man in this room that can take me right now. Step the fuck down Garrett."

Firming his lips, Garrett glanced quickly up and over Eli's shoulder. He was looking at someone, but Eli didn't dare turn to check who.

"Just... don't do anything stupid," Garrett cautioned, and backed a step.

That singular moment of hesitation was all Eli needed. He was shoving past Garrett in the next instant, his shoulder brushing against the guy's chest as he passed.

"Second door on the left!" Cass called after him. "But what are you going to do?! You can't just..."

Ducking down, Eli's feet ate up the short distance to the open bedroom door. He made sure to stay low, so as not to bump Shelby as he made his way inside. Behind him, came the stomping of more than one pair of feet, coupled with the opening of multiple other doors along the hall.

Eli passed through the threshold without a backwards glance. Spinning around quickly, he used one hand to shove the door closed while still holding onto Shelby with the other. It didn't take more than a second to drop his hand fro the knob to the lock and flip it.

The rapid pounding of a heavy fist against the wooden door came next, along with Liam's muffled growl.

"What the hell do you think you're doing?" Liam demanded, and then Cass was pressing in as well, her voice muffled.

"Shelby? You okay in there?" She asked.

Eli stepped back, still balancing Shelby on his shoulder. His chest was heaving and his blood was racing through his system.

Lifting her head, Shelby huffed a breath.

"I'm fine!" She called, and then lowered her voice. "I'm sorry, Eli. I'm sorry for everything."

"That's alright," Eli managed, and pursed his lips a moment before continuing, "You can fix everything, no problem."

Striding over to the bed now, he rolled her off of his shoulder. Her body landed with a gentle flop on the mattress. The covers were mussed, like she'd already slept here.

Shoving a hunk of flaming red hair back from her forehead, Shelby glanced up into his face.

"I shouldn't have kept the DNA thing from you," she sputtered. "I should..."

"Like I said," Eli cut her off and sliced a hand through the air. "You can fix it. No issues here."

Pausing, Shelby's mouth dropped and her brow raised. Eli could see that brilliant fast brain of hers working overtime. She was running through every possible scenario, and coming up empty. He'd stumped her for a split second and that pleased him somehow. Pleased him, and gave him hope.

"And how can I do that?" She asked carefully, her eyes narrowing on his face.

"By staying right here," he answered, and gestured to the room around them. "Because there's no way in hell you're going on that mission."

At his back, a fist pounded hard on the door. It was big and heavy and masculine. It had Eli's back going up.

"Eli!" Liam growled. "You're gonna need to open this shit and come on out."

Looking down at Shelby then, Eli cocked his head.

"He thinks he runs things all of a sudden," Eli told her, rolling his shoulders. "Because we're related by blood."

"I don't think..." Shelby tried, but Eli was already whirling away.

The incessant fist pounding continued. Liam was not letting up.

Striding over to the locked bedroom door, Eli sucked in a breath and leaned close to the wood.

"Cass?" He asked between knocks.

The pounding ceased, and there was a muffled argument. After a beat, Cass spoke, "Yeah Eli," she said. "I'm here."

"Is Liam standing next to you?" Eli asked.

"Yeah," Cass answered. "Why?"

"You remember how you asked me if I ever remembered anything about our dad?" Eli reminded her, and before she could answer he continued, "Liam is our brother."

"What?!" Cass screeched.

"Fuck," Liam spat.

With a knowing smirk, Eli listened. A chorus of groans and scandalized hissing ensued. Cass would make quick work of them all now, Eli knew. She'd sit the lot of them down and grill them for hours.

Satisfied with himself, Eli straightened abruptly and whirled away. There would be no more knocking. Stalking back over to the bed, he stared down at Shelby and folded his arms across his chest.

Shelby gaped at him.

"That fucker has a thing or two to learn," Eli stated, jerking a thumb over his shoulder. "About having a little sister. It's best he gets started right away."

"What did you just do?" Shelby whispered.

"I told my sister a very important piece of information," Eli offered. "Right after I found out about it. Because you don't keep things like that from the people that you love. You don't keep things like that from the people who have your loyalty."

Shelby's face fell and he knew he'd hit home. Her eyes grew glassy and she sucked in a sharp breath before turning her face away.

"I'm sorry," she croaked.

Eli's heart squeezed like a vice inside his chest. He wanted to be angry with her.

Hell, after that stunt she pulled in there, he was livid. But staring down at her now, with those freckles dusting across the bridge of her pixie nose, he couldn't help it. He was weak for her. He was an absolute fool for Shelby.

With a sigh, Eli sat down heavily on the mattress beside her. His hand came up to stroke along her arm, trailing upwards to her neck, where he brushed more flaming red hair back over her shoulder.

He'd had his face buried in that exact spot enough times to make him ache for just one more. He remembered the way she smelled. The way she tasted was even better.

"Shelby…" Eli trailed off, his eyes crawling over the side of her face. *I fucking love you.*

"I should've told you right away," Shelby said, her eyes fixed on the bed beneath them. "I should've told you *before* I even ran the test. I'm so sorry. Hannah came to me and she had the suspicion and I figured if the test came back negative then why put you through all that. It's a sorry excuse, I know."

Nodding, Eli firmed his lips. She was rambling and apologizing and all the while he couldn't stop himself from touching her. His fingers twined in her hair, tugged on the ends, itched to do more.

"I forgive you," he interrupted finally, and had her glancing up at him.

"You do?" She asked, her face twisting with the question.

Again, Eli gave a single nod. His hand stilled in her hair then, and his eyes danced to hers.

Shelby swallowed. He watched the delicate bob in her throat. The nerves. The uncertainty.

It had his whole body priming. Because there was something here still. There was something electric and commanding between them.

"Shelby," he whispered. "I have a secret to tell you."

"You do?" Shelby exhaled the question, her eyes bouncing between Eli's mouth and his eyes.

His brow rose then as he recognized that look. She wanted him. After everything, she *still* fucking wanted him.

Leaning in, he brought their lips within inches of each other. "I would forgive you for anything," he breathed. "The real question is, can you forgive me?"

"Forgive you?" Shelby frowned ever so slightly.

Licking her lips, she let her eyes flutter shut. It made Eli want to jump out of his skin. It made him want to shove her back onto the bed and crawl on top of her.

But in that moment, he held himself back. He balanced on the edge of a wire, and forced himself to stay in control.

Their mouths hovered, half-open, breathing, not touching, but wanting to.

"For dragging you into all of this," he explained. "I'm no good for you, but I can't stay away. I'm a bad man, and I know it. But I can't stop myself from wanting you, from falling for you. Can you forgive me?"

Sucking in a ragged breath, Shelby's eyes opened and locked on Eli's.

"What was that last part?" She whispered.

"Forgive me."

"No." Shelby gave her head the slightest shake. "The part before that."

Eli smiled, slow and sure, as his hands came up to wrap her neck.

"I'm falling for you," he said and brought their bodies that much closer together. "Already fallen, actually."

"Huh." Shelby licked her lips, her hands coming up to brace flat against his chest. "I am too, falling, that is… fallen."

Closing the gap between them, Eli pressed his lips to Shelby's. Slow. Deep. Heart exploding.

Greedily, he swallowed her gasps, first one tiny noise and then another.

His hands gripped the back of her neck, turning from gentle to demanding. His tongue darted out to taste and test.

Easing her back onto the mattress, Eli did what he'd wanted to do from the moment he'd seen her again. He crawled on top of her, pinning her down with his hips and his chest.

Shelby arched up beneath him. Her hands circled his shoulders, then dragged and scraped down his back.

Leaning up on one arm, Eli broke their kiss only long enough to pull his shirt off over his head. Shelby's eyes flew open and she did the same.

Suddenly, they were a pair of frantic bodies. Hurried. Rushing.

Stripping themselves and each other of every item of clothing, they panted and gasped. Pants and belts and zippers and boxers, until Eli's naked skin slid over Shelby's naked skin.

Moaning, she bit at the lobe of his ear. Eli's hips jumped and his chest rumbled its response.

But then she was sighing, and spreading her legs for him. Eli's hand snaked out and gripped the soft flesh of her thigh. Holding her in place, he tasted her lips, then the skin of her jaw and then that delicate hollow along her throat.

"Eli," Shelby hissed his name, and suddenly he was there.

Pushing inside of her, Eli squeezed his eyes shut and groaned. It was a million sensations and just one sensation all at the same time.

"Shit," Eli spat before burying his face in her neck. "Fuck, Shelby."

But he couldn't stop. He didn't stop. His body did what a

man's body is called to do. He pulled out just far enough to have her whimpering, before pushing fully back inside.

His lungs were burning and his muscles were straining as she wrapped her legs around his waist and hung on.

With every thrust, he felt himself building.

Shelby was making these delicious little sounds and squeezing him so fucking tight, he thought he might scream.

Biting down hard on his lower lip, Eli worked and rolled his hips, pushing the both of them higher, faster, harder... until Shelby was clenching around him and crying out in his ear.

*Fuuuuuuuck.*

Then Eli was seeing stars. His breath hitched and caught in his lungs as he tripped and sailed over the edge. Shoving into her, Eli let himself go. Heart pounding. Body spasming. Brain blitzing.

He let himself feel every single second of it.

He let himself feel with every single piece of his body, mind, and soul.

Until they were just two gasping breaths in the quiet. Until they were just two heartbeats beating as one.

"Shelby," Eli whispered. "You gotta promise me you'll stay here, where it's safe. You've gotta promise me."

"I promise." Shelby panted her reply. "I love you."

CHAPTER FORTY-TWO_
ELI

"I ALREADY TOLD YOU ELI," LIAM WAS SAYING. "THERE ARE *TWO* reasons that women lie. It's like you don't even listen."

Liam's voice echoed strangely in the underground tunnel, with its low ceilings and miles of cracked concrete. It was like a never-ending tube, filled with the stomp of boots and huff of breathing.

That didn't seem to deter the guy from talking though, which was unusual. Liam being talkative was becoming a thing.

Eli's boots slapped against the cement and his hands tightened on his rifle.

"I remember," he huffed finally, hoping Liam would decide to shut up.

No such luck though.

"One is *to* you," Liam stated. "And the other is…"

"*For* you. Yeah, yeah," Eli grumbled. "I got it."

"Hey fellas," Shelby said, from her position walking in front of them. "I can hear you."

"Well that's good then," Eli spat, still bitter. "We're all well aware of what sort of lying you do."

With a huff, she kept her face forward, but it was like Eli could feel her rolling her eyes. They were nearing the end of the tunnel, just about ready to step out into the forest.

It was dim in the tunnel but not completely dark. Davey (who was currently in the lead) had a small lantern hanging from his pack. Shelby was following the light, and the rest of them were following Shelby.

"Mia lied too," Davey announced with a shrug from the front. "So did I. We all do it."

"Shut the fuck up," Eli snapped. "This is different."

None of these men were marching with the woman they loved straight into the lion's den. They weren't about to offer her up on a silver platter to an unknown fate hundreds of feet below the ground.

"This *all women lie* thing isn't making me feel so good," Malik called fom the rear. "I think I may need to sit the whole girlfriend thing out."

"You could be gay," Davey suggested. "It's probably less drama."

Huffing a laugh, Liam gave a grunt. "It's so not less drama."

Twisting to shoot his newly discovered brother a look over his shoulder, Eli arched a brow.

"How would you know?" He asked.

Liam pursed his lips and gave a shrug, but offered no verbal explanation. The group of them fell to silence once more.

They were nearing the end of the tunnel now, Eli could smell the change in the stale air.

Coming to a stop, Davey reached for his small lantern and

switched it off. The already claustrophobic space fell to almost complete darkness. At the end of the corridor though, in the distance, you could see a circle of light.

That meant the moon was out, and the fog had gone.

"No more talking," Davey said quietly. "From here on out, we're silent. Got it?"

Everyone dipped their heads in acknowledgement, because mostly the reminder was for Shelby.

She didn't say anything, but Eli swore he could feel her tension. It made him want to step up to her and wrap her in his arms. It made him want to toss her over his shoulder like he'd done three days ago and lock her in her bedroom.

But he couldn't.

Because Shelby had volunteered for this mission, and practically everyone supported her. Uriah Linfield, Lena, Hannah, Davey, Cole, Mia, Malik… hell, even Liam had given her the nod. The only holdouts had been Cass, Garrett and himself.

So over the past three days, they'd prepped for the inevitable. Liam got covered in code tattoos and injected with a microchip. Eli walked them through what he knew of the underground base, the protocol for approach and gaining access.

Uriah and Malik sent a digital "proof of life" photo of Mia to Edward Vanpell. When the guy opened the file and downloaded it, he unknowingly downloaded some fancy bit of spyware along with it. Now Malik was 99% certain the chip they'd inserted into Liam's hand would read the same as Vanpell's chip.

Only problem was they wouldn't know for sure until Liam

actually tried to gain access to the underground base. And that part was next.

Walking along now in a single-file line, Eli watched as Shelby's silhouette became steadily more defined in front of him. Breathing in, he smelled the fresh air of the forest at night. Damp moss. The rustle of pine needles overhead.

Before too long, they were creeping out into the open.

It was quiet and cool. They'd done a drone flyover the night before, so they knew Vanpell's troops were posted up about two miles to the east of this location, but still, you never knew what you would find.

Eli's eyes scanned the area around them, packed with the towering tall trunks of trees and narrow overgrown paths made by deer and other animals.

Davey was moving steadily up in front, keeping his steps perhaps a bit slower than usual for Shelby who trailed along directly behind him. Eli swallowed the lump in his throat and pushed his nerves down into the pit of his stomach. He hated this. He didn't want to do this. But here they all were just the same.

And the next several miles of hiking didn't provide him with any relief. Nope. In fact, they seemed to creep by at a snail's pace.

Stepping off the trail finally, Davey turned to face them. He leaned back against the trunk of a tree and pulled a small map from his pocket. Eli reached out and pushed Shelby into the brush and then stepped off the trail himself. The others followed suit.

After a solid minute of silent contemplating, Davey folded the map up carefully and slid it back into his pocket. Bringing his rifle up, he nodded once.

"Jeep should be stashed in the clearing a hundred yards from here," he spoke quietly. "I'll go in first."

Nodding, Eli wrapped a hand around Shelby's arm and held her in place. The rest of the guys stalked back onto the game trail and moved off into the darkness. After a beat, Eli guided her to follow.

They'd gone over the location of this thing a hundred times it seemed but still, finding just the right clearing in a thick forest was not a simple matter. The Jeep should be hidden beneath a tarp about fifty yards from an old dirt road that lay to its west. That road would then lead to a gravel driveway, which would take them to an asphalt highway. The only issue was that all those major landmarks were to the west of the Jeep and their team was approaching from the east.

In front of him now, Shelby walked along the narrow trail. Branches scraped at their legs as they passed. Dead leaves crunched underfoot.

Controlling his breathing, Eli kept his rifle clutched in both hands now, the barrel pointing slightly to his left. His heart gave a steady thump, but stopped cold when heard the clicking of half a dozen rifles.

Shelby stopped dead in her tracks in front of him. Her body tensed and she began backpedaling fast.

"You lose!" A voice echoed in the woods, and was followed by a long cackle.

Quickly, Eli lifted his weapon to aim at the tree branches above him. The sound was coming from high up in the trees.

"Oh for fuck's sake!" Davey called suddenly. "Come down here you old bastard."

"Cookie!" Liam barked. "You son-of-a-bitch we weren't sure if you'd make it."

With a trembling sigh, Eli blew out a breath and lowered his gun. His heart was pounding in his ears. His fingers were tingling.

In front of him, Shelby dropped her hands to her knees and shook her head at the ground.

Stepping close to her, Eli ran a palm along her back. Uriah had made a radio call to the compound a few days ago, but the exchange was in brief snippets of code. In the end, no one was entirely sure if Cookie and Ace would make it to their location in time.

But apparently, they had.

"You should know better than to approach like that," Cookie's voice echoed through the trees. "Your sniper skills suck. You need a tune up."

"My heart could use a tune up," Malik grumbled. "You may have to restart it after that."

Laughter pattered throughout the woods then. Shelby straightened and so Eli urged her to begin walking again. He kept her close to him, his arm looped around her shoulders. When they made it to the clearing, the others were all standing around a black Jeep. It was armored, with gasoline canisters hooked to the roof rack and hanging off the back.

"Ace." Liam stepped up to a man dressed entirely in blackout fatigues and the pair of them slapped hands. "It's been a long time."

"Too long," Ace answered and flashed a bright smile. "You good? Baby here yet?"

"Not yet." Liam shook his head.

A few seconds later and the illustrious Cookie slid down

the trunk of a nearby tree. He was older and wiry. But when the others approached him, he pulled each of them in for a back-slapping hug.

Walking up to the side of the Jeep, Eli came to a halt. The tarp that had apparently hidden the thing was already pulled back. Parked just on the other side of it was yet another Jeep, this one was not armored. It must be what Cookie and Ace had traveled in from the compound.

"You all ready for this?" Liam asked and gestured around.

The men in the clearing gave a collective nod. Liam smiled, big and genuine and gleaming in the night.

"Then let's get it."

CHAPTER FORTY-THREE_
SHELBY

PUSHING UP TO SITTING BENEATH THE CANVAS TARP, SHELBY LET loose a groan.

The ground beneath her was cold and lumpy. The sleeping bag she'd shared with Eli didn't provide much cushion. She'd spent the night with half a dozen rocks poking into her spine.

Running a hand back through her tangle of brash red hair, Shelby glanced around.

The edge of the tarp was drifting slightly with the morning breeze and the sun was shining. It was early winter in Southern California. There was no snow on the ground here, and not a cloud in the intense blue sky.

The rest of the guys were awake already, and busy. This was the morning of day three. Last night, they'd officially arrived at their destination.

"Good morning." Eli's body came to crouch in front of the open end of the makeshift tent. They'd all slept side by side together, crammed beneath the tarp with only their bodies to keep them warm.

Bobbing her head in acknowledgement, Shelby swallowed.

"Good morning," she managed, and fought the twist in her belly.

When she'd first volunteered for this mission, she'd been so sure of herself. It was a logical choice for her to go. A woman was needed, and she was a doctor. She didn't have any children of her own to consider and she was comfortable with the team of men who would be on the mission.

But now... the reality of what she was about to do was finally sinking in. Her throat was constricting and her nerves were tingling.

Because just a mile or so down the hill from here, was a giant furniture distribution center. Its warehouse was an enormous building, once used to store bedroom sets and living room sofas. That's what everyone thought, anyway.

Its real purpose was never known to the general public. All those years before the war, it had been a cover used to hide the secret military bunker buried deep beneath it. Under its concrete slab lay a twisting network of tunnels and rooms and command centers.

And now, beneath the surface of the ground lay hundreds, possibly thousands, of people... men, women and children. They'd been taken below the surface, never to come out again. And Shelby was going to follow them.

"You don't have to do this," Eli murmured.

His intense hazel eyes traveled over her face before he crouched down and crawled under the tarp beside her. His butt plopped next to hers and his long arm snaked around her shoulders.

Pressing a slow kiss to the side of her head, Eli exhaled through his nostrils.

"Liam and I can go in alone," he offered finally. "We don't need you."

"You need me," Shelby countered, absorbing his closeness. "And I can do this."

"I wish you wouldn't," Eli again, pressing another kiss to her temple and talking against her skin.

"I know." Shelby pursed her lips and closed her eyes. "I'm sorry."

Another man might have said *that's okay, I forgive you*, but not Eli.

He wasn't okay with this, and he wouldn't tell her otherwise.

At the same time he recognized that he couldn't prevent her from going. He'd locked her in that bedroom for one night, he'd made love to her, and begged her not to make this choice. But when they both emerged the next day, and she'd made the choice anyway, he hadn't abandoned her.

His face had fallen and his jaw had ticked, but he stayed the course. He was going underground with her, and the sooner he and Liam got their part done, then the safer Shelby would be. That was the plan, anyway.

"I better clean up," Shelby announced. "I've got to brush my hair and get ready."

"No." Eli frowned and shook his head. "You've been out here for years on your own," he reminded her. "You need to look the part. In fact, we should smear some dirt on your face and rip your clothes."

Shelby's mouth parted, but then thinking better of it, she swallowed and looked away. This was real. Suddenly this was so very, very real.

"You okay?" Eli murmured.

"Yeah." Shelby dipped her head. "I'm fine."

Reaching for her shirt, Eli tugged and jerked until the cotton material split in several places. His hands traveled down to her jeans where he flicked out a small knife and cut a few tears.

"Now let's go outside and roll around a bit," he said.

Pressing her lips together, Shelby did just that. She crawled outside on her hands and knees until she reached the dirt and then rolled. Eli did the same.

Leaning up against a nearby tree, Liam watched quietly. Shelby could hear him chomping on something. When she got done and pushed up to standing she realized he was eating what appeared to be a granola bar, his brows were drawn together as his jaw ground and crunched.

Shelby noted that he was already a mess, covered in dirt and scratches. His blue jeans were caked in mud and his shirt was full of holes. Eli came to stand just beside her.

"Eat something," Cookie commanded. Sauntering over, he slapped a homemade granola bar in her hand.

"Thank you," Shelby murmured and ducked her head.

"I hear you're a fancy doctor or something," Cookie commented, bringing Shelby's eyes back over to his face.

"I am," she confirmed, and brought the bar up to take a bite.

"Don't forget the best weapon you've got is right here," he said, and tapped an index finger against the center of her forehead, right between her eyes.

Shelby blinked abruptly and rocked back a step. She couldn't help but huff a laugh and choke a bit on her granola bar.

Cookie arched a brow then and gave her a sly smile. "That's better," he murmured, and marched off.

"Was that my pep talk?" She called after him, but he just shrugged his shoulders and kept walking.

Slinging an arm around her then, Eli brought her in close against his side. A few feet away, Malik's fingers were flying across a laptop. No one said anything.

Glancing around, Shelby frowned. Davey and Ace were nowhere in sight. They were probably off somewhere, keeping lookout.

"Let's run through it a final time," Liam announced finally, and shoved off from his tree. His hands dusted together. The granola bar was gone.

Without lifting his head, Malik began to talk.

"So the chip in Liam's hand, coupled with the tattoos, should get you all inside," Malik offered, his fingers still flying. "I've got this data port that you'll need to connect to a computer on the inside. I'm guessing they're all hooked to the same server, if not… we might be screwed."

"We'll go to the main control room," Eli confirmed. "I'm sure one of those is hooked to a server."

"Good." Malik's head bobbed. "Let's hope that's the case. Once it's connected, then it needs to stay in place until I can hack inside and do my worst. You should know when I've succeeded because everyone in that place with a chip in their hand will drop."

"How long do you think that will take?" Liam asked.

"Minutes," Malik offered, then lifted a shoulder. "Hours… never… I can't be sure."

"And what about Liam?" Eli asked. "Will it wipe his memory too? He's got the chip."

Giving his head a brisk shake, Malik frowned.

"No," he said. "I've got control of his chip, and it's not actually connected to Vanpell's system. He should be fine."

"Alright." Liam stalked over to Shelby. "Anything else?"

The granola bar was almost gone now, and her palms were sweaty. Swiping them against her dirty pants, Shelby straightened her spine.

"I'll go wherever they take me," she said. "Once inside, I'll look for any signs of other women or children."

"What if they try to hurt you?" Liam asked.

Eli's arm tightened across her shoulders, and his body tensed.

Bringing a finger up to her temple, Shelby tapped her own head. "Then I'll use my best weapon," she answered, and had Cookie cackling from a few feet away.

"She'll be just fine!" Cookie called. "She'll be better off than you two idiots I'm sure."

"That's great Cook," Liam spat. "Real reassuring."

"I ain't here to wipe your ass," Cookie countered, and picked up a rifle. "I'm here to cover your ass, as best I can."

"I guess that'll have to do." Liam nodded, and then looked over at Malik. "You ready yet?"

Huffing a breath, Malik kept punching at his computer. His legs were crossed beneath him and the machine was balanced on his lap. His shoulder were hunched and his eyes locked on the screen.

A solid minute later, he blew out a breath and leaned back. Removing a small data port from the side of the laptop, Malik held the plastic device up over his head.

"Don't fuck this up," he stated, as Liam snatched the thing from him, and shoved it deep into his pocket.

"You either," Liam commented.

Turning to Eli and Shelby, Liam's face was grim. He adjusted the rifle slung over his shoulder and gave a tiny nod. Eli pulled Shelby into him and squeezed her tight. His heard was beating in his chest and his lips pressed against the top of her head briefly before all at once he stepped back and let her go.

"It's time," Liam confirmed, and stepped closer to lay a hand on Shelby's shoulder. "You good? You need to back out of this whole shit show?"

Tipping her chin up Shelby stared into Liam's dark eyes and steeled herself.

"I'm good," she told him. "Let's go save the world or something."

CHAPTER FORTY-FOUR_
ELI

Walking along the cracked asphalt, Eli's boots thumped against the ground. There was a silver metal guardrail on his right, and he kept close to it, although the structure itself provided no cover.

Keeping his head up, Eli scanned their surroundings. It was strange, following the path of an empty freeway, one he'd driven a time or two in his youth. The I-5, once crammed with zooming vehicles and rumbling semi-trucks, was now silent and still.

A little ways off in the distance, were the farming fields. No one was working them at the moment, from what he could tell.

On their immediate left, their destination loomed. The warehouse. Its stark white exterior walls gleamed bright in the sun.

"We'll take this next exit," Eli said, throwing the words over his shoulder.

"Okay," Shelby answered, she was walking just behind him.

Liam, who was stalking along directly behind her, said

nothing.

Clutching his rifle in his hands, Eli kept his eyes on a swivel. His heartbeat was steady, and measured, and slow.

"There aren't any men out in the fields," Shelby spoke quietly. "I thought you said they worked outside."

"They used to," Eli confirmed. "They could be inside right now, or maybe they marched as soldiers to the Wall."

"Probably a little of both," Liam added. "That's what I would've done, if I was in Vanpell's position."

Firming his lips, Eli tended to agree. There were definitely still men here, but they were all underground and staying put until the majority of Vanpell's force returned.

Veering further right, Eli followed the swinging circle of the freeway off-ramp. Overhead, the sun beat down, its rays warming the ragged material clinging to his shoulders and back. Even still, it was cold. If the wind would stop for just a few minutes, then it wouldn't be so bad. But it wasn't stopping.

He worried about the decision to leave Shelby's jacket behind. He worried she might get cold, either above ground, or below. But in the end they all thought it was best if she looked disheveled and dirty, like she'd just lived through hell, instead of protected behind a nice shiny wall for the past seven years.

And yet here Eli was, about to deliver her straight into danger.

Bringing his hand up absently, Eli pushed the heel of his palm against the ache in the center of his chest. For a split second, he wanted to change his mind. He wanted to wheel around, scoop her up and jog like a maniac in the opposite direction.

But it was too late.

There were too many lives depending on the three of them. There were too many people relying on them to succeed.

So before he knew it, he was stepping onto a cracked sidewalk and striding down an abandoned street. Before he could blink, before he could think, Eli was standing at the entrance to the warehouse, with nothing but a camera staring at him, its little round light glowing red.

Not bothering to look back, Eli wrapped his hand around the metal door handle and pulled it open. This one didn't have a lock, but they were being watched all the same. Shelby walked into the darkness first, followed quickly by Liam. Eli was last, his gut twisting as his heart rate began to climb.

The interior was dim, dank and vacant.

Hundreds of towering steel shelves stood in orderly rows, empty. Dust had collected on them, dulling their once shiny surface.

Standing still for a few seconds, Liam glanced around. No one approached them, which wasn't too unusual. Sometimes there were other men around, soldiers or field workers, and sometimes there weren't.

*In the north-east corner.* Eli said the words in his head, but he didn't dare say them out loud. They were being watched after all, and Liam had to look like he knew his way around.

Back at the Wall, they'd rehearsed this part enough times, if the guy fucked it up now, there was no undoing it. Liam was the one with the microchip *and* the tattoos, so he had to go first.

Shelby and Eli would follow him in, and therefore they wouldn't need to be scanned to gain entrance to the underground. It should work like a charm… or set off a million alarm bells delivering them to their eminent death. Either way, it was go time.

With a tick of his jaw, Liam strode off in the correct direction. Eli held back an exhale as Shelby took off after him. The dance had officially begun.

Weaving his way through the metal shelves, Shelby's boots tapped and echoed in the large space. Eli stalked after, all bunched shoulders and controlled breathing. The three of them pushed their way through a swinging doorway, into an employee lounge area, and then down a flight of stairs.

Coming to a stop at a solid steel door, Liam rolled up the sleeves of his filthy shirt and presented his arms, just like Eli had shown him. He didn't hesitate but Eli held his breath all the same.

The camera above the door stared down at them. Its light, like all the others, was a solid, steady red.

After the count of three, something changed. A tiny laser affixed to the upper corner of the wall did a sweep. Eli watched the familiar lights dance along Liam's skin. Clenching his teeth, he held perfectly still.

Then… click.

The door unlocked. When Liam reached for the handle, it opened easily beneath his palm. They were in.

Standing aside then, Liam pulled Shelby close to him and let Eli go first, as planned. In this way, the two men switched positions so Eli could take them where they needed to go.

Quietly, they traversed a short hall, which was illuminated by a single bulb set into the ceiling. At the far end was another flight of stairs, the first of three.

Down, down, down they went.

Their footsteps were a relentless thunder against the thick concrete walls. The sound set the rhythm for Eli's heart, which cinched tighter in his chest with each flight they descended. At the bottom, Eli stood aside and let Shelby and Liam brush past him.

Another position change. Another heavy steel door. Another camera. Another sweep with a laser.

And they were officially in.

Swinging that final door wide, Liam managed to keep a straight face when this time, there was a soldier waiting for them on the other side.

The man was one Eli recognized from a few brief interactions before. As a sweeper running an outside team, Eli had very rarely visited the bunker more than three or four times per year, and even when he did he was in and out in a day, but still, this guy's face was familiar.

"Holy shit," the soldier exhaled the words, his name was Clint. Green eyes wide and mouth gaping, the extent of the guy's brain function seemed to end there.

Shifting on his feet directly behind Shelby, Eli's jaw ticked as he bobbed his head. There wasn't a sweeper team left that had brought back a living woman in over three years. The guy's shock was clearly because of her presence and not because of Liam, or even Eli himself.

If anything, Shelby helped to distract from the fact that Eli was returning home after being MIA for months, without a chip in his hand, and accompanied by a soldier that no one would recognize if they looked too closely.

"It's been awhile," Eli managed finally, his voice tight. "Do you know if the handling protocol for women is still the same?"

"I… uh…" Clint blinked a few more times, his emerald-eyes stuck on Shelby, before giving his head a slight shake. "Yes, it should be."

Unable to stop himself, Eli's fingertips came up to brush against Shelby's lower back. It was taking all of his willpower to remain calm. He was battling against every instinct he had at this point, the instinct to protect what was his at all costs.

Turning on his heel, Clint strode off along the hallway. To his credit, he only glanced over his shoulder once.

Shooting Eli a quick look, Liam ducked his head and followed suit. Shelby went next, with Eli once again trailing behind.

They veered through familiar corridors and past closed doors. They passed more than one open room, filled with half empty desks and a few men quietly working.

When Shelby entered the space, the energy changed. Eli could feel the shock, hear the whispers, and see the gaping. But Clint didn't stop in his progress, and no one else said a word.

Before too long their little parade arrived in a small room that resembled a reception office but there was no one inside. No one manning the single wooden desk, or sliding papers into one of five metal file cabinets.

Striding over to the desk, Clint picked up an old style black telephone, complete with coiled cord and held it to his ear. His finger jabbed at a few buttons and he waited.

"Yes," Clint spoke into the receiver. "We have a Level 1E."

His eyes shot to Shelby then, as he listened to the voice on the other end of the line.

Standing off to the right, Liam turned slightly to one side, so that his face was in profile to the camera positioned in the upper corner of the room. He had five days' worth of beard growth to obscure him, and so far he could easily pass as one of the sweeper guys that Eli had on his old team. Most of them hadn't gone underground for years prior to their attack because there was just no need. Eli did all the paperwork and item transfers. But still...

"I know," Clint again, huffing a light laugh. "But I'm looking right at her. Are we still able to process them the same?"

Eli's lungs began to burn and his nostrils flared. Holding his breath, he strained to listen. The person on the other end of the line was talking about the handling of all those women, but no one other than Clint could hear what was being said.

For a split second, Eli wanted to break. He wanted to swing his rifle up, shoot Clint in the head and fucking run for the surface.

But then the guy was smiling, and ducking his head.

"Alright," Clint said. "Good. I'll send her in."

Hanging up the phone, he flashed them all a smile.

"It's all set," he confirmed and moved around the desk towards a heavy metal door not five feet away.

Liam and Eli exchanged a quick glance. This is it.

Shoving up the sleeves of his shirt, Clint presented the tattoos on his forearms, and waited for the lock on the door to click.

When the door swung slowly open of its own accord, there was no one waiting on the other side, just an empty corridor and a single light bulb flickering overhead.

"Go ahead," Clint urged, and motioned for Shelby to go in. "You'll be safe here."

Glancing back, Shelby locked eyes with Eli. Her beautiful

pale-blue gaze stabbed straight into him. Her mouth parted slightly, but no words came out. Eli's breath caught in his own throat, threatening to choke the life out of him.

This was the part they hadn't been able to rehearse.

This was the part where he let her go, without slamming his mouth to hers, without staking his claim. This was the part where he let himself be shattered into a million pieces, by doing nothing, by not putting up a fight.

Exhaling through his nostrils, Eli gave her a little nod. She was turning away from him already, and striding straight through the open threshold to the door, before he could change his mind, before he could say a word, she was gone.

Clint grabbed the heavy metal door and swung it shut. Just like that. Its slam was a like a bolt of lightning straight down Eli's spine. His body went stiff. His stomach twisted.

"Good find," Clint said and huffed another light laugh. "I wouldn't have believed it if I didn't see her for myself."

"Me either," a new voice entered the space, from somewhere just behind Eli.

Looking over his shoulder, Eli blanched. His lips parted as the the color drained from his cheeks.

"Rene," Eli sputtered the name, his eyes widening.

"Eli?" Rene's brow rose in quick surprise, and he took a jerking step forward. "I thought you were dead. I thought… holy shit. You're supposed to be dead! I watched your microchip flatline."

Swallowing, Eli grasped hard for composure. He needed to keep it together. He needed to play this off. Rotating fully towards the one man who could blow this entire thing out of the water, Eli tried for a cocky smirk.

"Not dead," Eli managed. "Not yet, at least."

HER FIRST FEW STEPS WERE TENTATIVE, UNSURE.

Shelby wrung her hands in front of her body and peered down the end of the empty hall. It was fairly well lit, with light bulbs hanging every few yards. The floor and walls were all concrete though, and vacant.

Forcing herself to keep moving, Shelby jumped when the overhead lights suddenly flickered.

"Hello?" Shelby raised her voice before glancing back over her shoulder.

The metal door was still shut. No one was there.

Turning back forward, Shelby's body stiffened and she let out a yelp. A woman was walking towards her now, her arms stretched out to Shelby, in welcome.

She had perfectly styled silky blonde hair that fell neatly to her shoulders, and a red lipstick smile framing straight white teeth. She was dressed in a navy-blue pencil skirt, white blouse and matching business jacket. As the woman approached, her black high heels tapped along the flooring.

"Welcome, welcome!" The woman said.

Coming to a stop in front of Shelby, the woman heaved an enormous sigh.

Shelby's mouth dropped then, and she stuttered. Even through the excessive makeup, and despite the light color of her eyes, this woman could be Mia's slightly older clone.

"Um… hello," Shelby gasped the words, as the woman leaned in and hugged her.

Expensive perfume flooded Shelby's nose. Channel. When the woman pulled back to arm's length, Shelby noted an American Flag pin attached to the lapel of her jacket.

"You must be exhausted," the woman stated and brandished that megawatt smile once more. "And hungry. I can't imagine the ordeal you've been through."

"Um…" Shelby didn't know what to say.

As she continued to gawk, she noted the recent split in the woman's lip and the slight swelling beneath her left eye. Makeup as extensive and thick as hers could only hide so much. Plus… she was very thin. When they'd embraced, Shelby had felt the bones of the woman's ribcage jutting out from her back.

"I'm Rachel Vanpell," the woman introduced herself. "And if you'll just follow me, then we'll try to make you comfortable."

"Alright," Shelby agreed and snapped her mouth shut.

With an encouraging little nod, Rachel rotated expertly on her heels and strode away.

The tap, tap of her shoes sounded eerily in the corridor, and Shelby wondered why she hadn't heard them before. She didn't have time to give it much thought though, as they were beeping their way through a closed door and down another hallway. No tattoos were used, she noted.

Glancing over her shoulder occasionally, Rachel Vanpell continued to talk.

"We'll get you cleaned up first thing, dear," Rachel said. "We have extra clothes here, and hot running water."

"Oh," Shelby replied, trying to remember the twists and turns as they headed further into the apparently empty underground. "Thank you."

"Then a good hearty meal," Rachel continued, facing forward. "We have vegetable soup, and bread."

Coming to a stop at a closed door, Rachel Vanpell glanced up into the camera positioned over it. The red light was steady and staring.

After a moment, the door clicked. Rachel pulled it open and stood aside, gesturing for Shelby to go first.

"You first, dear," Rachel said and smiled.

## CHAPTER FORTY-SIX_
## ELI

"W‌HAT THE HELL HAPPENED?" R‌ENE STRODE OVER AND WRAPPED Eli in a tight hug. His meaty hand slapped right between Eli's shoulder blades and together the two men rocked a bit to one side.

After a moment's hesitation, Eli's hands came up and he returned the hug.

His heart was hammering in his chest, but he kept his cool and clapped Rene on the shoulders. Dust from Eli's clothes puffed into the air as their chests pressed together.

Eli's eyes shot to Liam, whose face remained plain. Not two feet away, Clint was frowning.

Pulling back then, Rene gave him a once over. His brown eyes were wide with wonder. He gave his head a little shake.

"Your entire team got wiped out," he stated. "We watched the microchip readings fall one by one. What the hell happened?"

"We came under attack," Eli explained. "We found a woman."

Blowing out a breath, Rene stepped back and ran his

hands up through his mousy-brown hair. "I heard about the woman," he confirmed. "That's why I came over. I was hoping to see her before you sent her in."

"She's already been admitted," Clint offered. "But she was definitely real."

"That's incredible," Rene again. "Did you find her in Hermiston? And how the hell did you survive? Everyone on your team flatlined."

"Yeah." Eli huffed. "We found her in Hermiston."

Rene's eyes narrowed, then dropped down to study Eli's right hand. A tiny pink scar covered the place where the microchip had been inserted so many years before… an insertion that Rene himself had been witness to… the one where he'd been holding Eli down.

When the guy's gaze popped back up to Eli's face… he knew.

Pop.

A single gunshot rang out in the room, causing Eli's breath to clog in his throat and his stomach to clench. Stumbling back, Eli reached for his weapon. Rene's eyes went wide then, and he threw a look over his shoulder.

Liam was already on the move. He'd been the one to fire the gun. He'd been the one to make the shot.

Shoving his handgun back into its holster, Liam was closing the distance between himself and Clint. The guy's eyes were as round as saucers as he backpedaled.

The camera above the door was demolished and smoking. The red light that had been steadily recording them only seconds earlier was gone. That's what Liam had hit.

"Remove their chips!" Liam shouted, as Clint scrambled for the handgun at his side.

Everything sped up then. Everything happened at once.

Clint backed himself into the wooden desk, still fumbling at his side. The legs jolted and scraped across the concrete floor. Liam rushed forward, the glint of his knife flashing, just before Clint screamed.

Eli didn't hesitate.

Before Rene had a chance to turn back towards him, Eli was jerking his own knife from its sheath and lunging forward.

"Eli!" Rene screamed, and yanked out his gun. "Stop!"

Pop. Pop.

The rounds went wide as Eli tackled his old friend to the ground. There was the rush of breath. The clenching of teeth. Rene's finger squeezed the trigger again.

Pop.

Bringing the hilt of his knife down hard on Rene's gun hand, Eli heard the crunch and snap of bone. The guy cried out, but he did not stop kicking, he did not stop struggling.

Somewhere above them, papers and pencils flew from the wooden desk, scattering and rolling and fluttering to the ground. Clint was screaming. Liam was silent. Eli clenched his teeth and bore down.

All the while Rene twisted and writhed, trying to fight Eli off.

"Hold." Eli bit out the word as he slammed the hilt of the knife down again. "Still." And again.

Gasping, Rene's hand fell limp. The gun skidded across the concrete floor.

Scrambling up, Eli climbed onto Rene's chest and dug both of his knees into the guy's shoulders. Rene stared up at him, eyes wide and questioning. His body bucked and twisted.

"Fuck!" Rene growled. "Eli!"

Chest heaving, sweat dripping, Eli flipped the knife around so it was blade side down and began digging for that microchip.

Rene howled as his right hand burst with blood. Clint fell silent.

Liam was jumping down to the floor in the next second. His large hands came to wrap Rene's arm in an effort to keep him still. Even so, Eli was forced to dig around with the point of the knife in search of the microchip.

It took way too long, with Rene screaming and cursing and fighting before Eli was able to fish the thing out. Then all at once, Rene was gone. His eyes rolled into the back of his head and his body went limp.

"Let's go," Liam spat, and shoved up to standing. "Now!"

With a quick nod, Eli fought the adrenaline now coursing through his system and got up. Shoving his knife back into its sheath, he took two steps back, his eyes on the bloody mess that was now his old friend. He was alive right? It was just the chip removal that had knocked him out, right?

"We don't have much time," Liam hissed.

Grabbing for Eli's chest, Liam twisted the material of Eli's shirt in his hand and gave him a quick shake.

"The computer room," he demanded. "Lead me to it."

Coming to his senses, Eli ripped his eyes off Rene and settled on Liam. When his brother gave him a nod, he nodded back.

## CHAPTER FORTY-SEVEN_
### SHELBY

Blinking, Shelby stepped through the door and came to a stop.

She was in a well-appointed sitting room, with thick beige carpeting and elegant gray leather wingback chairs. There was a glass top coffee table in the center, and a mantle on one wall, like the kind that would go over a fireplace, except there was no fireplace there.

A heavy oil painting was placed front and center, with a familiar man depicted in a navy-blue suit. It was Vice President Vanpell... or rather President Vanpell now. Shelby recognized him from before the war, when he was running for office.

"Please dear," Rachel urged at her back. "Have a seat."

Rising from their positions seated in the wingback chairs, three other women stood and gave her wide smiles.

After a beat, Shelby forced a smile back.

They were all too thin, their skin was tinged gray. Much like Rachel, the women were wearing business skirt suits with stockings and conservative heels. Unlike Rachel, they didn't wear any makeup. Their faces, though gaunt, were not bruised in the way Mrs. Vanpell's seemed to be.

"It's so fortunate that you've made it to us," one woman said.

"Yes, a miracle that you've survived," another added, nodding her head.

"Poor thing," the third one stated, and turned a too bright smile on Rachel. "Are we sure she's not… sick?"

"Now, Mrs. Jameson…" Rachel tisked her disapproval and came to stand beside Shelby. "Our microchip will cure any illness she may have contracted up there. You know perfectly well, that down here, we are all immune."

"Of course." Mrs. Jameson ducked her head and bit at her lower lip.

Urging Shelby to take a seat, Rachel gave her a single nod before sitting down herself. As one, the other three women in the room also sat. Legs together, ankles tucked behind ankles, hands folded carefully in each and every lap.

It was something out of a Stepford nightmare. Shelby didn't know what to make of it.

After an agonizing thirty seconds of silence, wherein all of the women simply stared at Shelby, Rachel Vanpell cleared her throat.

"We'll get her cleaned up first," she announced. "And then provide her with a meal."

"Yes," one woman (a brunette) answered, but she did not move from her position.

"So…" Shelby glanced nervously around. "Are there many other women here?"

Still smiling, the women glanced at each other before nodding eagerly.

"Oh yes," Rachel stated. "You will be perfectly safe here. Our glorious President, my husband, has provided protection for us all."

Pursing her lips, Shelby blinked and waited, but no further information came. Sucking in a breath, she tried again.

"I heard rumors that there were children here," she ventured. "Do you have any children?"

Maintaining their smiles, the women looked amongst each other before nodding.

"Oh yes," Rachel stated. "Our microchip implantation efforts have been successful on thousands of children. Thanks to our glorious President, we are able to provide a safe and healthy environment for all of our people. This place is the only one of its kind left on Earth."

Frowning, Shelby felt a trickle of sweat slip down her spine. Something was not right here. The room fell into an awkward silence once more. The smiles on the women's faces grew tighter and more strained.

Lifting her head, Shelby noted the various cameras positioned all around the room. When she returned her attention back to the women, one of them was slowly rubbing her hands together in her lap. Her fingers threaded themselves together, clenched, then released.

It was Mrs. Jameson, a woman who appeared to be somewhere in her late-60s. Her hair was short, with gray streaks. Her light-blue eyes were intense and locked entirely on Shelby.

Shelby's eyes dropped to the woman's movement. She was rubbing the spot where a microchip would be implanted, like it hurt, like it was dosing her. Mouth parting slightly, the woman looked as though she wanted to say something, but then suddenly, she snapped her mouth closed again. Her jaw ticked. Her throat bobbed.

Shelby's eyes darted around, her stomach sinking.

"Are you all…"

"However did you survive the nuclear fallout dear?" Mrs. Jameson rushed the words out, then gritted her teeth.

The other women took a collective inhale.

"Nuclear fallout?" Shelby's eyes danced between the woman's busy hands and her face. "There was *no* nuclear fallout. There's nothing wrong with the Earth at all. It's perfectly safe to go outside."

"No dear." Rachel Vanpell leaned forward then, and placed a hot palm on Shelby's thigh. "I'm sorry, but that just isn't true."

"But…"

"*No* dear." Rachel Vanpell squeezed so hard that her fingernails dug into Shelby's leg. "And I think it's time for you to get cleaned up. We'll need to insert that microchip to protect you right away."

Shelby's mouth dropped. Her eyes flew about the room. These women were misinformed. They were trapped here, clearly malnourished and afraid.

Rachel Vanpell rose from her seat and the other women look worriedly at the painting of President Vanpell.

"I don't understand," Shelby began, but then Mrs. Jameson passed out.

Leaping to her feet, Shelby moved forward.

"Don't touch her!" The brunette cried and leapt between them. "You're sick!"

"I'm…" Shelby shook her head, but then the door behind her gave a sharp click, and ever so slowly, it swung open.

CHAPTER FORTY-EIGHT_
ELI

"This way," Eli said.

Whirling away, he picked up to a jog and rushed from the room. Liam's shot had taken out the camera and so the attack hadn't been recorded, but the removal of the two microchips would show up on some warning system somewhere.

Jogging down the hall, Eli took the rifle slung over his shoulder and brought it around in front of him.

He didn't have to look back to know Liam was keeping pace and doing the same. To get to the computer room where Eli had done those recordings, they would have to travel down two long corridors and pass not one, but two reception areas.

As they approached the first room, Eli had to choose between walking calmly into it like nothing had happened, and just full on taking the place by storm.

His lungs were heaving and his body was primed, but as he ran his brain clicked through scenarios. The fact that this place was currently understaffed (most of the soldiers were far away from here, laying siege to the Wall) was the deciding factor.

Slowing his steps suddenly, Eli glanced behind him at Liam. The guy slammed to a halt as well and up a nod.

Shoulders working, chests expanding, Eli and Liam switched positions in the hallway. The camera above the door had a steady red light, and after the count of three, the laser did a sweep of Liam's forearms.

Much to Eli's relief, the lock on the door clicked. Liam rolled his shoulder and strolled in. Sucking in a steadying breach, Eli composed his features and followed.

The room was quiet and well lit, just as they'd found it several minutes before, when they'd been escorting Shelby. A single soldier sat at a wide wooden desk, flipping through a book. The computer monitor on his desk is the one that showed the hallway, but he wasn't paying attention to it. He hadn't seen them running. He hadn't received any alarm.

As Liam and Eli strolled past, he didn't even look up.

On the far side of the room, Eli pushed through a door into another long corridor. Liam was just behind him. The tap of their boots felt like a pounding echo, matching the harsh hissing of their breathing.

"The next room is a hub," Eli whispered. "There should be five doors. Take the second one from your left, labeled BROADCAST."

"You sure?" Liam hissed.

"Yeah," Eli confirmed, and dropped back to switch their positions. "I'm sure."

The next metal door was the same as the last. Steady red light. Camera. Laser sweep. Door click.

Liam strode in first with Eli hot on his heels. There were

five soldiers waiting inside, and *this* time, none of them were sitting at a desk.

"Hey." One of them stepped forward and raised a hand. "We need to check your…"

He never got a chance to finish his sentence. Liam slammed the butt of his gun up into the guy's chin, and shit went south real quick.

The four other soldiers drew their weapons and sucked back.

Pop. Pop. Pop. Pop. Pop.

Bullets sprayed the space.

Ducking low, Liam raced for the second door on his left, while Eli swung his rifle up and returned fire.

Pop. Pop. Pop. Pop. Pop.

Two of the soldiers dove behind a desk, and flipped it on its side. One staggered back and collapsed to the floor. Another crouched beside him, screaming.

Pop. Pop. Pop.

"Get that door open!" Eli called, as lightning hot pain lanced through his arm.

Liam was already standing in front of the metal door. The steady camera light and laser did their thing, and much to Eli's astonishment the damn door clicked open.

Pop. Pop. Pop. Pop. Pop.

Shots zinged through the air. Eli could feel the whoosh as bullets flew past his cheek. But then Liam was tearing the door open and darting inside, Eli turned and dove through the threshold. The metal door closed behind them with a click.

"We need to keep them out!" Eli called as his hands gripped the silver handle.

Pulling back with all his might, he felt the moment a soldier gripped it on the other side. The door kept making a clicking sound as the thing tried to unlock. But when the guy on the other side twisted and yanked at the handle, Eli jerked the damn thing shut once more.

"Fuck!" Liam spat. "Hold it as long as you can!"

Sweat burst along Eli's forehead and upper lip. His heart hammered in his chest as every muscle in his body strained. The handle twisted in his hands and for a split second the door heaved and opened a crack.

With a grunt, Eli yanked it back shut and the lock clicked. Hands came up to slap and bang against the door from the other side. Behind him, Liam swore.

"I guess any computer will do," Liam growled.

They were in the giant computer room. They'd made it. Eli didn't dare turn to look. His entire focus was on the handle he clutched in his sweaty hands.

The wheels of an office chair rolled along the ground then, and Liam sat with a slam. There was the tap of a keyboard and the snap of plastic.

"There," he announced. "Data port is in."

The door handle beneath Eli's grip jumped.

"Shit!" He cried, his arm muscles vibrating. He could feel it all the way up in his shoulder "How long will it take?"

Racing up beside him now, Liam grabbed the handle over top of Eli's hands and, leaning back, he added his weight to the door. The men on the other side shouted and pounded their fists against the metal. The door clicked heaved, then shut and locked.

"In five more seconds," Eli panted. "They'll be at it again."

"Let go," Liam told him. "We'll take turns holding it."

"Fuck," Eli hissed and wriggled his hands out from beneath his brothers. "Shit."

"You're bleeding," Liam spat. "You get hit?"

As the handle beneath Liam's hands twisted once more and he fought against the men trying to pull it open, Eli looked down at his own body. Blood had soaked through the sleeve of his shirt. Wrapping a hand around his upper arm, Eli hissed as pain lanced through him.

"Yeah," he said, and looked to Liam. "I guess so."

"How bad is it?" Liam demanded, not taking his focus from the door.

"Not bad," Eli answered, although he truly didn't know.

Blood continued to soak and spread through the material of his shirt, but the adrenaline coursing through his body kept the pain at a manageable level.

"My turn," Eli said and stepped back up beside his brother.

"Not yet." Liam shook his head. "Let's look at your arm."

"No," Eli countered and wrapped his hands over Liam's on the handle. "I'm fine."

"Just rest a minute," Liam argued. "Show me your fucking arm."

"I'm. Fine." Eli gritted out, and it was in that moment he realized the attack on the other side of the door had stopped.

Eyes zooming to Liam's face, Eli raised a brow.

"Been longer than five seconds," he offered.

"They could be getting reinforcements," Liam suggested.

"All of them at once?" Eli pursed his lips and ever so carefully, he released the door handle.

After a solid thirty seconds of waiting, Liam did the same. Together, the pair of them stood there, shoulders heaving, chests screaming, stomachs twisting.

Easing back, Eli turned to the computers stacked everywhere in the room and glanced at the monitors. They showed lines of data and spreadsheets and bar graphs and things he didn't understand.

"I don't know how to work this system. I can't get it to show footage of that room," Eli admitted.

"Only one way to find out what's on the other side," Liam stated and sucked in a breath.

Before Eli could protest, the guy drew his handgun from his side and pushed the door open a crack. Eli jerked his weapon from his side and bit back a scream of pain. His arm was well and truly fucked.

Silence. Nothing.

With a glance back, Liam tipped his chin up.

Stalking over to him, Eli brought his weapon up and tried not to wince at the throbbing in his arm. For a few seconds, he rocked on the balls of his feet, tense and ready. Sweat dripped from his forehead.

Pushing the door a few inches wider, Liam kept his body hugging tight against the metal. The further he pushed it, the harder Eli's heart pounded. But then he saw the first hand, limp and open on the ground, then arm attached to it, then the head, then the body.

The soldiers were out. On the ground. Unconscious and unmoving.

Liam's gaze shot to Eli, and in that moment, the fucker outright grinned.

"Holy. Shit." Liam whispered. "It fucking worked."

CHAPTER FORTY-NINE_
ELI

"Shelby." Eli's eyes widened and his heart stopped in his chest. "We've got to find Shelby."

This time Eli didn't wait for the nod. He didn't wait for an affirmative or any other reaction from his brother. He picked up his feet and he ran.

Out of the room with all the bodies, down the corridors of silence, not stopping until he got to the door where he'd last seen her alive.

Clint and Rene lay useless on the ground. Blood was everywhere. Paper and crap from the desk was everywhere.

Jogging past the bodies, Eli stopped at the metal door and looked up. The camera above it was completely destroyed. Liam's shot had done its job… maybe too well.

"How the hell are we going to open it?" Eli hissed, panic beginning to take over his chest.

On the ground a few feet away, Rene let out a soft groan. Still lying beside the desk, Clint rolled onto his side.

"They're coming to," Liam announced with a frown.

"How are we going to open this fucking door!" Eli shouted, gesturing wildly at the camera.

Liam swallowed and glanced around the room. He didn't know. He hadn't thought that far ahead.

Diving for the handle, Eli attempted to shove it down, then yank it up. The metal thing wouldn't budge in his palm. His arm vibrated with pain but he hardly noticed.

The laser scanner was still in its position, waiting to scan.

Dropping his rifle to the ground, Eli jerkily rolled up his sleeves, one soaked in blood and one not. Presenting his tattoo covered forearms, he held his breath and waited.

*Come on. Come on. Come on.*

Still. Nothing.

Without the camera to trigger the sweep, there was no way to unlock the door. Shelby was trapped. He couldn't get to her.

"What..." Rene smacked his lips together and pushed slowly up to sitting. "What happened?"

"Fuck!" Eli slammed a desperate fist against the metal door again and again. "Fuck!"

"We'll find a way!" Liam called.

Coming up beside him, Liam looped an arm around Eli's waist and tried to pull him back from the door. "We'll get it open," he promised.

Eli wanted to scream. He wanted to shove his brother off of him and kick down the fucking door. But then the handle dipped of its own accord and the damn thing pushed wide.

Stumbling back, Eli gaped.

"Is anyone there?" Shelby's voice came out timid at first. "Eli? Liam?"

Breaking from Liam, Eli jumped for the door and ripped it wide.

Shelby was standing there, just like he'd left her. Messy red hair, dirt smudged all over that pixie nose of hers. Gathering her into his arms, Eli lifted her off her feet and buried his face in her neck.

He'd be a complete little bitch if he cried right now. He'd never ever be able to live it down.

"Shelby," he gasped her name into her neck. "Thank God. You're okay. You're alright."

"I am," she whispered, and wrapped her arms around him. "You've got to come and see. I need the both of you to come and see."

Wriggling against him, Shelby fought her way down to her feet, but couldn't quite make it out of Eli's embrace. He kept his hand tight on her wrist so when she turned back down the hall, he followed.

"There's thousands of people down here, Eli," Shelby rushed. "Thousands and thousands. They're underfed, malnourished, but they're alive."

"They've been living underground this entire time?" Liam's voice carried from just behind Eli, he was tracking along with them, keeping pace.

"Yes, apparently they were told there was nuclear fallout and they had to stay underground," Shelby explained.

Arriving at a door, she pulled it open easily and walked through. That's when Eli's breath caught in his throat and he stuttered to a stop. His hand dropped from hers and he stared.

So many women. There were so many women crammed into the hall, rubbing their foreheads and talking to one another.

"Oh my God," Eli breathed out the words as Liam slammed to a stop behind him.

"They're confused." Shelby gestured around. "The microchip wiped their memories. They don't know who they are or why they're here. We need to get them above ground. And there's more. There's so many more further in. We can't lose any of them. What should we do?"

"I don't…" Liam stammered. "I don't think we thought this part through."

"We can radio for Malik now, right?" Shelby asked. "Can he contact Commander Linfield? We need support."

"Yes." Liam slapped a hand down on Eli's shoulder, causing pain to shoot through his arm and nearly level him. "I guess we can."

"Ow, fuck," Eli spat and sucked in a breath.

"He's been shot," Liam stated.

"I'm fine." Eli brushed him off.

Shelby whirled to him with a critical eye, her fingers already reaching out to explore.

Just then, Eli's gaze shot up and past Shelby's head. For a moment, the world stopped.

He couldn't hear anything, couldn't smell anything, couldn't see anything save for that one woman.

"Mrs. Jameson?" Eli's voice came out on a rasp as his heart jump started in his chest. "Charlotte?"

The woman did not look up at the sound of her name, but Eli *knew* it was her.

He recognized the woman who'd stepped in to be more of a mother to him than his own mother ever thought about being. He recognized the woman who'd taken in a couple of stray kids that her own beloved son had dragged home from high school. He recognized the woman that he'd thought had died in the war, Garrett's mother… she was alive.

Pushing through the crowd as gently as he could, Eli stopped in front of Charlotte Jameson and looked down into her sweet face.

"I know you," he said, and held back the tears that wanted to burn his eyes. "You're name is Charlotte, and you're my mother. I'm so happy that I've found you."

Looking up at him, Charlotte tilted her head and gave him a smile.

"I am?" She said and laughed.

Stepping forward, Eli wrapped her in an enveloping hug. Charlotte (just like when he'd first met her) didn't hesitate to hug him back.

"You are," he said. "And your other two kids are going to be so, so happy to see you."

## SIX MONTHS LATER

Staring down at the tiny bundle in his arms, Liam let himself marvel. This little being. This human, only a few moths old now, belonged to him. Or rather, he belonged to her. He belonged to Flynn Mae.

"Do you want me to take her?" Hannah whispered. She was sitting just beside him, in a row of white wooden chairs all lined up along the grass.

"No." Liam frowned down at his daughter and pursed his lips. "No, I've got her. Don't I baby? Daddy's got you."

Leaning against him, Hannah's golden hair tumbled onto Liam's shoulder, and she let loose a contented sigh.

All around them, their friends sat murmuring and laughing. There were several rows of chairs all facing the wooden arbor that the girls had spent the past few days covering with fresh spring flowers.

Up in front, Uriah sat in full uniform with Lena wedged beside him, trying unsuccessfully to keep Ian from wriggling out of his seat.

Jameson and Cass were next, with Jameson's mother, Charlotte beaming between them. She still didn't remember who she was, but she was alive and she was here. Her husband, apparently, hadn't survived Vanpell's microchip implantation, not many people did.

On the other side of the aisle, Mia brushed back her blonde hair and patted a hand against her growing belly. Her mother, Rachel Vanpell, was here too.

Unlike so many of the others, she did have her memories back already. Thankfully though, she didn't have to be afraid anymore, because her husband, President Edward Vanpell, had been shot dead. They didn't tolerate women-beating pieces of shit inside the Wall.

Next to her, Davey sat straight-backed and serious, like a guard dog hovering close to the two women. Liam eyed the back of the guy's head, and when Cookie leaned up and pinched Davey on the ear, both of them outright laughed.

In the next second, Ace delivered a well timed elbow to Cookie's side. The squawk that followed had everyone rippling with laughter.

"Settle down, settle down," Cole announced.

He was standing at the head of the aisle, positioned under the arbor with Eli by his side. He'd been picked to officiate this thing, and Liam was glad. Cole was good at this. He was good at talking and making speeches.

"Here she comes," Eli whispered, and everyone fell to silence.

Rotating slightly in his seat, Liam looked over his shoulder.

Shelby was there, her brash red hair framing her face. The wedding gown that Cass had slaved over, fell perfectly from Shelby's body. All women were beautiful in their wedding dress, Liam realized. There was just something special about it.

"Please rise," Cole announced, and had everyone shifting.

Coming to his feet, Liam held his baby daughter to his chest and bounced her slightly. Jameson had giving him a few tips... okay a LOT of tips about babies. The key was movement, apparently. Lots of constant movement, and you weren't allowed to sleep, or put the baby down... ever.

Which for whatever reason, was fine by Liam. He never thought he'd be a good dad. He never thought he could do it. But turns out... he was wrong.

As Shelby walked down the aisle, all eyes followed her. Hannah glanced at Liam slyly and smiled.

Liam's heart expanded even bigger than before and, as always, he frowned at the feeling. So much fucking feeling. He couldn't fathom it.

But then he looked up to the top of the aisle and saw his baby brother's face. Liam nodded, almost to himself. The guy was starstruck by bride... absolutely gone. And Liam recognized that feeling too.

"You may take your seats," Cole announced, as Shelby looped her arm in Eli's elbow and they faced away from the crowd.

Sitting down now, Liam did a quick sweep of the space. They were in the middle of the Wall. Rolling green lawns.

Bright blue sky overhead. Warm spring breeze rustling the women's hair.

His daughter was asleep in his arms and his wife was content by his side. His brother was standing at an altar in front of all of their friends and family, feeling like the luckiest man on the planet.

But Liam knew the truth. *He* was the luckiest guy on the planet. Him.

"Life is good," Liam murmured quietly, and listened to his baby girl sigh. "Life is good."

ACKNOWLEDGMENTS_


Sara Mae and Emily - thank you for Beta Reading.

Mom - life is a roller coaster right now, thanks for riding it with me.

Readers - you guys keep me going... seriously. Much love. See you on the next series! Keep reading.

Standalone novels:

VANISH ME

The Captive Series:

THE CAPTIVE BORN - Book One

THE CAPTIVE MISSING - Book Two

THE CAPTIVE RISING - Book Three

Outlasting Series:

OUTLASTING AFTER - Book One

CHASING TRUTH - Book Two

SURVIVING THE WALL - Book Three

BREAKING BEFORE - Book Four

TAKING TOMORROW - Book Five

FINDING FOREVER - Book Six